Poppy Done
to Death

Poppy Done to Death

Charlaine Harris

St. Martin's Minotaur
New York

www.minotaurbooks.com

Library of Congress Cataloging-in-Publication Data

Harris, Charlaine.
    Poppy done to death / Charlaine Harris.—1st St. Martin's
Minotaur ed.
        p. cm.
    ISBN 0-312-27764-4
    1. Teagarden, Aurora Roe (Fictitious character)—Fiction.
2. Women librarians—Fiction.   3. Group reading—Fiction.
4. Georgia—Fiction.   I. Title.

PS3558.A6427P67   2003
813'.54—dc21

                                                              2003043137

First Edition: August 2003

10 9 8 7 6 5 4 3 2 1

To my wonderful "second family," Christine and Gregg, Bill and Nancy, Joe and Misty, and Tom and Lori. My luck could not have been better.

Acknowledgments

My thanks for the advice of wonderful people like John Ertl, Kate Buker, the Reverend Gary Nowlin, and Michael Silverling. I may not have always used their information and advice correctly, but that fault is only mine. Special thanks to Ann Hilgeman and all the other real Uppity Women.

Poppy Done
to Death

Prologue

I paid almost no attention at all to the last conversation I had with my stepsister-in-law, Poppy Queensland. Though I liked Poppy—more or less—my main feeling when she called was one of irritation. I was only five years older than Poppy, but she made me feel like a Victorian grandmother, and when she told me she was going to foul up our plans, I felt very . . . miffed. Doesn't that sound grumpy?

"Listen," said Poppy. As always, she sounded imperative and excited. Poppy always made her own life sound more important and exciting than anyone else's (mine, for example). "I'm going to be late this morning, so you two just go on. I'll meet you there. Save me a place."

Later, I figured that Poppy called me about 10:30, because I was almost ready to leave my house to get her, and then Melinda. Poppy and Melinda were the wives of my stepbrothers. Since I'd acquired my new family well into my adulthood, we didn't have any shared history, and it was taking us a long time to get comfortable. I generally just introduced Poppy and Melinda as my sisters-in-law, to avoid this complicated explanation. In our small Georgia town, Lawrenceton, most often no explanation was required. Lawrenceton is gradually being swallowed by the Atlanta metroplex, but here we still generally know all our family histories.

With the portable phone clasped to my ear, I peered into my bathroom mirror to see if I'd gotten my cheeks evenly pink. But I was too busy thinking that this change of plans was inexplicable and exasperating. "Everything okay?" I asked, wondering if maybe little Chase was sick, or Poppy's hot-water heater had exploded. Surely only something pretty serious would keep Poppy from this meeting of the Uppity Women, because Poppy was supposed to be inducted into the club this morning. That was a big event in the life of a Lawrenceton woman. Poppy, though not a native, had lived in Lawrenceton since she was a teen, and she surely understood the honor being done her.

Even my mother had never been asked to be an Uppity Woman, though my grandmother had been a member. My mother had always been deemed too focused on her business. (At least that was how my mother explained it.) I was trying awful hard not to be even a little bit smug. It wasn't often I did anything that made my successful and authoritative mother look at me admiringly.

I think my mother had worked so hard to establish herself— in a business dominated by men—that she didn't really see the use in lobbying to join an organization made up mostly of homemaking women. Those were the conditions that had existed when she plunged into the workforce to make a living for her tiny family—me. Things had changed now. But you were tapped to join Uppity Women before you were forty-five, or you didn't join.

What did it take to be an Uppity Woman? The qualifications weren't exactly spelled out. It was more like they were generally understood. You had to have demonstrated strong-mindedness, and a high degree of resilience. You had to be intelligent, or at least shrewd. You had to be willing to speak out, though that was not an absolute requirement. You couldn't have any big attitude about what you were: Jewish, or black, or Presbyterian. You didn't have to have money, but you had to be willing to make an effort to dress appropriately for the meetings. (You would think an organization that encouraged independent women would be really flexible about clothing, but such was not the case.)

You didn't have to be absolutely Nice. The southern standard of niceness was this: You'd never been convicted of anything, you didn't look at other's women's husbands too openly. You wrote your thank-you notes and were polite to your elders. You had to take a keen interest in your children's upbringing. And you made sure your family was fed adequately. There were sideways and byways in this "nice" thing, but those were the general have-tos. Poppy was teetering on the edge of not being "nice" enough for the club, and since there had been an Uppity Woman in the forties who'd been just barely acquitted of murdering her husband, that was really saying something.

I shuddered. It was time to think of the positive.

At least we didn't have to wear hats, as Uppity Women had in the fifties. I would have drawn the line at wearing a hat. Nothing makes me look sillier, whether I wear my hair down (because it's long and really curly and wavy) or whether I wear it up (which makes my head look huge). I was glad that the Episcopal church no longer required women to wear hats or veils to Sunday service. I would have had to look like an idiot every week.

I'd been mentally digressing, and I'd missed what Poppy said. "What? What was that?" I asked.

But Poppy said, "It's not important. We're all fine; I just have to take care of something before I get there. See you later."

"See you," I said cheerfully. "What are you wearing to the meeting?" Melinda had asked me to check, because Poppy had a proclivity toward flamboyance in her clothing taste. But I could hardly make Poppy change outfits, as I'd pointed out to Melinda. So I'm not sure why I stretched the conversation out a little more. Maybe I felt guilty for having tuned her out, however briefly; maybe it would have made a difference if I'd listened carefully.

Maybe not.

"Oh, I guess I'll wear that olive green dress with the matching sweater? And my brown heels. I swear, I think whoever invented panty hose was in league with the devil. I won't let John David in the room when I'm putting them on. You look like an idiot when you're wiggling around, trying to get them to stretch enough."

"I agree. Well, we'll see you at the meeting." She wasn't even dressed yet, I noted.

"Okay, you and Melinda hold up the family banner till I get there."

That felt strange, but almost good, having a family banner to hold up, even though my inclusion was artificial. My long-divorced mother, Aida Brattle Teagarden, had married widower John Queensland four years ago. Now Melinda and Poppy were her daughters-in-law, married to John's two sons, Avery and John David. I liked all of the Queenslands, though they certainly were a diverse group.

Probably John's oldest son, Avery, was my least favorite. But Melinda, Avery's wife and mother of their two little Queenslands, was becoming a true friend. At first, I had tended to prefer Poppy, of my two new step in-laws. She was entertaining, bright, and had an original and lively mind. But Melinda, much more prosaic and occasionally given to dim moments, had improved on acquaintance, while Poppy and the way she lived her life had begun to give me pause. Melinda had matured and focused, and she'd broken through her shyness to express her opinions. She was no longer so intimidated by my mother, either. Poppy, who didn't seem to be scared of anything, took chances, big chances. Unpleasant chances.

So, while I enjoyed Poppy's company—she could have made the Devil laugh—I held part of myself away from her, afraid of the intimacy that would make her loss even more painful. Frankly, I figured she and John David would divorce within the next year or so.

What actually happened was much worse.

Chapter One

Melinda sat next to me at the table nearest the door. We'd kept a chair open for Poppy the whole meeting, but she'd never shown up. The room was full of Uppity Women, and they'd all turned to look at us when Poppy's name had been called and we'd had to say she wasn't there. The other Uppities saw a very short woman in her mid-thirties with a ridiculous amount of brown hair and a wonderful pair of green-rimmed glasses, and a taller, very slim, black-haired woman of the same age, who had a narrow and agreeable face. (I was the shorter of the two.) I am sure all the Uppities who could see that far noticed that we had matching expressions, compounded of social smiles and grim eyes. I, personally, planned to rake Poppy over the hottest coals I could find. The president of Uppity Women, Teresa Stanton, was giving us a basilisk glare.

"Then we'll continue the meeting with our book discussion," Teresa said, her voice clipped and businesslike. Teresa, aggressively well groomed, had that chin-length haircut that swings forward when you bend your head, as she did now to check the agenda. Her hair always did what it was told, in sharp contrast to mine. I was sure Teresa's hair was scared not to mind.

Melinda and I sat through the book discussion in mortified silence, but we tried to look interested and as though we were thinking deep thoughts. I don't know what Melinda's policy was, but mine was to keep silent so I wouldn't draw any more attention. I looked around the room, at the circular tables filled with well-dressed, intelligent women, and I decided that if none of them had ever been disappointed by a relative, they were a lucky bunch. After all, a woman hadn't shown up for a big-deal, high-pressure social engagement. Surely that was not such a rarity.

I muttered as much to Melinda, between the book discussion and lunch, and she widened her dark eyes at me. "You're right," she said instantly, sounding relieved. "We'll go by and see her after this is over, though. She can't do this to us again."

See? Even Melinda was taking it personally, and she's much more well balanced than I.

We scooted out of the dining room as quickly as we politely could after Teresa had dismissed the meeting. But we were waylaid by Mrs. Cole Stewart, who inquired in her deep southern voice where Poppy was. We could only shake our heads in ignorance and mutter a lame excuse. Mrs. Cole Stewart was seventy-five, white-haired, and all of a hundred pounds, and she was absolutely terrifying. From her affronted stare, we clearly received the message that we were being charged with guilt by association.

When we got to my Volvo, Melinda said, "We're going over there and have a few words with her."

I didn't say no. In fact, I'd never considered any other course of action. "Oh, yeah," I said grimly. I was so focused on having a few choice words with Poppy that I couldn't enjoy the clear, chilly November day, and November is one of my favorites. If we passed anyone we should have waved at, we never noticed it.

"It isn't as if she does a lot of work around the house," Melinda said suddenly, apropos of nothing. But I nodded, understanding the extended thought. Poppy didn't work outside the home anymore, she had one baby, and she didn't even take very good care of the house, though she did take good care of the baby. She should have been able to manage what was on her plate, as my mother would have put it.

As I'd half-expected, when we got to Poppy's and saw that her car was still parked in the carport, Melinda quailed. "You go in there, Roe," she said. "I'm liable to get so mad, I might mention a whole lot of other things besides the topic at hand."

We exchanged a meaningful glance, the kind that encompassed a whole conversation.

I swung my legs out of the car. I noticed something on the ground by my feet, two long straps of embroidered cloth.

"Oh crap," I said, glad only Melinda was there to hear me. I tossed them into the car for Melinda to look at, and I marched to the front door. I was mentally loaded for bear. "Poppy!" I called as I turned the doorknob of the front door of the house. The door opened. Unlocked. Since by now I knew Poppy had already had company that morning, I was not so startled by this.

I stepped into the foyer and called again. But the house was quiet. Moosie, Poppy's cat, came to see what was happening. Moosie was a pale sylph compared to my huge feline basketball, Madeleine. The cat meowed in an agitated way and ran from hall to kitchen and back again. I'd never seen Moosie act so jittery. He was Poppy's pampered pet, a declawed half Siamese she'd adopted from the animal shelter. Moosie was not allowed out the front door, only out the sliding glass back door, which led into a backyard enclosed all the way around with a six-foot-high privacy fence. After Moosie stropped my ankles a couple of times, I registered the fact that the sensation was sticky. I looked down and saw that my hose were stained.

"Moosie, what have you been into?" I asked. Several unpleasant possibilities crossed my mind. The cat began cleaning himself vigorously, licking at the dark patch on his side. He didn't seem hurt or anything, just, well, catty. "Where's Poppy?" I asked. "Where's your momma?" I know that's disgusting, but when you're alone with animals, you get that way.

Poppy and John David actually had a human child, Chase, as well as the cat, but they'd had the cat longer.

"Hey, Poppy!" I yelled up the stairs. Maybe she'd gotten in the shower after her visitor left. But why would she? Even for Poppy, missing such an important engagement was very unusual. And if she'd been up to her usual shenanigans . . . I had to press my lips together to hold in my anger.

I stomped up the stairs, yelling Poppy's name the whole time. She'd missed Uppity Women, and she'd missed lunch, and, by golly, I wanted to know why.

The master bedroom looked as though she'd just stepped out. The bed was made and her bathrobe was tossed across the foot of the bed. Poppy's bedroom slippers, the slide-in kind, were in a little heap on the floor. Her brush was tossed down on her dressing table, clogged with red-gold hair.

"Poppy?" I said, less certainly this time. The bathroom door was wide open, and I could see the shower enclosure. The wall was dry. It had been quite awhile since Poppy had showered. I could see my reflection in the huge mirror that topped the two sinks, and I looked scared. My glasses were sliding down my nose, which is a very insignificant feature of my face. I'd worn the green-rimmed ones today to offset my bronze-colored jacket and tobacco brown sheath, and I took a little moment to reflect that autumn colors were really my best.

Well, I could think about myself any old time, but right now I needed to be searching. I went back down the stairs faster than I'd gone up. Melinda, waiting out in my Volvo, would be wondering what had happened to me. I, however, was wondering why the central heating was roaring away on this cool but moderate day, and why I was feeling a draft of chilly air despite the heating system's best attempts.

I muttered a less ladylike word under my breath as I strode farther down the entrance hall to the kitchen, though *striding* is a moot word to use when you're four eleven. Moosie wove in and out between my ankles and darted ahead when it suited him. The kitchen was a mess; although big and bright, it was scattered with dishes and crumbs and pieces of mail and baby bottles and car keys and the St. James Altar Guild schedule— a normal kitchen, in other words. To my left, dividing the room in half, was a breakfast bar. On the other side of it was a family dining table, positioned by the sliding glass doors so Poppy and John David could look outside while they ate. A mug of coffee was on the breakfast bar. It was full. I laid my finger against the side of it. Cold.

Over the top of the breakfast bar, I could see that the sliding glass door was open. This was the source of the intruding cool air. A sharp-edged wind from the east was gusting into the kitchen.

My scalp began to prickle.

I stepped through the narrow passage between the end of the breakfast bar and the refrigerator and looked to my right. Poppy was lying on the floor just inside the open sliding glass door. One of her brown pumps had fallen off her narrow foot. Her sweater and skirt were covered in blotches.

A spray of blood had dried on the glass of the doors.

I could hear a radio playing from the house behind Poppy's.

The tune wafted over the high privacy fence. I could hear someone splashing through the water of a pool: Cara Embler, doing her laps, as she did every day, unless her pool was actually frozen. Poppy, who had laughed about Cara's adherence to such an uncomfortable regimen, would never laugh again. The processes of life and living, continuing in the houses all around us, had come to dead stop here in this house on Swanson Lane.

Moosie sat by Poppy's pathetic, horrible body. He said, "Reow." He pressed against her side. His food bowl, on a mat by the breakfast bar, was empty.

Now I knew how Moosie's fur had gotten stained. He'd been trying to rouse Poppy, maybe so she would feed him.

Suddenly, I had to escape from that suburban kitchen with its horrible secret. I flew out of the house, slamming the front door behind me. I had a fleeting impulse to scoop up Moosie, but taking charge of him was too much for me at that second. I dashed down the sidewalk to the curb, where Melinda was waiting. I was making the "phone" signal as I hurried, little finger and thumb pointing to mouth and ear, respectively. Melinda had turned on the cell phone by the time I got to her car.

"Nine one one," I said, gasping for breath. Melinda gave me a sharp look, but she punched in the number as I'd asked and then passed the phone to me. Did I mention that Melinda has a ton of good sense?

"The nature of your emergency?" said a distant voice.

"I'm at Eight-oh-eight Swanson Lane," I said. "This is Aurora Teagarden. My sister-in-law has been killed."

I never did remember the rest of that conversation. When I was sure they were coming, I pressed the button that ended the conversation, and I began to try to explain to Melinda.

But instead, I flashed on the deep wounds on Poppy's

hands, wounds incurred when she was defending her life, and I leaned over to avoid the car, my dress, and the phone while I threw up.

For the sixth or seventh time, I explained very carefully why Melinda and I had gone to Poppy's house. Because the city police made the house off-limits instantly, Melinda and I drove right down to the police station, and from there I called my mother at Select Realty, her agency. It was a difficult conversation, over my cell phone in a public place, but one that had to be completed. Her husband, John, had had one heart attack already. Mother was terrified of another, and the news about his favorite daughter-in-law might trigger one. Mother was right to worry about that, and she thought of a few more things to worry her before we'd finished our conversation.

"Who'll tell John David?" Mother asked. "Tell me it doesn't have to be John." John David was John's second son, and the husband of the late Poppy.

"Where is he, Mother? Do you know?" The police had been asking me that quite persistently. If John David wasn't at his company headquarters in Atlanta, I didn't know where he'd be. He'd been a pharmaceuticals salesman for the first few years of his marriage, but recently he'd gotten a job at company headquarters in the Public Relations division. John David had always been good at turning an attractive face to the world.

"John David? He's at work, I guess. Two o'clock on a Monday afternoon, where else would he be?"

"Do you have that phone number and address handy?"

I could hear little efficient sounds as Mother wheeled through her Rolodex. She rattled off a number, and I wrote it on a scrap of paper and handed it to the policewoman sitting across the desk. "That's the same number," the detective said, and I nodded.

"Will they let you go tell him?" Mother asked.

"I think the police will tell John David," I said. "If they can find him."

"What do you mean?"

"I already gave them that number. The police called, and the people there told the police that John David left work early today. Before noon."

"Then where could he be?"

"I guess they'd like to know that, too," I said, figuring a number of other shoes were about to drop.

After an appreciable pause, my mother said, "That would kill John." Another pause: I could practically hear her thinking. "Aurora, I've got to go, before he hears about this some other way. You know someone's bound to call the house and tell him there are a lot of police cars around John David's house. Wait! Roe, where's the baby?"

My face must have changed dramatically, because the detective stood up abruptly, sending her chair skidding a couple of feet.

"I don't know where the baby is," I said numbly. I couldn't believe I'd forgotten about Chase, who was only eleven months old. "I don't know. Maybe Melinda . . ." I swiveled on the hard chair, looking for my remaining sister-in-law. The next instant, I was on my feet. The detective said something, but I didn't listen as I searched for Melinda, my heels click-clacking on the linoleum floor.

She was in a cubicle with Detective Arthur Smith, whom I knew all too well. I stuck my head in. "Roe?" she said, already apprehensive.

"Where's the baby? Where's Chase?"

She looked at me blankly. "Why, John David dropped him

off at my house this morning. My sitter is keeping my two and Chase, so Poppy and I . . ." And then her face crumpled all over again.

I hotfooted it back to the telephone, which I'd stupidly left on the desk. "Chase is at Melinda's," I told my mother. I was limp with relief. "Evidently, John David took him over there this morning."

"So John David was in town this morning. At least we know that." My mother had already absorbed Chase's safety and was moving on to other ramifications. "Listen, Roe, you've got my cell-phone number." I had it all right, tattooed on my brain. "Call me the *minute* you know where John David is. I've got to get to your stepfather."

I thought my mother was a wee bit affected in calling John my stepfather, and she did on every possible occasion. After all, I'd been in my early thirties when John, a widower, had married Mother. He'd been a friend of mine before he'd dated my mother, and I felt a mixture of different obligations and attitudes toward John. I certainly never addressed him as "Stepdad."

I hung up and faced the woman who'd been taking my statement. Her name was Cathy Trumble, and I'd never met her before. Detective Trumble was stocky and graying, with an easy-care curly hairdo and sharp, pale eyes behind rimless glasses. She was a real professional, I guess; I had no clue as to how she felt about the information I was giving her—the death of Poppy Queensland, my brother-in-law's absence—or anything at all. It was like talking to a piece of stainless steel.

"How come you don't have a cubicle?" I asked. I had been wandering off in my own mental world while Detective Trumble was typing into a computer, and she was a little nonplussed by my question. The Sparling County Law Enforcement Center housed the sheriff's office, the town police, and the jail. In the world of SPACOLEC, detectives got their own little space with head-high carpeted dividers.

"I just got hired," she explained. She seemed startled into answering the question.

I recalled Sally Allison's story in the paper about the county having to increase its law-enforcement budget because of increased population, which had led directly to increased crime. Okay, Detective Cathy Trumble was the result. "Where do you live?" I asked, trying to be sociable. With a mother who made a living in real estate, it was a question that was second nature.

"And you had planned this lunch date with your sisters for how long?" she asked pointedly.

Okay, we weren't going to be best friends.

"They're my sisters-in-law, sort of once removed," I said for what felt like the millionth time. "We've been planning to go to the Uppity Women together for a month. Melinda just joined three months ago, and I've been a member for a about half a year."

"And Poppy?"

"Oh, she'd gone as our guest twice. But today she was going to be inducted. Somebody had died to let her in," I explained.

The clear eyes fixed me in their stare. I felt like I'd been caught in the headlights. "Somebody had died?" she said.

For the first time, I regretted not being questioned by Arthur. "Well, to get in Uppity Women—it's really the Uppity Women's Reading and Lunch Club, but everyone calls it Uppity Women—you have to fill a vacancy, because the bylaws limit membership to thirty," I told Cathy Trumble. "You have to be nominated, and if they vote yes, you get on the list. The list is limited to five. Then when a member dies, the top person on the list replaces that member. Etheline Plummer died for me."

"I understand," Detective Trumble said unwillingly. She looked a little dazed.

"So when Linda Burdine Buckle died two weeks ago," I said, "it was Poppy's turn." I patted at my cheeks with a soggy Kleenex.

"What do Uppity Women do?" Detective Trumble asked, though she sounded as though she didn't want to hear the answer.

"Well, we talk about local politics and then we decide how we're going to handle local issues. We have representatives at every city council meeting and school board meeting, and they give reports to the club. We decide whom we're going to back in the primaries, and how we're going to do it. And then we have a book we've all read that we discuss, and then we eat lunch."

This didn't seem extraordinary to me, but Trumble gave a kind of sigh and looked down at her desk. "So, you have a political agenda, and a literary agenda, and a social . . ."

I nodded.

"You all read, what? Like from the Oprah Book Club? Like *The Lovely Bones*?"

"Um, no."

"Well, what was this month's book?"

"*The Sublime and the Ridiculous: Economic Currents in the Southeast.* By a professor at the University of Georgia? She was supposed to come down to speak to us about it, but she got the flu." I had read every word, but it hadn't been easy.

The look Trumble gave me would have frozen a pond. "Could you just tell me what you've been doing, say last evening and this morning?" Detective Trumble asked, her voice hard despite the thinnest overlay of courtesy.

"Last night won't do you any good," I said, surprised she'd even tack that on. "She wasn't killed till this morning."

"How do you know that?" Trumble leaned forward, her eyes sharp and intent.

"About twenty different ways. First off, I talked to her this morning. Then, her clothes. She was wearing the right clothes."

" 'The right clothes'?"

"For the meeting. Poppy usually dressed a little extreme for Lawrenceton, and Melinda and I warned her that she had to look like Missy Matron for this crowd, at least till they got to know her. So I wanted to check on what she was planning on wearing. And she told me. And it was the outfit I found her in."

Trumble nodded. Good. This was the kind of fact she liked.

"So, this *morning,* I got up at six-thirty, showered, had coffee, read the paper, got a phone call from Melinda." I inclined my head toward the cubicle where Arthur was "interviewing" Melinda. "We talked for maybe five minutes. I got dressed. Then I called the vet to make an appointment for my cat, and I called Sears because the ice maker on my refrigerator is acting up, and I called work to find out when I could pick up my schedule for this month, and I called my friend Sally to ask her out for her birthday."

Detective Trumble was gaping at me. "You made all those calls this morning?"

"Well, yes. It's my phone-call morning."

"Your 'phone-call morning.' "

Gosh, she seemed big on repetition. "Yes, my phone-call morning. I don't go to work till the afternoon on most Mondays, so I make all my phone calls early. I have a list."

She shook her head slightly, as if she were shaking off raindrops. "Okay," she said. "So, when would you estimate these phone calls were finished?"

"Let's see. The vet opens at eight-thirty, so I probably began around then." Though I found it hard to believe, I again wished I were being questioned by Arthur. He knew Lawrenceton, and he knew me, and he would not make such heavy weather out of this. "You know, they don't want to see Madeleine, so making the appointment takes awhile. The new receptionist is better about it than the old one, though."

"Madeleine."

I am not a ditz—at least I don't think I am; I just daydream a lot—so I was getting a wee bit tired of feeling like an airhead. "My cat. Madeleine. Had to go to the vet."

"Your cat's a real handful?" Comprehension was dawning. Perhaps she was a cat owner. I thought of Moosie, and wondered who was watching him. He wasn't supposed to go out of the house. I was willing to bet the police had let him out. I was mad at myself for not telling them Moosie had been declawed before Poppy adopted her, so she wasn't an outdoors kind of cat. I explained to the detective. To my surprise, she called the house right away.

When she hung up, she looked concerned. "Our team searching the house says none of them has seen a cat."

"Oh no. That's awful. That cat is declawed; he can't make it outside that fence."

"I'll have the patrol cars look out for him, and I'll alert the pound in case anyone brings him in. Give me a description before you leave. Now, let's get back to this morning. You said your sister-in-law called you later, after you'd finished making all your phone calls?"

"Yes. The phone rang while I was getting ready to go. Poppy said Melinda and I should go on ahead, that she'd meet us there."

"And she gave no reason for this?"

"No." I hesitated. "She said there was something she had to take care of, and she sounded as though it was something unexpected, but other than that, no." There'd been the moments of my inattention, but that was for my conscience alone, not for Detective Trumble's consumption. Nothing could be done about it now. "She just said there was something she had to take care of," I repeated.

Arthur came out of his cubicle and beckoned to Detective Trumble, who pushed up from her desk and met him on middle ground. Possibly she thought I couldn't hear her because I was rooting around in my purse.

"Is this a fair example of a southern belle?" she murmured to my former boyfriend. I glanced up, to see her tilting her head toward me.

"Aurora?" Surprise made him a little louder than he'd intended.

"She's a moron. Her brains are scattered over several miles of bad road."

"Then she's hiding something," he said flatly.

Darn that Arthur.

I saw Melinda leaning out of Arthur's cubicle, making little gestures at me behind his back. So far, the new detective hadn't caught sight of Melinda, but she would soon. I shook my head violently then pasted a sweet smile on my face as Arthur leaned to one side to fix me with a glare. The minute my lips moved, I realized a sweet smile was wildly inappropriate, and I wiped my face clean, trying to come up with an expression that wouldn't be worse.

Arthur made his way through desks and chairs on the way to Trumble's area, and even I could read the reluctance in his gait. His whole demeanor was that of a man who'd just quit smoking but was obliged to tour the Marlboro factory.

The Marlboro factory would be me.

I should have been pleased, because God knows I'd hoped for years Arthur would get over his confused feelings about me, and he definitely had. I just didn't know why I had to be categorized as "bad" in the process. Possibly this was a childish thought and I would be ashamed of it later. I hoped so.

"What are you up to?" he asked without preamble.

"My sister-in-law got killed, Arthur. I'm not 'up to' anything."

"Uh-huh. Anytime you pull that fluff-headed southern eccentric routine, you're putting out a smoke screen. I take this real serious, Roe. There's no give in this."

I considered my options. I looked over at Melinda again. I shrugged. She looked relieved. I was taking the burden of concealment away from her.

"We found something in the driveway when we were sitting and waiting," I said. I looked up. Why on earth couldn't Arthur sit down in Detective Trumble's seat, so I wouldn't have to strain like this? I looked down at my hands clasped on my purse, rotated my head to ease my neck.

"What did you find?"

"Ah, a baby pacifier."

"Whose was it?" Arthur asked, his voice quite gentle. I could believe he wasn't mad until I looked back up at him.

"I'm not sure," I said.

"You're sure."

"No, I'm not."

"Your sister-in-law Melinda saw it, too."

"Yes."

"And you agreed not to tell us?"

"No," I protested. "We just don't know for sure whose it was."

"I think you have a real good idea."

This was the part that was impossible to explain. I tried to think of how to get around it. I had a stroke of genius—at least it seemed to be at that moment. "It's just a Binky," I said. I pulled it out of my purse and handed it to Arthur.

20

He turned it over and over in his fingers. It was a blue Binky, and there were millions just like it.

"It could even be her baby's," he said. "Maybe it fell out of one of the family cars."

Melinda had left the cubicle and inched closer to hear all this, and she looked profoundly relieved. Arthur was fairly irritated to see her when he turned around. He sighed. "Do you confirm this, Mrs. Queensland?" he asked. Melinda nodded.

"That's where we found it. It could have come from anywhere. Roe just picked it up on her way into the house because she assumed it was Chase's."

Bless Melinda's heart. I couldn't have done better myself.

Then Melinda almost ruined it by shooting me a triumphant glance that practically screamed, But there's more that we've concealed! I felt as if my purse were smoking, the contents were so hot.

"If that's all, Detectives, we need to go to our family," I said quickly. "Melinda's got the baby at her house with her kids, and we have to see to John, and Avery will want to know all about it."

"Where will you be going? In case we need to talk to you again?" Arthur was nothing if not tenacious.

"We'll be going to my house first, to check in on the kids and the baby-sitter," Melinda said briskly. She was glad to be back on familiar ground, where she knew what was what and she could be her normal efficient self. "Then we'll go over to John and Aida's house, I'm sure. You have Roe's cell number and mine, and the house numbers, so we'd like to hear as soon as possible if you find out anything."

The next thing I knew, we were in the parking lot of the SPACOLEC complex, and Melinda and I were hugging each other and crying. This was unprecedented, and maybe we were

21

both a little relieved when we separated to dig in our purses for tissues.

"They'll find out," Melinda said.

"Yes, they will. But at least it won't have been us who told them."

"I don't know why that makes me feel better," Melinda said, giving a few hiccupping sobs, "but it does. You know if that Arthur Smith finds out we're lying, he'll make it hard on us, and Avery will never forgive me."

I nodded grimly. If Melinda thought Avery was the most frightening thing facing her, she'd never seen my mother angry.

"What should we do with them?"

I pulled the cloth straps out of my purse and glared at them. They were cute as the dickens. They'd been embroidered by Poppy, who was fond of needlework, for the sons of Cartland ("Bubba") Sewell and my friend Lizanne. The boys, Brandon and Davis, were now—well, Brandon was a toddler, and Davis was sitting up. The straps, which snapped into a circle, were designed to run through the plastic loop on a pacifier, so when the baby dropped the pacifier, it wouldn't fall to the floor. You could run the strap around the baby's neck, or around the brace of a car seat, or whatever. Brandon's had his name and little bunnies embroidered on it, while Davis's had footballs and his initials. Lizanne had loved them when Poppy had given them to her; I remembered the day she'd opened the little package. And I'd found them on the ground in Poppy's driveway. Melinda and I exchanged a long glance, and I stuffed them back into my purse.

I drove to Melinda and Avery's house, trying to be extra careful, because I was all too aware of how dazed I was. I waited out in the driveway while Melinda ran in to check on the kids, tell the baby-sitter what had happened, and change shoes.

22

Highly polished flats replaced the pumps she'd been wearing. I liked Melinda more and more as I spent time with her, and not the smallest reason was her practical nature.

"Where's Robin?" she asked as we parked in front of my mother's house.

"He's in Austin," I explained. "He got nominated for some award, so he's going to the mystery writers' convention where they give it out. He asked me if I wanted to go, but . . ." I shrugged. "The convention's over, but he's doing some signings on the way back. He should be home on Wednesday, in time to pick up his mother at the airport."

"You didn't want to go with him?" she asked shyly. My relationship with Robin Crusoe, fiction and true crime writer, was new enough that the family was delicate about making any assumptions.

"I kind of did," I said. "But he was going to be with a lot of people he knows really well, and I haven't been with him very long."

She nodded. You had to have a pretty firm footing in a relationship to be dragged into a massive "meet the friends" situation. "Still, he asked," she said.

It was my turn to nod. We both knew what that meant, too.

That was our last pleasant moment for the rest of the day. Our sister-in-law had died a terrible death, a violent death, and John David still hadn't been located. Poppy's parents had to be called, which awful job Avery agreed to undertake. All the Queensland men were tall and attractive. Avery was certainly the most handsome CPA in Lawrenceton, but his personality did not live up to his face, which could have been devilish if there'd been any spark in it. Avery was one of those men always described as "steady," which is what you want in an accountant, of course. He was the older brother, and had been a year ahead of me in high school. Instead of playing football like John David, Avery had played tennis; instead of being elected class president, Avery had been editor of the school paper. He'd added to the local gene pool by marrying Melinda, who'd grown up in Groton, a few miles away.

Poppy had gone to high school in Lawrenceton. She and John David had been five years behind me at the local school, which in those days had meant I was hardly aware of their existence. Her parents, who'd had her late in life, had moved to a retirement community a couple of hours' drive away after she'd graduated. Poppy's father, Marvin Wynn, had been the local Lutheran minister, and his wife, Sandy, had worked in the registrar's office at the local junior college. The whole community had pitied these righteous people when Poppy, their only child, reached her teen years.

But she'd never been arrested or gotten pregnant, those two grim incidents typical of wild teen years. And by the time she'd gone to college, she'd more or less settled into a relationship with John David Queensland. It had been a tumultuous one, and they'd broken up and reconciled more times than any onlooker could count. Neither Poppy nor John David had been faithful during the off-seasons, and maybe not even when they were supposed to be going steady. This pattern seemed to have continued even after they'd eventually married, five years after they'd graduated from college and begun pursuing their careers. Amazingly, Poppy had been a great elementary school teacher. I'd heard how good she was from more than one set of parents. And John David seemed to be able to talk almost any doctor into buying his company's pharmaceuticals.

After Poppy had had Chase, almost any onlooker would have been excused for assuming that life had settled down for these two former wild kids.

Not so.

Though I'd always liked Poppy, and had often admired her terrifying habit of saying exactly what she thought, I didn't approve of some aspects of her marriage. To me, marriage is the chance to put away the trappings of a single life and concentrate on making one good thing work really well. The cornerstone of this would have to be—in my view—faithfulness. There have to be some assumptions you make when you agree to bind your life to another person's, and the basic assumption and maybe the most important of all is that this person will get your exclusive attention.

Poppy had had at least two flings that I knew about, and I would not have been surprised to hear there had been more. I had tried—real hard—not to judge Poppy, to enjoy the part of her I liked and ignore the part that made me queasy. I behaved this way for several reasons. The most important reason was that I was also bound to her by marriage, my mother's marriage, and to make a family work, you have to be willing to keep your mouth shut and park your judgments by the door. The last thing in the world I wanted to do was complicate my mother's life by causing trouble in our new family.

Another reason was my attempt to live my religion. When I'd dated our priest, Aubrey, he'd commented once or twice on my ardent wish not to cause trouble by speaking up about other people's behavior. "You have to take a stand for what you believe," he'd said. Well, that was true. What was the point of having beliefs if you didn't express them and live them?

"I don't have to take a stand by telling other people they're wrong," I'd protested. "What business is it of mine?"

"If you love them, it's your business," he'd said firmly. "If their misbehavior is intruding on the happiness and well-being of others, it's your business."

I don't know what Aubrey would have said about Poppy and

John David, because I never asked him. I always felt I had so many weaknesses myself that the last thing I should do was point out other people's flaws to them. So I never mentioned their infidelities to John David or Poppy, and I didn't want them to discuss those affairs with me.

For sure, I didn't want that.

When other people would try to tell me what my in-laws were doing, I'd just hurry the subject right past my nose.

Avery interrupted these unwelcome memories to tell us that Poppy's parents were on their way to Lawrenceton. John, my mother, Melinda, and I were sitting around the table in the kitchen, coffee mugs in front of us . . . trying. Trying to think what to do next. Trying not to talk about where John David might be. Trying not to think about what to do with Chase, a baby with a dead mother and a missing father.

"At least he's weaned," Melinda muttered to herself.

I raised an eyebrow at her.

"I bet Avery and I end up with him," she said, then tried to sound happier about it. "He's a sweet baby, but . . ." She struggled to keep the words "I already have my hands full" locked down in her throat. "Poppy's parents are too old, Avery's dad and your mom are too old, and I can't picture John David raising a kid by himself, can you?"

No, I couldn't.

"Poppy was a good mother," Melinda said quietly. "You wouldn't think so, but she was."

I nodded. "Poppy had a lot of good qualities."

"What—excuse me, Roe, but I need to know—what actually happened to her?" Melinda asked, keeping her voice hushed.

"I think someone stabbed her," I said, not meeting Melinda's dark eyes. I was actually quite sure about that, but I'm no coroner, and I wasn't going to give any final judgment on Poppy's death.

Melinda made a little sound of horror, and I winced in sympathy. How scared Poppy must have been . . . how much it must have hurt. Had she hoped Melinda and I would come to save her, arrive in the nick of time?

I snatched my mind away from this fruitless conjecture and gave myself a good scolding. Poppy must have died very quickly, perhaps within a scant few seconds. Melinda pushed back from the table and left the room. Avery followed her. After a moment, I could hear the murmur of their voices coming from the living room.

My mother was watching John like a hawk, on the alert for signs of heart trouble. John was staring down at the table, studying a tablet open to a blank page. He'd stated his intention of starting a list of people he needed to contact, like the funeral home and the church, but he'd stalled. I knew that couldn't wait any longer. I went upstairs, carrying the cordless phone into my old bedroom. I called Aubrey's house.

"Hello." It was the cool, composed voice of Emily, Aubrey's wife.

"Emily, this is Aurora." I sounded just as calm and sweet. We couldn't stand each other.

"Hey, how are you?'

"Well, I'm fine, thanks, but we have a family trouble, and if Aubrey is handy . . ."

"Roe, he's over at the country club, playing golf. Jeff Mayo asked him to make up a foursome. You know, Monday's supposed to be his day off. . . ." Her voice trailed away delicately.

Bitch.

"Yes, and if my sister-in-law hadn't been murdered, I wouldn't dream of disturbing him," I said somewhat less sweetly.

A long silence.

"He has his cell phone," Emily admitted. "Let me give you that number."

"Thank you so much," I said with no expression at all. Why couldn't I have dated a vet, or a bartender, or a farmer? Why had I dated a cop and a minister before I met my first and now deceased husband, Martin Bartell?

Who shows up in emergencies? Policemen and preachers!

I repeated the number to make sure I'd gotten it right, then bid Emily good-bye. I knew she would set the drums beating to alert the Women of the Church to the imminence of a funeral meal. Emily always did her duty.

I took a deep breath and called Aubrey before I could change my mind.

I don't like cell phones, and I almost never turn mine on; to me, it's an emergency tool, like a car jack or a rifle. But today I was really glad our priest had one.

He said he'd be at the house in thirty minutes.

Chapter Two

Aubrey made it in forty minutes, and he was wearing his black shirt and dog collar when he rang the doorbell. Aubrey had had very dark hair when I met him, and he was graying heavily now. He'd shaved his mustache the year before, which had changed his appearance drastically. And he'd gained a few pounds, even though he played golf, tennis, and ran three times a week. Still, Aubrey was an attractive man, and Emily was very watchful around the single female members of the congregation—and some of the married ones, for that matter.

Take Poppy, for example. Emily had always been markedly cold toward Poppy, who had laughed it off.

I took a ragged breath and hugged Aubrey out of sheer thankfulness for his presence. Then I took him into the kitchen.

Somehow, the appearance of the priest gave weight and substance to the fact of Poppy's death. If the priest showed up, it had to be true. Aubrey's arrival was both a shock and a relief.

I wandered in and out of the kitchen, keeping a sharp eye on John. He looked good, considering the horror of the day. He was practically vibrating with worry over John David's absence. I thought he would not feel the impact of Poppy's death until he could be sure of his son's whereabouts and safety.

John had to be aware that we were all thinking that until John David showed up to establish his innocence, he was the chief suspect in his wife's murder.

Even John had to be thinking that.

Where the hell could John David be? I walked through the kitchen, the dining room, the formal living room, back through the family room. Then I made the circuit again. I noticed my pattern was irritating the hell out of Avery, but that was just his bad luck. It helped me think.

If I were John David, and I'd left work early, and my wife was busy, and my son was safely at his aunt's house . . . I'd go visit my mistress. The answer popped into my mind with the air of finality your subconscious reserves for sure things. Whom had John David been seeing lately? I could feel my upper lip wrinkle with faint disgust at even considering such a question. I made myself comb through the half-heard rumors.

There was Patty Cloud, who'd worked for my mother for several years before becoming Mother's second in command. I'd never cared for Patty, who was a cold and manipulative woman. There was Romney Burns, the daughter of a murdered detective in the Lawrenceton Police Department. There was Linda Pocock Erhardt, whose bridesmaid I'd been; Linda, divorced for many years, had two daughters in high school, and I knew she should be at work today. She was a nurse for my doctor, Pincus Zelman.

I felt much better now that I had a mission. I slipped out of my mother's house and into my car and began touring the town. I'd never driven through Lawrenceton hunting down love nests before, and I felt queasy about doing it now. I know I'm not such a wonderful moral person. But somehow, the slipping and creeping, the surreptitiousness of it, the deceiving . . . well, I had to shrug and sigh all over again at my own censoriousness.

Linda's car, as I'd expected, was parked behind the doctor's office. And there was a phalanx of vehicles in the parking lot. I was 98 percent sure that Linda was inside taking temperatures and blood pressures, just as she ought to be. I called my mother's office and asked for Patty, and when she came to the phone, I told her my mother wouldn't be in for the rest of the day. Patty replied in a puzzled sort of way, saying that my mother had already called her to let her know that very thing, and I laughed weakly. "Guess we got our signals crossed in all the confusion," I said, and Patty said, "Um-hum" in a loathsomely skeptical way.

That left the least palatable alternative.

Linda and Patty were both strong women, veterans of the divorce wars, and both quite capable of making their own decisions. Romney Burns was neither of those things. Romney's apartment was a duplex, and I spotted John David's car immediately, parked in the neighbor's driveway. I assumed the neighbors were at work and that this was John David's way of casting up a smoke screen. How subtle.

Romney was a lot younger than John David. Romney was—well, she had to be less than twenty-six, I rapidly figured. And she'd lost her father less than two years before. Sandy-haired and fair, Romney had shed the weight she'd carried in high school by the time she graduated from college and returned to Lawrenceton, where she'd gotten a poor-paying white-collar job in the financial aid office of the junior college. Mother had told me Romney was the financial aid officer's assistant.

I hoped they didn't have any loan emergencies at Sparling

Junior College today, because it looked like Romney was home.

I took a deep and unwilling breath before knocking on the shabby door. I would rather have been pulling my eyebrow hairs out one by one than doing this.

Naturally, Romney answered. Her light hair was a real mess, and she was clothed only in a bathrobe. It took her a second to recognize me, and when she did, she looked disgruntled. I hadn't been her father's favorite person, either.

"What are you doing here?" she snapped. She had to realize that seeing John David's sister-in-law at her door meant bad things.

"John David needs to get his clothes on and get out here right now," I said, abandoning any attempt to put a polite gloss on the situation.

"Who?" she blustered, but she discarded that quickly. Then she straightened. "Well, maybe I better come, too, since I might be a member of the family before too long," she said, both defensive and proud.

"Oh bull," I said. "This is the third place I tried to find John David, honey. Not the first."

I saw comprehension leak into her eyes as she struggled to maintain her position. "He loves me," she said.

"Right, that's why you two are walking down Main Street arm in arm," I said, and turned my back on her. The door slammed behind me. Big surprise.

"What the hell is this about?" John David said when he joined me. He was put back together pretty well, as far as clothing goes, but his composure had big holes in it. John David had a more florid coloring than his father and brother, and fairer hair. He was a powerfully built man, and a handsome one. But I didn't like him anymore, and in my eyes, he would always be ugly.

"John David," I said slowly, suddenly realizing I'd condemned myself to breaking the news. "How long have you been here?"

"What business is it of yours?"

We faced each other, standing by my car.

"Believe me, it's my business. Tell me."

John David was no fool, and he'd picked up on the undertone.

"I've been here since I drove back from the office at eleven," he said. His voice was even. "Now, you tell me what's happened."

"It's Poppy." I met his eyes squarely.

His face began to crumple. I swear that he looked as though this were news to him.

"Poppy was attacked in your house after you left this morning."

"So she's in the hospital?" There was a desperate hopefulness on his face.

"No," I said. No point stringing this out. I took a deep breath. "She didn't survive."

He scanned my face for any sign that what I was saying wasn't true, that my words might have some other meaning.

He knew before he asked, but I guess he had to. "You mean she's dead," he said.

"Yes," I said. "When Melinda and I went to check on her, she was gone. I called the police. I'm very sorry."

Then I had to hold this man I didn't even like anymore. I had to put my arms around him and keep him from sinking to the ground while he wept. I could smell the scents of his deodorant and his aftershave, the laundry detergent that Poppy had used on his clothes—and the smell of Romney. It was intimate and disgusting.

There really was nothing more to say.

When he calmed a little bit, I told him he had to go to the police.

"Why?" he said blankly.

"They're looking for you."

"Well, now you've found me."

"They're looking for *you*."

That got his attention.

"You mean that they think I might have killed her?"

"They need to rule it out," I said, which was as diplomatically as I could phrase it.

"I'll have to tell them where I was."

"Yes, absolutely."

"You think I need a lawyer before I go in?" he asked, which was the most sensible thought he'd voiced.

"I think it wouldn't hurt," I said slowly.

"I'll call Bubba," he said, and whipped his cell phone out of his pocket.

"Oh no," I said without thinking.

He stared at me.

I shook my head vehemently.

"You just call someone else, not Cartland Sewell," I said. I was hoping the earth would open up and swallow not me but John David.

If he could look any worse, he did. "All right," he said after a deadly silence. "I'll call Bryan Pascoe."

Bryan Pascoe was the toughest, meanest criminal lawyer in the county. I don't know how much that was saying, but Bryan was local, and he was tough, and he knew his law. He was around Avery's age, I thought, which meant he was a year or so older than I. I knew him only by sight. Many of the Uppity Women hoped that Bryan would become a judge in the next couple of years.

Luckily, Pascoe was not in court, and his secretary put John

34

David through. John David tried to explain the situation, but he broke down in tears. To my acute discomfort, he pressed the telephone into my hands.

"Mr. Pascoe," I said, because I had no choice. "This is John David's sister-in-law, Aurora Teagarden."

"Of course, I remember you. I hope your mother is well?" The lawyer had one of those wonderful voices—deep, smooth, authoritative.

"She's fine," I assured him. "But we have trouble."

"People who call me always do. What can I do for you on this beautiful fall day?"

"Um. Well, this is the situation." I explained it to him as rapidly and concisely as I could while John David lay over the hood of my car, weeping. I was so glad Romney didn't come out of her duplex that I could hardly contain myself. Staying inside was incredibly smart of the girl, because I would have pounded her into a pulp. I didn't have any sympathy or tact to spare.

"Good summary," Bryan said, and I felt like he'd poured syrup on my pancakes and cut them up for me. "Lucky for both of us, I just had a client cancellation. I can meet John David at SPACOLEC in forty-five minutes."

I started to ask Bryan Pascoe what the hell I was supposed to do with my brother-in-law in the meantime, but that was hardly the lawyer's problem. "See you there in forty-five minutes, right outside the front doors," I said, and hung up.

"Okay, John David." I tried to sound bracing and authoritative. I turned off his phone and stuck it into his pocket. "We need to get into my car, now." I worried about leaving John David's car where it was, but I figured I couldn't take care of every little thing. I'd have to get Melinda or Avery to come pick it up pretty quick, because as soon as the news of Poppy's death was widely known, that car in that location might as well have a big scarlet *A* printed on the trunk. I fished John David's keys out of his pants, got his car key off his key ring, and slipped it under the floor mat on the driver's side. Then I called Avery and gave him the heads-up on the car. At least Avery understood completely without me having to explain every little detail.

I wrangled John David into the front seat of my car, fastened his seat belt, and ran around to get in the driver's seat. It would take me all of fifteen minutes, if I drove slowly, to get to the SPACOLEC complex. What could I do for thirty minutes?

"I need to go by the house," John David said. "I need to see where it happened."

"No," I said. "You don't need to go there right now. For one thing, the police are sure to still be there. For another thing, the site needs to be cleaned up before you get in. I can tell you about it. It happened in your patio doorway. Someone came to your back door. He probably got into your backyard through one of the gates." Or maybe Poppy was trying to flee into the backyard when her attacker caught up with her, having entered from the front door? But wouldn't she have pitched forward in that case? She'd been lying on her back with her legs outside the door. No, the attack had come from in front of her when she was facing out the glass door. "She died real quick. She was stabbed."

John David insisted again that he wanted to go home, and I told him flatly that I wouldn't take him, that the first place he was going was to SPACOLEC, and that he better tell them all the truth. I listened to the words coming out of my mouth, and to my terrified delight, I sounded exactly like my mother.

"This will ruin Romney," he said, speaking so quietly, it was almost to himself.

"Poppy is more important right now than Romney Burns's reputation."

36

"I'm just saying," he said, placating me with a gesture of his hand that meant, Level out.

I had taken so many deep breaths, I thought I might hyperventilate. I drove very slowly and took the longest route I could imagine, but still we arrived at SPACOLEC before thirty minutes had elapsed.

Scared a policeman would spot John David in my car before the lawyer arrived, I drove out to Fuller Gospel Church and parked for a moment under the huge live oak in the old church's parking lot. The sun danced through the changing leaves as they flickered in a chilly wind. It was an oddly beautiful moment, and one I knew I would never forget—the grieving and faithless man beside me, the country church, the light among the dancing leaves.

Bryan Pascoe wasn't at all what I'd expected. Since everyone seems tall to me, I was surprised to notice that next to John David, he was actually a small man, perhaps five seven. He shook hands with me gravely and then turned all his attention to my brother-in-law.

While the lawyer listened to John David, I was able to examine him more closely. Bryan Pascoe had ash-blond hair and light blue eyes. He had the narrowest, straightest nose I'd ever seen in my life; it made him look sharp and arrogant. I didn't know him well enough to know if that was true. Right away, he told us to call him Bryan, and then he asked John David to tell him exactly what he'd done today.

"Got up at six-forty-five, usual time," John David began. His voice was dull. "Poppy stayed in bed until Chase started crying about seven. She fed him and changed him and packed his diaper bag for the day. We didn't talk much. She wasn't much of a morning person. I knew I was supposed to take Chase over to Melinda and Avery's, because it was Poppy's club day. Poppy asked me if I was going to be home on time today, because she was thinking of fixing pork chops for supper. She didn't often feel like that." For a minute, John David's mouth twisted. "She took Chase in to brush his teeth; he doesn't have many, so it just takes a second." He clamped his lips shut, and his eyes, too, holding the memory in or blocking it out—I wasn't sure which. "Poppy said since she didn't have to get ready until nine, she might get back in bed and snooze awhile longer. Since I was taking care of Chase this morning, I had to leave at seven-forty-five to get to work before nine, so I had to go then. I put Chase in my car—we've got a car seat in both cars—and I dropped him off at my brother's house. You know Avery and Melinda?"

Bryan Pascoe nodded. "I've met Avery," he said. "Go on."

"I talked to Melinda for a minute. Avery had already left for work. Melinda was worried because the sitter was late, and she couldn't leave the kids alone long enough to shower. I drove into Atlanta to work, usual terrible traffic. I got to work right at nine. I worked until about eleven." His faced reddened. "Then I told them I was feeling sick and needed to go home, so I drove back to Lawrenceton. I didn't go home. I went over to Romney Burns's house. She'd taken the afternoon off, too. I've been there ever since I got back to town, which would have been about eleven-forty-five, give or take a little. Traffic was a lot lighter coming back."

This was certainly a simple-enough account.

Bryan took John David through the morning's activities and their timetable once more, quickly. Maybe the contrast was clearer because John David and I were so stunned, but I had to admire the lawyer's clarity and focus.

Then Bryan took my hand, much to my surprise. "And you, young lady," he said gravely, though I was sure he was only a year or two older than I, "tell me what your part in all this was."

Once again, I told him a compressed version.

"The Uppity Women," he said with a smile. "My ex-wife is an Uppity Woman."

By that time, he was shepherding us into the building, and I took a step back. "I'm not going in," I said.

"Of course, you need to get back to the family," Bryan Pascoe said, his voice warm and understanding, but his thick blond eyebrows flew up.

"I need *not* to go in here with him," I said emphatically, though unclearly. "I'm a widow," I pointed out, and though John David still looked dazed and uncomprehending, Bryan Pascoe immediately grasped my point. Any unmarried woman would be doubly suspect if she accompanied John David on this day, of all days. "Good thinking. I'll talk to you later," he said, and he and John David marched into the complex, ready to plunge into the business of justice.

Since I had to go back to the house and explain all this to John Queensland, I wondered who would have the easier time of it.

On my way back to Mother's, I stopped by the library to explain the situation and beg for some time off. Still in my nice dress, with my good pumps on, I was much admired before the condolences started rolling in. Perry Allison and Lillian Schmidt both gave me hugs, which I appreciated. After I'd accepted the first wave of sympathy, Perry said, "Oh, by the way, there's a young man here waiting for you."

Those words were not exactly the thrill they might have been. "Not my stepson?" I asked, peering in all directions so I could hide if I saw Barrett coming.

"No, no, this one's younger." Perry, who was resplendent

today in deep green cargo pants and a chocolate brown shirt, pointed at the magazine area, and I looked at the young man sitting at the round table with a *Gaming* magazine in front of him. He was easily five nine, and he was broad-shouldered. His teenage-chic clothes had started out expensive, but now they were definitely on the grimy side. His skin was not perfect—teenage spottiness had hit him pretty hard—but it was deeply tan, and his hair had been dyed a bright metallic gold. His face looked familiar; there was something about the nose and mouth that made alarm bells sound in my head.

"I know him," I muttered. "Who is he?"

He glanced up, and his gaze returned to me after passing me over once. He got up slowly, closing the magazine and tossing it back on the rack.

"Want me to stay?" Perry asked as the teenager came over. I didn't answer him, because a hope had begun to grow in me, one I could scarcely bring myself to admit.

"Sis?" the boy said.

Oh my God—his voice had changed.

Peering up at him, I said, "Phillip?"

The next instant, muscular arms lifted me into the air and the oddly familiar face was grinning up at me.

"My brother," I said proudly to the gaping Perry. "This is my brother."

Once Phillip had replaced me on the floor, I pushed my glasses up on the bridge of my nose and grinned back at him.

"Are my dad and Betty Jo here in Lawrenceton?" I asked, amazed that I hadn't known of such a trip.

"Ah, no." He might as well have had the word *apprehensive* tattooed on his forehead. Hmmm.

My coworker reminded me he was present by making a little noise in his throat. "Phillip, this is Perry," I said, sure I was

40

making Perry's day. The arrival of a long-unseen brother was great news for Lawrenceton's gossip mill.

Perry shook Phillip's hand solemnly, said he was glad to meet any brother of mine, and then found something to do on the other side of the library. Perry was not insensitive to atmosphere. After an awkward moment, I suggested to my brother that we go outside to the employees' parking lot to have a little talk. It was cooler, and gusty; I was sure it was going to rain. Phillip was wearing a tank top under an unbuttoned flannel shirt, and the breeze was way too brisk for his ensemble. His flesh looked goosey.

"I'm truly happy to see you, but you better explain why you're here," I said, trying not to sound too stern.

"Things haven't been going too good at home," he admitted, shoving his hands down in his pockets. He'd hinted as much in his E-mails, so I shouldn't have been surprised.

"Dad couldn't keep his—" I stopped abruptly and substituted a milder phrase. "Dad was not faithful to Betty Jo?"

"Right," my half brother mumbled.

"I guess some things don't change." I tried not to sound bitter. "Listen, Phillip, please tell me they know where you are."

"Ah, not exactly." He tried to smile at me, but it didn't work.

"How'd you get here?"

"Well, a friend of mine's big brother was driving to Dallas, so I told him if he'd take me along, I'd split the gas."

"This brother didn't know how old you are?"

"Uh, no."

Sure he had. He had helped a fourteen-year-old runaway. Or was Phillip fifteen now? Yes, just barely.

"And after you got to Dallas?"

"I, uh, hitched a ride with a truck driver to Texarkana."

"He was okay?" Phillip wasn't meeting my eyes.

"He was okay. The next guy wasn't." Phillip was just shivering from cold, I hoped. After giving him a good look, I was sure.

I took a deep, deep breath, trying to keep it silent. "Do I need to take you to the doctor?" I asked very gently. "There're lots of specialists in Atlanta; they don't know you or me, and they'd never see us again."

"No," Phillip said, his face brick red. "I get what you're saying, but it didn't come to that. It was pretty intense, though." He may have thought he was smiling, but it was a grimace, compounded of fear, embarrassment, and humiliation.

"Where'd you end up?"

"I just made it partway to Memphis with the bad guy. I got another ride into the city."

"Okay." I was biting the inside of my mouth to keep my face calm. "What then?"

"Uh, I went to the college campus—you know, the University of Memphis? And I found the Student Center, and I read the notices on the bulletin board."

I wondered how he had learned to do that.

"And in those notices, there was one from two girls who needed a guy to ride with them to Birmingham. They were scared they'd have a flat tire or something, and I can at least change a flat tire. I think. Anyway, Britta never had one."

Britta. Hmm. "So they took you as far as Birmingham."

"Yeah." If possible, Phillip's face was an even deeper red. I was willing to bet those girls hadn't known his true age, either, and I was thinking even more grimly that Phillip might need a blood test. "So from Birmingham, I just rode the bus."

"I'm glad you had the money left for that."

"Uh, Britta and Margery chipped in on it."

"You had a lot of adventures," I said, smiling so I wouldn't scream. He was lucky to be alive.

"Yeah. I think, you know, I did okay." He seemed to know

that sounding any more boastful than that would get him a good slap on the wrist.

"And all this time your parents haven't known where you were?"

He nodded.

I could not even imagine how they were feeling.

"How long has that been?" I asked in a voice I just barely managed to keep even.

"Uh, let's see. Two and a half days to Dallas, a half day to get the ride with Mr. Hammond, then the ride to Texarkana, where I helped him unload the truck, and then the other guy, the one in the pickup, that lasted about two hours, and I hid in the woods. . . ."

I could feel all the blood draining from my face, and I sat down on the hood of Perry's car, which was the closest.

"Hey, Roe, don't look so . . . It wasn't as bad as you're probably thinking. I'd just . . . I'd never imagined . . . He probably wouldn't have actually, uh, forced me. . . . I just freaked."

"That's okay. That's what people do when they're faced with a scary situation. Hiding was the best way to make sure you were safe," I said reasonably, thinking I would even try calling the Psychic Friends hot line to find out who this individual was who had ripped a hole out of my brother's life. And then I'd rip a hole out of his.

"Now," I said briskly, "I think you've gotten up to four days?"

"I think so. Anyway, I did get a ride with a chartered busload of people who were going to the gambling boats at Tunica—you know, right below Memphis? But I got them to drop me off in Memphis, because I thought I probably had a better chance at getting a ride in a city. And then I met Britta and Margery."

"So, your mom and dad haven't known where you were for six days, give or take a day?"

43

"Uh, well, I called them, you know."

I closed my eyes. Thank God.

"I called them with my phone card, from pay phones. I'm almost out of minutes on it now. I just told them I was okay. I didn't tell them I was coming to you."

And it had never occurred to them, because they hadn't called me to ask me to be on the lookout. For some reason, that made me angry. My half brother is missing, and my own father can't call me and let me know?

I realized, looking up at his young face, that Phillip was exhausted. Though I hadn't been around for much of Phillip's youth, due to my father's taking him far away from me—on purpose—when Phillip was in elementary school, I was sure that Phillip had had as sheltered and middle-class an upbringing as his parents could provide in Southern California.

"Maybe they'll let you stay for a while," I said. "I sure would like that."

"I'm sorry they wouldn't come to your wedding, or your husband's funeral," Phillip said miserably. "I really liked Mr. Bartell, when I met him. I tried to make them let me come by myself, but they wouldn't listen."

"Hey, bud, that's okay," I said. Of course it hadn't been, but his parents' bad behavior wasn't Phillip's fault. Martin had uncomfortably excused his son, Barrett, who had done pretty much the same thing, but Martin had been quick to become angry with my father and Betty Jo: Of course, he could see that my father had hurt me. Martin and I had stopped in to see them when we'd taken a trip to California. The visit had been very uncomfortable; the only highlight had been seeing Phillip.

That had been what—a year and a half ago? I figured Phillip had grown five inches in that time.

"We need to talk a little more about your trip later, and we need to call your folks, and we need to put your clothes in the wash, and you, too. You don't have any other clothes?" I was trying to sound mature and in charge, but I'd used up a lot of whatever authority I possessed when I was dealing with my errant brother-in-law.

"Uh, I left my backpack when I got out of the truck so fast," he confessed, his eyes sliding away.

"Then we'll take care of the clothes situation."

"Uh, Roe, you dating now? Mom said there was something in a gossip column in one of the movie magazines."

"Ugh. I didn't know that. I'm sure not important enough to rate that, so it must be because of Robin Crusoe, the man I'm dating. He's a writer. I knew him a long time ago, and he came back to Lawrenceton a couple of months back and we started going out."

"I read *Whimsical Death*." That was Robin's nonfiction book, which had made a lot of money and spread his name everywhere. "So I can just hang somewhere else when he's staying over," Phillip told me with a man-of-the-world air.

"We'll talk about that later. It's not going to be a problem. And Robin's out of town right now anyway." But I had to call him, and right away. Robin would be hurt if I didn't tell him about Poppy as soon as possible. "Now, let me go inside and let them know I have to take the rest of the afternoon off, and we'll go over to my new house. I told you I'd moved, right?"

"Sure."

"Okay, then." I still had my purse clutched in my left hand. I dug out my car keys and pointed out the Volvo to my brother. "You go wait in there while I run in for just a second."

"Okay," he said.

I started in the back door of the library, wondering what kind of fool I was to give my car keys to a wandering teenager, and I prayed with all my heart that he would be there when I came back.

Explaining to Sam wasn't easy, but then talking to Sam was becoming increasingly difficult. Sam was getting crankier as he got older, and since he was only in his early fifties, he had a lot of room to spare. He'd lost his perfect secretary a few months before, and he hadn't replaced her. He couldn't find anyone who even gave a hint that someday she might be almost as good as the lamented Patricia. I wondered how Sam's wife was taking his prolonged grief. I didn't know her very well, but Marva had been a junior high algebra teacher a long time, and I didn't think she'd put up with much foolishness.

To my overwhelming relief, Phillip was in the car when I opened the door. Not only was he in the car but he was sound asleep. His head was tilted back on the cushion, and when I slid into the driver's seat, I noticed that Phillip had a few long hairs on his chin. I almost burst into tears, and that would have been terrible. I drove to my house as gently as anyone can drive, and when we got there, I maneuvered my little brother (now only chronologically smaller) into the kitchen from the garage, and then into the guest bedroom. He was just barely awake.

"You get into the shower, and then you climb in the bed. I'll wash your clothes while you're asleep," I said. "I'll even call your mother for you, if that's okay."

"Would you?" Phillip was transparently grateful for that. I probably should not have offered, but I couldn't let them worry a minute longer than necessary about their son, and he was clearly in no shape for an emotional confrontation.

I kept a robe hanging in the closet in the guest room. I pointed it out to Phillip, who looked at it as if he'd never seen such a garment before. I left to give him a little privacy, and in a short time I heard the shower running—and running, and running, and running. Just when I was about to go into the bathroom to see if he'd drowned, the water cut off. I caught a glimpse of Phillip shuffling from the bathroom back into the bedroom, the robe swathed around him. His clothes—and two towels—were in a heap on the floor of the steamy bathroom, and I automatically went through the pockets of his grimy blue jeans so I wouldn't wash anything I wasn't supposed to.

I fished out his wallet, a couple of wadded tissues, a pocketknife, some loose change, and two sealed condoms.

Okay, I was horrified. Legally, my brother couldn't even drive by himself!

I had to sit down and collect myself for a minute. I was reacting as if I were Phillip's mother—and I was old enough to be Phillip's mother—but I *wasn't*. I was his big sister. Phillip had a perfectly functional mother, who admittedly thought I was the devil incarnate, but other than that, she seemed to be a reasonable woman.

I realized that in all the fluster of his arrival I hadn't asked Phillip exactly why he'd turned up on my doorstep. He'd said that my dad had cheated on his mother, which was all too easy to imagine, but that just didn't seem like a motivation for hitchhiking across the country. I thought something more must have happened for Phillip to taken such drastic action . . . though it probably hadn't seemed as scary to Phillip as it would to me, I suddenly realized. At his age, maybe Phillip didn't appreciate the evils of the world.

On the other hand, he had discovered at the age of six that bad things could and did happen to him, and I didn't know if that was a lesson that could be forgotten, no matter how young the learner. When he'd lived in Atlanta, I'd kept him for the weekend fairly often, so my dad and Betty Jo could have some couple time. And I'd enjoyed that a lot. But one weekend, Phillip had been abducted while he'd been staying with me, and he would have been killed in a horrible way if I hadn't shown up when I did; actually, if it hadn't been for Robin, Phillip and I both would have been killed. I'd bought us a little time, and the crisis had passed, but since then, my dad and Betty Jo had acted as though I'd caused the incident. They'd maintained that seeing me would further traumatize Phillip, and by moving to California and finding jobs there, they'd made sure I'd have to keep my distance. I'd only renewed unmonitored contact with my brother when he'd gotten his own computer. The first person he'd sent an E-mail to—after about twenty of his best friends—had been me. I'd been so proud.

It was time to face the music, whatever tune might be playing today. I looked up my dad's home number and punched it in.

"Hello?" The voice was Betty Jo's, and she was strung tightly.

"It's Aurora," I said. "I have Phillip."

"Oh thank God!" Betty Jo burst into tears. "Phil, pick up the other phone. Phillip's at your daughter's!"

"Is he okay?" my father asked.

"He seems to be fine. He's asleep right now." I hesitated, then decided Phillip's adventures were his to relate. "I told him I was calling you."

"How did he get there? What—did you ask him to come see you? We checked his computer, and we found out he'd been sending you E-mails."

Strike. I rolled my eyes, though no one was there to get the effect. "Then you know that I didn't invite him here. I would never do that without talking to you first. As far as I can tell, this was completely his idea. He said there was trouble at home." Counterstrike.

There was a long period of silence, way over there in California.

"Well, not to get into it now," my dad began, and Betty Jo

said sharply, "He walked in on Phil while Phil was sticking it to another woman. Well, not even a woman. A *girl*."

This was more than I wanted to know, but it did explain Phillip's extreme reaction. I was willing to bet Phillip knew the girl.

"You two have to work out your own problems. I don't want to hear the graphic details," I said flatly. "Let Phillip stay here for a while, okay? I'd love to have him, and this house is big."

"But you have a boyfriend now," Betty Jo protested.

"If you're accusing me of setting a bad example by perhaps sleeping with my steady friend from time to time, well, I think Phillip already knows about the birds and the bees. Especially in view of what you just told me." Hell, he already *engages* in sex, I thought.

"He would have this week off for Thanksgiving anyway," Betty Jo said. For once, she sounded subdued. "So, maybe if he could stay for a week . . . we may work things out, at least decide what we're going to do."

"That might be a good thing," my father said cautiously. "Thanks, Doll."

I hated being called "Doll." But he'd always called me that, and he wasn't going to change now.

"If you need longer, he can go to school here," I said, as if accomplishing that would be a snap of the fingers. Of course, I hadn't the faintest clue how to enroll a teenager for school, but how hard could it be?

"Okay," said Betty Jo. "Okay." She sounded as though she were trying to persuade herself that this was a good idea. "I can't believe he went all the way across the country on his own. When I think of what could have happened to him . . ."

"Roe, thanks," my father said. For the first time, he talked to me like I was an adult. "I know you'll take care of him. I bet he just needs someone to talk to."

"I'll bet that's it," I said, trying to sound reassuring. "He'll be fine. I'll watch out for him."

"No new murders, right?" my father asked nervously.

Not since this morning.

"No, Dad," I said, as if that was silliest idea I'd ever heard. "Ha ha ha."

"Say hello to your mother for us," Betty Jo said, a sop toward courtesy. "And have Phillip call us himself the minute he gets up."

"He has a lot to answer for," my father said grimly.

"So do you!" Betty Jo told him. "Good-bye, Roe."

I was so glad to end the conversation, I almost danced.

Chapter Three

The rest of my family was probably wondering where I was. I made a face in my bedroom mirror. When I'd gotten up that morning, my most pressing problem had been whether or not my only pair of intact panty hose was clean.

While Phillip slept, I'd checked Robin's itinerary and then called him at a store called Murder by the Book, in Houston. The young man who'd answered the phone had been very civil about getting Robin to the phone as soon as he'd been convinced I actually knew Robin and was not a crazed fan who'd dreamed up a clever way to talk to him.

"Did you win?" I asked him.

"No," Robin said, though he sounded cheerful. "But the panel was standing room only, and my signing line went out of the room. Awards are nice, but sales are better."

"How's your signing at the bookstore going?"

"Just about to get under way. I'm signing with Margaret Maron, and the store is jam-packed."

So he had a group of people waiting for him.

"I just have some things I had to tell you," I said anxiously.

"You're all right?" His voice was suddenly sharp. "Your step-father okay?"

"I'm fine, Robin," I said, my voice soft. "And John is healthy. But John David's wife, Poppy? She got killed this morning."

"In a car?" he said cautiously.

"No, she was murdered."

"Oh, I'm so sorry. From your voice, I'm betting you found her."

"I'm afraid so."

"Shall I come home right now?"

"Bless you for offering. But there's more."

A long pause. "I'm listening," he said, just when I was about to ask if he'd hung up. "Did you get arrested?" He wasn't entirely joking.

"My brother Phillip is here."

"Your brother? Oh, sure! The little guy who was staying with you all those years ago! Hasn't he been living in Pomona? What's he doing in Lawrenceton?"

"He's at least five eight or nine now," I said. "And he got here by running away from home."

"Uh-oh. You talked to your dad and the new wife?"

"She's not so new now, and my dad cheated on her. Phillip walked in on this little episode," I said. "That's supposed to be the reason he ran away, but I'm finding that a little, I don't know, extreme."

"So, what do you think the real reason is?"

"Maybe time will tell. He's going to stay here for at least a week."

"Hmm. Okay."

"Yeah, I know," I said. "He needs this right now."

"No problem. If you don't need me instantly, I'll just do two more signings tomorrow, one in Austin and one in Dallas, and then I'll fly home from there."

"I sure will be glad to see you," I said. "But you keep up with your signing schedule." I was flattered and delighted that Robin would offer to do that, but at the same time, it scared me. Had we rushed into this comfortable intimacy? I had just adjusted to being alone in my widowhood when Robin had unexpectedly returned to Lawrenceton. It hadn't taken long to resume our relationship of a few years ago. Though I hadn't yet brought myself to discuss my doubts with Robin, I had been thinking the past couple of weeks that we might have hurried things too much. But the minute Robin had left for his convention, I'd missed him. Now I found myself looking forward to his return, not only for the pleasure of his physical presence but because I'd be glad to have his support and his insight—especially in matters regarding Phillip. After all, Robin had been a teenage boy once upon a time.

"I have to go sign some books," Robin said gently.

The doorbell chimed. "And I have to go answer the door," I told him. "Just let me know when you're coming in, and I'll pick you up at the airport."

"I left my car there so I could bring my mother back with me," he reminded me. "Her plane gets in right after mine. I'll call you when I'm back."

When I remembered that Robin would not exactly be at my disposal when he returned, I was so distracted by my disappointment that I answered the door without looking through the peephole. That was a bad habit, and one I'd have to break. When I'd lived out in the country, I'd heard every visitor before they'd gotten to the door, and I'd had time to look out the window to find out who it was. Town living was different.

Bubba Sewell, my lawyer (and possibly my next state representative), was looming in my doorway. Cartland Sewell was a big man anyway, and he'd put on the pounds since he'd married my beautiful friend Lizanne.

"Is it true?" he asked.

"Hello. Glad to see you. Why don't you come in," I said, waving my hand down the hall. I knew I sounded pissed off, and I was.

"I'm a little too upset for the amenities, Aurora," he said. When he was in the house, I got a better look at him. Bubba had been crying. I reminded myself to call him Cartland; since he'd gotten into politics, Cartland had been the name of choice.

"What's put a bee in your bonnet?"

"Poppy," he said. He seemed to have trouble getting the name out.

I looked at him for a long moment. "So the rumor is true."

"Yeah, it's true. I was actually thinking of . . ."

"You weren't going to leave Lizanne?" I sounded every bit as horrified as I felt. "You idiot!"

Cartland looked as though he was thinking of slapping me. And I would almost have deserved it if he had; not that I think hitting is ever excusable, but I'd been unbearably tactless.

"Poppy was so wonderful," he said. "She was so beautiful, and she was . . . in intimate moments . . . she, ah . . ."

"Don't want to know," I said. "Too much information!"

He looked a little embarrassed. "Sorry. But you just don't know," he said. "She was everything to me. I wanted her to run off with me."

"Meaning an end to your political ambitions, your marriage, and your relationship with your children?"

"I could have patched things up politically, eventually," he said, sounding as if he really believed it. "Lizanne and I don't get along anyway. And how could she stop me from having a relationship with my own sons?"

54

"There's still a lot you don't know about Lizanne, if you believe that."

"Roe, Lizanne is a great woman, and she's beautiful and peaceful and she's a good mother to the boys, but . . ." He waved his hands in frustration.

"But what?" I snapped.

"But Lizanne's so *dumb!*" he said. It was as if the words had been ripped out of him.

I opened my mouth to rebut his blunt assessment, but I made myself think over what he'd said. Poppy hadn't exactly been a rocket scientist, but she was shrewd, and practical, and a follower of world and local events. And she was articulate in voicing her ideas and opinions. That's why she'd been tapped to be an Uppity Woman. Poppy was—had been—a very different animal than Lizanne, who admittedly had very limited interests. Lizanne's intellectual boundaries had never seemed to bother any man before, as I reminded Cartland now.

"You know as well as I know, Roe, that being attracted to someone physically is not the same as being her constant companion."

"But you're not Lizanne's constant companion. You go out almost every night to this or that meeting, and everyone knows you're counting on a political future."

"And the reason I did all that was at least partly to get away from Lizanne."

"I've never heard of anyone running for office to avoid a spouse." Cartland wanted to be our next state representative.

"I've done a lot of things lately I never thought I'd do."

I didn't like the sound of that. I took a step away from him. "When did you last see Poppy?"

"I saw her last night. John David was going to be at some meeting, so I stopped by."

"How'd you get in?"

"Went to the front door. I figured it might as well be an open visit, since it wasn't going to last that long, not with John David due back within the hour. I helped her bathe Chase," he said tenderly.

I could have beaten him on the head with a baseball bat. I was willing to bet Lizanne could have used some help bathing Brandon and Davis. Why did this man think he was any smarter than his wife? And I'd been considering voting for this jerk!

"When did you leave?" I asked after an appreciable pause to regain control.

"I guess about . . . eight-thirty. She was wearing a bathrobe, since she'd gotten wet bathing Chase," he said dreamily. "Her hair was all curly from the humidity in the bathroom. She told me she'd think about divorcing John David. I think she would have done it."

"And who do you think killed her?" I asked, conversationally throwing cold water on his fantasies.

"Her husband," Cartland said, and he didn't look like an overweight lawyer anymore. He looked dangerous. "I know it was John David."

"And how do you know that?"

"She must have told him," Cartland said reasonably. "She must have told him she was going to leave him for me, and he killed her for it."

"Where were you all morning?"

"Oh for God's sake, Roe! I went to my office and worked until about eleven, when I left to speak at the Rotary Club in Mecklinburg." Mecklinburg was about fifteen miles away. "I was there, in front of about forty people, for the next hour and a half."

I was going to have to talk to Lizanne soon, and I dreaded it. Those embroidered straps were still stuffed into my purse, and if Lizanne hadn't gone to Poppy's house and thrown them down in the driveway to let Poppy know she knew the situation, I was a Jersey girl.

"Okay, get out."

"What?"

"Get out. I've listened to as much as I'm going to."

Cartland looked stunned. "But Roe, I was trying to explain—"

"Go to hell. You've just told me you've been cheating on your wife, who is a good friend of mine, with the wife of my brother-in-law; and you are evidently assuming that your wife would be happy to raise two sons of yours on her own, while you raise John David's boy! You actually think Poppy would have left John David? You're a moron! Get out! And keep your grief to yourself!"

I had herded Cartland to the front door, snapping at his heels like a sheepdog, and now he left in something of a hurry. I slammed the door shut and glowered at it.

For a few minutes, I hovered outside Phillip's door, afraid we might have wakened him. But there was no movement from the room, no rustle of sheets. Struck with the sudden fear that he'd crawled out of the window, I opened the door a crack, and was reassured by the sight of a big bare foot hanging off the end of the bed.

I eased the door shut as silently as I could, then I hovered in the hall, trying to think of what I should do next.

Amazingly, it was only 5:00 P.M. Since it was November, the daylight was almost gone, but I thought of some errands I needed to run. I hastily wrote a note and stuck it to Phillip's doorknob. After checking his clean clothes for sizes, I pitched them back in the dryer and set off for the small branch of Davidson's that Lawrenceton was proud to have. I got my brother a package of underwear, a bundle of socks, a pair of jeans and a pair of khakis, and two shirts, a T-shirt and a nice sports shirt, and a jacket. Crossing over to Wal-Mart, I quickly purchased a comb and brush, a toothbrush, and a razor and some shaving cream. I grabbed some gloves, too; his hands had been bare.

Satisfied that I could clothe and clean him, I made one more stop, at the grocery store. I had a dim awareness that teenage boys ate a lot, but I wasn't really sure what they ate a lot of. I got some frozen pizzas, some Bagel Bites, and some egg rolls. I got some milk, too, and a bottle of soda.

By the time I'd unloaded all this booty and folded Phillip's dry clothes, it was seven o'clock. I called Mother to find out what was happening. She sounded exhausted and tearful, and she said John wasn't feeling very well. After a long, long "interview" with Arthur Smith, John David had arrived at the house to assume his role as chief mourner. Mother thanked me from the heart for running him to ground and getting him to go into SPACOLEC with Bryan Pascoe. "Avery was really angry for a while, but I think he sees now that you were right," Mother said.

"I'm sorry if you've had to take the fallout from people who were really mad at me," I said. The thought did cross my mind that it seemed to take very little to make Avery angry with me. "I had to stay with Phillip, to get him straightened out."

"I do wish all this hadn't happened at the same time." I knew Mother had to have been really distressed even, to voice that much complaint about something that simply couldn't be helped. "John told Avery that you'd done more practical things to help our family than had even occurred to him. John, that is."

"That was sweet of John," I said, abruptly aware of how fond I was of my stepfather. He was a better man than my real father. I felt cold and disloyal for that thought instantly, but I made myself face it and admit it was true. God wasn't going to strike me dead for admitting my own father wasn't a perfect man.

"How long is the boy staying?' my mother asked. Her voice was a little stiff. She had always had a hard time with the existence of another child of my father's, but I hoped she would get over it right now.

"I think at least for this week. He's out for Thanksgiving break now. I got the impression that things are going pretty badly between Dad and Betty Jo." No point in spelling out my father's peccadilloes. As far as my mother was concerned, it was an old story. "Phillip got caught up in the middle of that. He made his way over here, and I hope he can stay for a while. He's so big now, Mother, you wouldn't recognize him."

"Just like Phil, messing up a second chance to get it right," my mother said.

This was such a vulnerable way to put it, and her voice was so unhappy, it was hard for me to believe I was listening to the same stiff-backed woman who had created her own fortune after my dad had left her. The shock of Poppy's death had cracked Mother wide open.

"Have Poppy's parents come in yet?"

"No, they'll be here in about an hour, I think. Then poor John will have to go through another emotional scene."

"Why?"

"Well, he feels obligated."

"No, Mother. John David is obligated, not his dad. You make John go to bed, tell him John David and Avery can handle the Wynns. In fact, they can all go to Avery and Melinda's. For that matter, I can put the Wynns up. I have another bedroom, and all I have to do is go make the bed."

That would make my life even even more confusing, but I wanted to help my mother any way I could.

"I'll give you a call back on that. But you're right," she said resolutely. "John needs to rest more than he needs to worry. Avery and Melinda are perfectly capable of handling whatever comes up. And poor John, he keeps thinking that he and John David are so alike because John lost his first wife and now John David's lost his . . . but the situation is totally different. Tell me, where was John David when you tracked him down?"

"Ah, he was visiting a friend." I closed my eyes at my own stupidity. That had sounded pretty lame.

"Visiting a friend, in the afternoon of a workday." My mother's eyebrows were probably arched clear up to her hairline. "I'll be willing to bet the friend is pretty and female and wasn't wearing work clothes when she opened the door."

I winced. "Well . . ."

"You don't need to say anything else," Mother said. "And Poppy, bless her heart, was just as bad. People these days are just like rabbits. Everything's sex. No duty, no loyalty. By the way, where's Robin?"

I didn't like her thought association there, and she was not the first person who'd asked me today where Robin was. We weren't engaged and we weren't talking about marriage. We weren't a locked-in official couple.

"He's in Houston. He'll be back day after tomorrow," I said, sounding just as stiff as my mother.

"Do you think he and Phillip will get along?"

"Mother, you have enough to worry about right now. I believe I can handle Phillip and Robin."

"You're right. Well, let me go. I have to convince John he's not responsible for the whole social process surrounding Poppy's death, and I have to remind John David that he *is*."

"Good luck, Mother. I'll be there when I can. Remember, if the Wynns need a place to stay, the door is open. Just let me know thirty minutes ahead of time."

"Thanks, baby. I'll talk to you soon."

Because I couldn't seem to sit still, I went to the third bedroom and made the bed, just in case. If the Wynns drove in from their retirement community in the next hour, it would be at least another hour after that before they'd be ready to retire, and they might well want to go see Poppy's body. Could they? Or would her body have already been sent to Atlanta for autopsy?

I just didn't know.

I yawned, a big jaw-cracking yawn. I'd run out of steam.

Phillip shambled into the living room and plopped down on the couch opposite my chair. He was looking much better, and he was smiling.

"Thanks for the clothes and stuff," he said. "It was neat to find the bags in the room when I woke up."

I was glad I'd passed a rack of those drawstring flannel pants at Wal-Mart, because that was what Phillip was wearing, the pants and the sleeveless T-shirt he'd had on under his flannel shirt.

"I was glad to do it."

"Listen, what's happening about your sister-in-law?" he asked.

I told him what the situation was, and he was openmouthed at the awfulness of the adult world. Moments like this reminded me how young my brother really was.

"I'll bet you're hungry," I said.

"Oh," he said. "Oh, yes. Just point me at the kitchen. I can fix stuff myself."

"Has your mom been working these past few years?" I felt guilty for not knowing this basic fact about Phillip's life.

"Yeah, ever since we moved to Pomona, she's worked at an insurance company as a clerk."

"I talked to her."

He froze in the act of turning on the oven. He'd already

found the box of Bagel Bites in the freezer compartment. "Um, how is she?" There were so many layers to his voice—guilt, anger, grief—it was hard to pick the dominant emotion.

"Glad you're okay. Relieved she knows where you are. Not too happy that you're with me."

"I'm sorry," he mumbled.

"You don't have to apologize. She wants you to be safe and happy more than anything."

"Then why can't they act like it?" he said furiously. "Why can't they act like parents, instead of switching partners like they were kids?"

This was a complex bunch of ideas. I was beginning to get the feeling that there was no simple way to raise a teenager, or even to answer the questions one might ask you. Was every conversation with my brother going to be as loaded as this one? The prospect was exhausting.

"People don't always do what I wish they would, either," I said. In fact, people stubbornly lived their lives as they wanted, without regard to me, to an amazing degree. I suppressed this observation, as I expected it wouldn't find favor with Phillip.

We talked for over an hour while Phillip ate (and ate, and ate). I told him about the possible arrival of Poppy's parents and introduced him to Madeleine, who came in while he was wiping his mouth with a napkin.

"Is that a cat?" he asked, regarding Madeleine with startled eyes.

"Sure," I said, trying not to sound offended. "She's really old, I know. . . ."

"She's really *fat*."

"Well, that, too. She doesn't get as much exercise as she used to, now that we live in town."

"She probably can't walk more than five feet," Phillip said scornfully.

"I guess she is a little dumpy," I said, wondering how long it had been since I'd actually looked at Madeleine and really evaluated her. "You know, she must be—let's see, when my friend Jane died and left me Madeleine, she was at least six years old. That was at least seven years ago. Wow, Madeleine, you *are* really old." I tended to forget between vet appointments.

"Almost as old as I am," my brother said.

That was a startling thought. I wondered if any of Madeleine's kittens were still alive. I scrabbled around in my memory for the names of the kind people who'd adopted them. That led to another thought, one I should have mentioned earlier.

"Oh, your mom said it was okay for you to stay this week," I told him.

Phillip hadn't asked, but he'd been anxious; I could see his shoulders relax. I scolded myself for not having told him sooner. A deep sigh left him, as if the weight of the world had squeezed the air out of his lungs.

"I'll clean up the kitchen this time," I told my brother, "but from now on, when you use it, you wash it. That's the rule."

"Thanks," he said. "I clean up at home, honest. Sometimes I vacuum and stuff, when it's on my list."

I'd done the few dishes, wiped down the kitchen surfaces, and straightened up the living room a little, when Phillip, who'd been wandering around, said, "He doesn't really look that different." He was looking at a newspaper article about Robin's latest book. I'd clipped it to give Robin when he returned.

"I don't think so, either," I said, trying to sound casual.

"And you guys are dating."

"Yes."

"Are you . . . um . . . really tight?"

"We're not dating each other exclusively," I said, though I hadn't dated anyone else since Robin had returned to town. On the other hand, I hadn't dated anyone before then, either. But we hadn't talked about exclusivity.

"If he asked you to marry him, what would you say?"

"I would say it's none of your business," I said, stating it more harshly than I'd intended. "No, I'm sorry I said that." Phillip's face had flushed. "Truly, Phillip, I married Martin really quickly, and though I'm not sorry and never have been, I guess now I feel a little . . . cautious about doing the same thing again." Then I felt like a hypocrite. I was as quick in making up my mind as I ever had been. I was just trying to put a mature face on for Phillip's benefit. But I knew I would never stop making up my mind quickly. That was my nature.

The Wynns pulled to the curb twenty minutes later. Avery, who'd called me to announce their arrival, had led them over in his car. He came inside for just a minute to reintroduce us. Avery looked awful, but then, I was sure I looked no better.

"The police are really asking questions," he whispered as he gave me a hug.

"Well, sure," I said, surprised. "That would be the way to find out who did such an awful thing to Poppy." Avery was speaking as though asking questions would lead to unpleasant revelations, when what we wanted, as a family, was the truth. But I was grateful to him for escorting the Wynns in and easing the way, so I tried to be friendly.

I had known the Wynns only slightly, and that when I was more or less a child, so it was almost like meeting them for the first time. Sandy and Marvin Wynn were into their seventies, but they were both healthy and lean as whips. They'd always eaten correctly, walked four miles a day, and done things like taking square-dancing classes, or tai chi for beginners. Poppy, their late-in-life and unexpected child, had not had a chance of being included in this harmonious twosome. As much as they seemed to care for their daughter, when she'd begun to act out in high school, the Wynns hadn't had a clue how to handle the problem. They'd clung to their sanity and hoped that Hurricane Poppy would lose its impetus in time.

Tonight, they were exhausted and grief-stricken and stunned. Somehow or other, they'd seen Poppy steered safely into the harbor of marriage and motherhood in suburbia, and now she had been killed in a horrible way, despite her achievement of a smooth life.

I had no idea what the Wynns needed. I didn't know whether to try to get them to talk, to hustle them into their bedroom, or to feed them. . . . I'd had enough experience with grief to know that its effects can be unpredictable.

Phillip shook their hands, though I don't think he registered with them. Sandy hugged me as though we were very close, which we had never been, and Marvin hugged me, too, murmuring into my ear that he was so grateful to me for putting them up; the drive had been so long and confusing. . . .

"Have you eaten?" I asked.

"Yes, I think we stopped a couple of hours ago," Sandy said. "I think we ate. I'm not hungry. Are you, Marvin?"

I remembered Marvin Wynn's hair as being red. Now it was snowy white. His face was lean and lined, and he had broad shoulders. He looked as though normally he could climb a mountain without breathing hard, and Sandy could probably drag a sled through the snow for a few miles. But right now, their faces were gray and sagging. Marvin shook his head. "No, not hungry."

I showed them the bathroom they would share with Phillip (which I had restored to its orderly state) and then their bedroom. I'd opened boxes of tissues and left them on the bedside tables. There was free closet space and a couple of free drawers, extra blankets at the foot of the bed.

"If you need anything during the night, just come get me," I said, showing them where my bedroom was. "Otherwise, there are cold drinks in the refrigerator, muffins in the bread box, and the coffeepot is right here."

"We don't drink coffee," Sandy said earnestly. "But thank you. We'll just wash up and go to bed, if that's okay."

"Anything you want is fine with me," I said. "Here's a key to the house. You may need it tomorrow." I put it out on the counter, making sure they couldn't miss it in the morning.

"You're being so kind," Sandy said, and her eyes overflowed. "Everyone is being so kind." Marvin had put their suitcases in the bedroom, and now he put his arm around his wife. They went into the small room I'd prepared for them. I heard the door close.

I stared after them, the memory of the misery I'd plumbed after my husband died yawning wide at my feet. I would be useless the next day if I let myself step over the brink back into that awful time. With all the will I had, I wrenched myself back into the here and now. My brother's alarmed face was staring at me. He really did look only fifteen at that second.

"Phillip, everything I told them—coffeepot, muffins, if you need me—I would have told you before we went to bed. Anything you want to ask?"

"Is there anything in the refrigerator you don't want me to eat? Anything you're saving for supper tomorrow night or something?"

"No, feel free. Eat me out of hearth and home." I could tell he was trying to be a great houseguest, and that touched me.

"What do we do tomorrow?" he asked.

"Tomorrow, I'm going to have to do stuff connected with

poor Poppy dying," I said. "And I have to work, too. In fact, I have to get up early in the morning and go to work. I'll leave a note here with my phone number on it. Why don't you use the computer in the study to send your folks an E-mail? The password is on a slip of pink paper in the drawer."

"The study? The room with all the windows and books?"

"Right. Sometimes Robin works in there, if his apartment gets to feeling too small. So don't rearrange the piles of books."

He snorted, as if that was ludicrous. "I'm not that much of a reader," he explained. "That book of Robin's was the first one I'd read in months. I'm not much on school, either."

Meaning, I gathered, that the day he touched books voluntarily was a day that should be marked on the calendar. I suppressed a sigh. It was hard to believe a brother of mine wasn't a reader. I had never been able to figure out what non-readers *did*. Maybe, during Phillip's stay, I'd find out.

I knew he had other pastimes. I was thinking, of course, of the condoms, and I thought about health issues. I tried to smile at him. "Tomorrow, you and I are going to talk about some stuff."

His smile faded. "Uh-oh."

"It won't be as bad as all that," I said. I hugged him, and just when I was about to let him go, I pulled him tighter instead. "Phillip, I'm so glad to see you. I was wondering if I'd ever get to see you again. I'm sorry you've been having a tough time. I'm happy you're here."

He patted my back awkwardly and made some indeterminate noises. I'd embarrassed the hell out of him, and he was fifteen and didn't know what to do about it. After a second or two, I realized he was crying. I could only guess at the correct response. I remained still, my arms around him, rubbing his back gently. He wiped his eyes on the shoulder of my sweater, a childish gesture that somehow won me over completely.

"Good night," he said in a clogged voice, then retreated to his room so quickly, I only glimpsed a reddened face.

"Good night!" I called after him, keeping my voice low so I wouldn't disturb Marvin and Sandy Wynn.

The silence sank into my bones. With a deep sense of relief, I went into my own bedroom. It had been a very long day, maybe twice as long as my days usually were, at least in terms of emotional content. Either Poppy's death or Phillip's arrival would have given me a full slate of thoughts and feelings, and to have both at one time had sent me into overload. I needed to sleep more than I needed anything, and the only thing that would have made my bed look more welcoming would have been a shock of red hair on the other pillow.

I sat on the side of the bed and realized that what I missed was not Robin exactly, and not sex exactly. And it wasn't missing Martin, either, though still at rare moments I felt I was being stabbed, the flash of grief was so intense. What I was missing at this moment was the state of being married. I missed having someone there to share the little moments of my day. I missed having someone someone to whom I was the most important person on earth. I missed being part of a team, whose job was always to back each other up.

Even the least perfect marriage has moments that are wonderful, and mine had been far from the least perfect.

I made myself go into my bathroom and begin my nightly routine. I was being ridiculous. My sister-in-law had died an awful death this morning, and here I was, blubbering about not having anyone to sleep with tonight. I was a ridiculous human being. I should know better, I told myself. There were far more terrifying things in the world, and one of those things was very close.

Somewhere in our town, tonight, a person was talking, or

brushing his teeth, or making love to a spouse. Yet that person knew he—or she—had committed murder. That person had knocked Poppy down with vicious blows. That person had watched the life drain out of one of the most vital women I'd ever known . . . and done nothing to help her.

Now that was something to brood about.

Chapter Four

I woke up when my alarm went off the next morning. It was 6:30, and the glass doors onto the patio showed me it was a beautiful day. I felt wonderful for about thirty seconds, until I remembered the events of the previous day, which had been a Monday.

The rest of the week wasn't going to be good.

Look on it as a challenge, I told myself briskly. Something rebellious within me muttered back that it was sick of challenges.

But I was now an official Uppity Woman, and I would not let a bad Monday ruin the rest of my week.

This new point of view got me through my morning shower and my simple hair/makeup/clothes routine. After I'd made my bed, I went out to see what I could do for my company before I left for work. I was only a part-time employee, but today I had to work six hours, and tomorrow, too.

A glance into Phillip's room told me he was still asleep. The

Wynns were already up and gone, their bedroom door left half-open. They'd positioned a note where I'd left the key, telling me that they were going out for breakfast, then over to my mother's, and probably from there to the police department.

John David should be with them, and I hoped he had realized that, too. I wondered if the police were going to let them into the house anytime soon. I also wondered if they had arranged for anyone to clean up the mess in Poppy's kitchen. I knew there were professional crime-scene cleanup teams in Los Angeles and other big cities, but there sure wasn't one in Lawrenceton, and I didn't think there was such a company in Atlanta. But if there was, would they come out to Lawrenceton? Wouldn't such a service cost a great deal?

I poured myself a cup of just-perked coffee and buttered my slice of toast, so deep in my thoughts that I hardly noticed what I was doing. I was really hooked on the idea of getting that house cleaned.

I decided I would be willing to pay the fee as my way of easing the burden on my mother's family. How could I find out? My Atlanta telephone book was an old one, scrounged from a friend in the city who'd been about to toss it. I wasn't sure what the Yellow Pages listing would be under. I would call SPACOLEC and ask Arthur if he'd heard about any such service. I wasn't real excited about initiating any contact with Arthur, in case he had a relapse into thinking he was in love with me, but it was probably the quickest way to get that information. I looked up the general number and punched it in. It was very early, but with a murder case going, Arthur would be at his desk, I was fairly sure.

While I was talking to the dispatcher, I spotted a small crumpled wad of paper on my polished wooden floor, under one of the barstools at the breakfast bar. I stooped to pick it up, frowning. I don't like littering, either inside or outside. In fact,

I've become kind of a crank about neatness, which my mother thinks is hilarious. While Arthur's extension rang, I flattened the little ball out.

The small piece of paper was a receipt from a gas station, the Grabbit Kwik, which was on the highway between Lawrenceton and the interstate. I shrugged, then walked around the counter so I could toss the slip into the garbage. I was mostly thinking about the phone call.

Then the time printed on the slip registered. Whoever had dropped it had gotten gas the morning before at 10:22, right about when I'd been talking to Poppy on the phone.

My fingers closed around the slip of paper. It had a slick feel, and the wrinkles in it looked gray.

"Hello?" Arthur's voice.

"Arthur, this is Roe."

After a moment's silence, Arthur said, "You call to confess?"

I laughed. I hoped that was the correct response. On the other hand, laughing about my sister-in-law's death was really outrageous. "No, it's not that easy," I said, trying to sound very sober. "I wanted to ask you if you knew of a crime-scene cleanup business in Atlanta? And if I could find someone willing to do that, when could they get into the house?"

"Yes, there's a crime cleanup business there," Arthur said. "The guy who started it up came by the office last week and left some cards. It's called Scene Clean, and this guy named Zachary Lee is the one who owns it. For all I know, he's the sole employee, too. He used to be a lab tech for the Atlanta Police Department."

"Thanks. Can you give me his number?"

Arthur dug up the card and read the information to me.

"Probably later this afternoon will be okay, as far as him getting in," Arthur said. "I think your hiring him is a good idea, if what I've read about crime-scene cleanup teams applies to

Zach Lee. It could very well be that John David's insurance will pay for the bill, or maybe crime victims' compensation."

"I never thought of that." I'd made up my mind to shoulder the cost, but if insurance would cover it, all to the good.

"I hope they can get the . . . well, the stains . . . out of that rug by the back door," Arthur said.

I found that comment somewhat odd. It was a second before I responded, "The one Poppy liked so much, the one she found at some flea market? Ah . . . I guess that would be a good thing. But all I care about is getting John David and Chase back into the house so they can get clothes and things they need."

"Sure." Arthur seemed to be coming out of his little fugue. "Well, let me know how it goes with Zachary Lee."

"Thanks," I said again. "I'll give this man a call after I check with John David." I started to say something about the Grabbit Kwik charge slip, and then I realized that by itself, it was meaningless. So, someone had stopped for gas between Atlanta and Lawrenceton? Lots of people did that every day. I needed to sit down and think of exactly who had been in my house, before this piece of paper acquired any significance.

"Roe, you're not close to John David, are you?"

I thought about it for a few seconds. "Nope, I guess not."

"If you knew something about him, in relation to Poppy's death, you'd tell me, wouldn't you?"

"Sure," I said promptly, before I could think twice. If I held back, it wouldn't be for the sake of John David, but for his father—as it happened, though, my conscience was clear. That's what I told Arthur.

He made a sort of noise in his throat, an unconvinced sound. "I'll let John David know about getting back in the house," he said. I thanked him again for the Scene Clean information, and my mind had already moved on to the slip on the counter in front of me before I hung up the phone, though I reminded myself to go back over that conversation when I didn't have anything else to worry about.

Who'd been in my house yesterday?

Marvin and Sandy Wynn, my brother, Phillip, and Cartland Sewell—the lawyer formerly known as Bubba. Oh, and Avery; he'd come in briefly, too. Could I have acquired the slip somehow? I pick up things all the time, because I hate litter. My purse is always full of other people's grocery store receipts, rubber bands, paper clips—all sorts of detritus that people leave lying around. It was faintly possible that I'd picked up the receipt myself, stuck it in my pocket or purse for later disposal.

But I tended to discount that theory. For one thing, I would not have rolled it into a ball. I would have folded it. That's just what I do. For another thing, yesterday had been kind of a tense day, what with the newness of being an Uppity Woman, Poppy's tardiness, and then the awful shock of finding her body, and I didn't think my mind had even registered litter all day long.

So, most likely, one of the people who'd come into my house had dropped the receipt. And none of them was supposed to have been anywhere around Grabbit Kwik at that hour of the morning. Marvin and Sandy Wynn were supposedly in their retirement condominium, almost three hours away. Melinda was with me. Cartland was in Mecklinburg, making a speech. Avery was—where had Avery been? At work, exactly where he was supposed to be, most likely. At least Melinda hadn't mentioned Avery being scheduled to do anything out of the ordinary.

But without saying anything to anyone else, I needed to check on all these people, just for my own peace of mind. I could think of no reason why anyone would have wanted Poppy dead, not any reason that made sense to me. I didn't really think John David would marry Romney Burns, now that he was a widower, no matter what Romney might imagine. It was somewhat easier to believe Cartland would have divorced Liz to marry Poppy (which reminded me that I was going to have to have another unpleasant conversation today). But I found myself reluctant to believe that such activity would have been reciprocated: Would Poppy have left John David, cleaved to Cartland? That was hard to imagine.

And Poppy's parents—having gone through so much hell to bring her up, it was highly unlikely they'd have snuffed her out.

My brother Phillip had been on a bus. Or so he said. No witnesses, at least none that he could produce quickly, I was sure. But why on earth would he have been interested in killing Poppy, a woman he didn't even know? Besides, he wouldn't have needed a receipt for gas. He had no vehicle.

Avery seemed happy enough with Melinda. Why would he have laid a hand on his sister-in-law?

But just at a surface level, Avery had had a better chance than anyone to be on that road at that time. He had a secretary, but she only came in in the afternoon. Avery shared a suite of offices, and the secretary, with another CPA, but essentially he worked by himself.

Someone had dropped that receipt on my floor, and none of the people who could have done it should have done it. I just didn't want to imagine that one of them was capable of driving a knife into Poppy.

As I dialed the Atlanta number, I realized something else was bothering me, but for the life of me, I couldn't put my finger on it.

"Scene Clean," said a happy male voice.

I introduced myself and explained the situation.

"Of course, I'd be glad to help you out," Zachary Lee said enthusiastically. I wondered if I were his first customer. "But I have to have the home owner's written permission, you understand. And the responsibility for the bill?"

"I'll be responsible," I said firmly. I could ask John David about the insurance coverage some other time. "Mr. Queensland can give you written permission, and I'll meet you there this afternoon at four, unless I call you and tell you otherwise." I gave the cheerful Mr. Lee my phone numbers, house and cell, John David's number, and the address on Swanson Lane.

Phillip staggered into the bathroom as I hung up. I was relieved to see him, because I had to go to work and we had to discuss what he would do while I was gone. I began to make a list while I waited for him to emerge; he seemed to be taking yet another marathon shower.

I scrawled a number of items on an old envelope. I'd number them later. "When Memorial Service or Funeral?" I wrote, and then, "T'giving." Entries under that included, "turkey," "celery," "sweet pot.," "cran sauce." Mother had invited me over to have Thanksgiving dinner with her and John, Melinda and Avery had been scheduled to go to Melinda's parents' home in Groton, and Poppy and John David had been wavering between accepting an invitation from some college friends or throwing in with my mother's plans. Now, of course, all these arrangements would be in disarray. Poppy's murder—and, to a much lesser extent, the unexpected presence of Phillip—naturally would alter the next few days beyond all recognition. No one in the family would want to think about the holiday, but we would all have to.

I was supposed to work today and tomorrow, though the library would be closed Thursday and Friday. Lawrenceton more or less shuts down on Thanksgiving, though not as much as it used to when I was a kid.

Phillip emerged from the steamy bathroom, wearing the bathrobe again. I was glad to see he looked pretty alert. When I offered toast or cereal, he said he didn't normally eat breakfast right after he rose. I bit my tongue to keep from pointing out he'd been up for a good thirty minutes in the shower, and he poured a glass of orange juice and sat by me on one of the high stools at the counter.

"You look ready for work," he observed. "So, what's my agenda for today?"

"If you left the bathroom in a mess, you need to go in and clean it. Remember, the Wynns are staying here," I said. Phillip looked distinctly alarmed and unhappy at continuing to live in such close proximity to unknown old people who were in the middle of such a crisis. Tough.

"Also," I said, "here is a pad and a pen. There are going to be lots of phone calls today. Please write down each one: the time, the caller, and the message. Here's my phone number at work. Every two hours, call me and let me hear the list. Some of these I'll have to act on pretty quickly. Now, there's a remote possibility people will bring food by here if they hear the Wynns are staying with me. You accept the dish, write down any instructions about heating or refrigerating it, and who brought it."

Phillip nodded. He seemed a little dazed.

"Here's the remote control for the TV. Here's the remote for the DVD player." I went over to the television cabinet and opened a door. "Here are my DVDs." I went into the kitchen, opened a drawer, extracted a key from a plastic tray. "Here's another key to the house. If you leave, please write a note saying where you've gone and when you'll be back. Do you have a watch?"

Phillip shook his head.

"Okay." I handed him a watch that had been Martin's. I'd

come across it that morning when I was putting on my makeup. It wasn't an expensive watch; it was the one he'd been wearing when we got married, and I'd given him a fancier one our first Christmas together. Martin had chucked this watch in a drawer and I'd automatically packed it when I moved. It was just a mass-produced watch; there were probably millions identical to it. It was absurd to feel a pang over a bit of assembly-line metal that ran on a battery.

Phillip gave me a sharp look as he slid the watch on his arm. "I won't break it," he said defensively. My face must have been showing more than I'd thought.

"I don't think you will," I said, and hugged him, much to his surprise. "And the world won't end if you do." I hoped I wasn't being too demanding. Not only would someone performing all those little tasks be genuinely helpful; I would know where Phillip was. I'd given him a key because I wanted to show I trusted him. I wasn't sure I really did. I could not stop Phillip if he decided to leave while I was at work, and it would be ludicrous to try to find a baby-sitter for him. No, this was sink-or-swim time for my brother and me.

I just hoped we'd both survive.

Janie Spellman was working the check-in desk when I came out of the employees' lounge, my lipstick fresh and my mind preoccupied. Janie gave me a brilliant smile as she loaded books on the cart. I regarded our newest staff member with both grudging admiration and envy. When Janie had gone to school, she'd learned computer systems as a matter of course, and she could help younger patrons far more knowledgeably than I. But Janie should have gotten a job somewhere else for a couple of years before she came back to Lawrenceton. She was always getting shocked. People who had been her revered elders when she'd been in high school and college were always startling her by checking out reading material that didn't jibe with her idea of what they should be reading. People she'd gone to high school with were not always particularly happy to see her. And children said and did things that could horrify the most jaded librarian, much less a young woman who'd so recently been a child herself.

Janie was also quite anxious about her single status. Though there was no discernable reason for her to be desperate, she was, and spread her nets unwisely. For one thing, Janie had cast her eyes at Perry Allison. Perry was at least fifteen years older, and I knew he was gay, but this was something Janie had not yet figured out—to be honest, it was fairly recent news to Perry himself.

Perry wasn't the only male Janie had set her sights on. Robin Crusoe was another. I was getting a little miffed about that. In fact, I was miffed at this very moment. Robin, who was supposed to be completing his postconvention book tour, was standing with his elbows on the desk behind which Janie stood, and he was smiling at her entirely too broadly. And she was simpering back at him.

I felt a rush of irritation, chased by a big dash of insecurity. I turned on my heel and went back into the employees' lounge. My hands were balled into fists and I was breathing deeply. I was being childish and unreasonable. Jealousy was beneath my dignity, and it was unattractive, too. What was wrong with me? I was one big emotional storm. This truly didn't seem like me, yet I was undeniably enraged. Janie's and Robin's shared smile had given me an utterly baseless sense of betrayal. I was so angry that I wished, not for the first time, that I were a lesbian. But a female couple probably had their share of lovers' spats, too. After all, it wasn't *men* I was unhappy with; it was vulnerability. I'd just had enough pain for a while.

I knew that I had a better life than maybe 90 percent of the women in the world, and I wasn't trying to be Pitiful Pearl. But after the little hurts of life that almost everyone sustains, I'd more or less just gotten through the staggering shock of losing my husband. More pain was something I hadn't signed up for when I'd succumbed to—okay, welcomed—the revival of my relationship with Robin.

"Eff him," I said. My spine straightened. That felt good. I swung a fist up and shook it. "*Eff* him." That felt better. I was pleasurably shocked at myself.

"Eff who?" asked my boss.

"Robin," I said after I'd jumped maybe a mile. "He's out there flirting with Janie. I just don't need that today. Actually, I don't need that any day. I need *security*. I need *devotion*." I couldn't believe I was saying this to my boss. I had known Sam forever, and I won't say we hadn't experienced some mind-to-mind talks, because we had. But he had never been anywhere close to the top of my list of confidants.

Sam patted me awkwardly on the shoulder. "Sorry about your sister-in-law," he said. I came out of my selfish absorption to register Sam's appearance. He looked awful. He was drawn and pale, and he'd visibly lost weight.

"What's up with you, Sam?" I asked with well-merited concern. I realized for the first time that Sam's problems amounted to more than missing his secretary. Sam looked really sick. In a way, I wasn't surprised.

Sam, who was in the neighborhood of fifty, had to juggle more balls than I could ever keep in the air. The city, the county, the state, the employees, the patrons—all of them had a stake in the library, and all wanted to have their say. The building maintenance, the book budget, hiring and firing . . . and on the home front, two girls who must be in their early twenties by now, and a wife named Marva, who could do simply anything, which I found almost unforgivable.

"I didn't sleep well," Sam said. Maybe if he hadn't slept well for a month, I might have accepted his appearance, but not after one night. "Marva is stenciling a design around the top of our bedroom walls, which she just finished painting."

See what I mean?

"So I had to sleep in the guest bedroom, and the bed there leaves a lot to be desired. Plus, even with the bedroom door closed, I could still smell the paint, and it just makes me sick."

Marva had been married to Sam for thirty years, so I was willing to bet she knew that. And yet she'd painted the bedroom in November, when the windows couldn't be opened. Big message there.

"I don't expect we can give each other any advice," I said, for lack of anything else to say.

"I guess not," he said. "Good luck to you, and again, I'm sorry about Poppy. She taught with Marva for a while and came over to the house from time to time. I liked her, no matter what anyone said."

That was typical Sam. Mr. Tactful.

I trailed back out into the library, determined to earn my money. I was supposed to be checking people in and out as they used our computers, and giving them extra direction if this was needed. I'd also be filling out the paperwork for our next book order while I sat at the desk. That part was fun, the little gush of excitement at all those wonderful books coming into our library, just waiting to be picked up and read. (See, I really am a librarian at heart.) But someone had to deal with questions like how much would be charged for printing out information our patrons had found on the Internet, or how to find out the greatest ocean depth recorded, or the best way to look up whether dromedaries have two humps and camels one (or vice versa).

Robin was still there, still leaning on the desk. See, this is why I believe in gun control; because if I'd had a gun, I wouldn't have had much control over my actions.

"Roe," he said, aiming his beautiful crinkly smile at me. It would have meant more—in fact, it would have melted my heart—if I hadn't seen him grinning at Janie just moments before. "I canceled the rest of my signings and came home last night."

"Robin," I said coolly. True librarians stay calm in the face of adversity.

He looked considerably taken aback.

"I thought you'd be happier to see me," he said uncertainly. "I thought I'd surprise you."

Janie was checking out books a little farther down the big desk.

"You seem to have found a way to keep busy while you waited," I remarked, and picked up the ringing phone. Porter Ziegler wanted to know how to get scum off the surface of his pond. I told him I'd find out, but I was registering Robin's reaction.

Robin looked a little guilty instantly. Not my imagination, then.

"Just passing the time till you came in," he said. "I know I shouldn't just come in and chatter to the librarians when they're at work. I guess I don't know that many people here in Lawrenceton yet."

And he was in Lawrenceton because of me was the subtext to that subtle plea for sympathy.

"Here I am," I said after considering several possible responses.

"Are you okay?"

He was sounding so sympathetic and caring, I felt like I was being a big idiot. Then Janie, having finished with the patron, sidled over and reached across the desk to finger Robin's coat, which was a very nice suede. In what I could only characterize as a coo, Janie said, "You're so snuggly in that coat!"

Gun control, I thought. Gun control.

"Let me leave you two to your discussion," I said lightly. I smiled at both of them with all the warmth of an alligator, then went to ask the reference librarian if she could find out about pond-scum removal. She thought for a minute and then gave me the phone number of the county agent. Porter Ziegler would surely find the answer from that individual, a man who seemed to know everything about the out-of-doors.

When I went back to the main desk, Robin was gone. Janie, looking a little sullen, was checking out some books for a bearded man who had made the library his second home. We had often speculated about Horton Aldrich. He was clean, and he never smelled, but he was noticeably shabby, and gaunt. The address he'd listed when he'd gotten his library card had turned out to be the address of the local Salvation Army store. Mr. Aldrich was prone to laugh to himself while he read the paper, which was maybe not so odd, considering the state of the world. He seldom talked directly to anyone, staff or patron, but he was nearly always through the doors right after they were unlocked, and he trotted out of them when the closing employee walked toward them with the key.

Today, Mr. Aldrich seemed to be in a jittery mood. I wondered what had happened to upset him. But he was so peculiar, I would have asked about his well-being only if he'd been bleeding or sobbing. My policy—my chickenhearted policy—about Mr. Aldrich was, Let him be. I always tried to smile at him, I tried not to look nervous when he decided to have a conversation with me, and I made sure no other patron hogged the Atlanta paper, thus preventing Mr. Horton from reading it right away, because I'd noticed that really made his day bad.

Everyone in the world wanted to use our computers today,

and the phone rang every time I put it down. I got about halfway through filling out the book order, when it should have taken me thirty minutes to do the whole thing. Phillip called at eleven o'clock, right on time, to tell me who'd phoned the house. He'd met Sandy and Marvin Wynn, who had come in briefly to retrieve an address book. Kind people had dropped off a cold-cut platter so the Wynns could have sandwiches whenever they were hungry, and a pie, though Phillip anxiously told me he didn't know what kind it was. But he swore he had the name and a description of the dish written down.

"You better have a sandwich and a piece of pie. Then you'll know what kind it is," I said.

"Shouldn't I save all this for Mr. and Mrs. Wynn?"

"Honey, I would say 'Sure' if I had any idea they were going to be eating, or caring what they ate," I said. "And you know there's no way two skinny older people like the Wynns are going to eat a whole platter of cold cuts, or a whole pie."

"Okay, that'll be lunch for me."

"Good. Who's called?"

There was a long list, including my mother (naturally), Melinda (no surprise), and Sally Allison, my friend, who was also a newspaper reporter. (Maybe I should say Sally Allison, the newspaper reporter, who was sometimes also my friend. That was definitely more accurate.) I remembered that I'd called Sally to ask her out to lunch, and I'd left a message for her to call me back. Cara Embler, Poppy's back-fence neighbor, and Teresa Stanton, president of the Uppity Women, had also tried to reach me. And, to my surprise, so had Bryan Pascoe.

Phillip seemed to be pleased that he'd been useful, and he was also happy to have HBO and MTV and lots of food. When I asked him about the state of the bathroom, there was a long moment of silence.

"Um, it'll be picked up within about ten minutes," he said defensively.

"Okay," I said, reminding myself again that I was not his mom. However, I was his older sister, and he needed to do what I asked of him. But for now, I backed off.

"I hope it's okay that I made a long-distance call on your phone?" he asked.

"Did you call your mother?"

"Okay, make that two long-distance calls."

"You called your mother and who else?"

"Um, Britta—you know, the girl who gave me a ride?"

I tried to give a mature, balanced answer. "Hell no" would not do. "Phillip, unless you're calling your parents, I don't think you should run up my phone bill," I said, keeping my voice calm and even.

"Hey, if I had any money, I'd pay you back!"

Okay, hostility alert.

"I know you would." Keep the voice calm and even, Roe. "But since you don't, you'd better hold off on the phone calls. Does Britta have an E-mail address?"

"Yeah."

"Okay, fine. E-mail her to your heart's content, but don't visit any Web sites you have to pay for."

After a silence, Phillip said, "Okay, I'll do that from now on."

I smiled at the patron standing at the counter, who beamed back. So that was a double-purpose smile. I was really pleased at ending the conversation with Phillip on a good note.

I noticed that Janie was staying away from me, which made me happy. I figured she wasn't as oblivious as she seemed. Perry came in to begin his work hours, and he gave me a pat on the shoulder.

"Sorry about Poppy," he said. Perry had had a troubled life, but he seemed to have found his foothold now. To my surprise,

I'd become his buddy, especially since his recent acknowledgment of his sexual orientation. I felt a little uncomfortable in the role, but I was so happy for Perry—and for his mother, Sally—when I watched his attitude grow more positive and cheerful, his demeanor more confident, I became resigned to assuming it.

"Had a great date last night," he said casually but very quietly.

"Local?"

"Yes," he said. "We went to the movies."

We talked about the film they'd seen, without Perry telling me his date's name. That was the norm in our conversations.

About fifteen minutes later, Perry's mom showed up. My friend Sally, who had always been incredibly put together, was beginning to look older. Although her hair color had once been easy to accept as natural, now that seemed increasingly unlikely. I didn't think she'd gained weight, but what she had was redistributing. She'd saved up for a face-lift, much to my surprise, but I had to wonder if she'd been to the right doctor. Her face looked smooth all right. But somehow, her skin didn't look like real skin.

Well, bless her heart. Sally had had a hard life, and she was doing her best.

"Son," she said coldly, looking at Perry.

"Hey, Mom," he said.

Uh-oh, trouble in paradise.

Sally asked me if I was ready to go to lunch. It was about 11:15, early for lunch.

"I didn't know we had a date," I said. "I called you to ask you out for your birthday, but we didn't ever get to set a date and time." Sally stared at me blankly. I became flustered. "Did I just forget? I can't believe it! I don't think I've ever just out-and-out forgotten a lunch date before." I rummaged around in my memory, trying to dredge up any conversation I'd had recently with Sally.

"Didn't we set up lunch for today when we talked yesterday?" Sally looked as surprised as I was.

"Sally, we didn't talk yesterday." I was sure of that. "I called you at work. You weren't at your desk. I left a voice-mail message."

"Of course we talked," Sally said. She looked more upset than the situation warranted. "I called you here, and you told me we would go to lunch on Tuesday, that you had something you wanted to tell me."

"Sally, that was weeks ago," I said, finally recalling the conversation. "That was right after I'd bought the new house, and I wanted to tell you I was moving."

Sally looked angry and frightened.

I turned to look at Perry, just because I had to put my eyes somewhere, and I couldn't bear to look at Sally. What on earth was happening?

Perry's face gave me a big hint.

"But today would be great," I said brightly. "Just let me go get my purse. I'll bet you did call, and I just got so upset with everything that's been happening to my family that I got all mixed up. You know me," I babbled on, walking rapidly back to the employee lounge. "I can't keep anything straight to save my soul."

I had planned on going home to lay eyes on my brother. I didn't think it was such a great idea, leaving him by himself all day. I wondered if I could combine two events in one.

I got my purse from my locker and went back out to the checkout desk, to find Sally glaring at Perry, who was looking miserable and defiant.

"I guess you know my son thinks he's gay," Sally said to me after we got in my car.

"Yes," I said cautiously.

"I must have been a terrible mother. I guess I shouldn't have divorced Steve. Or maybe Paul." Sally had been married to both Allison brothers. I'd hardly known Steve, but Paul had been a mine of emotional problems.

"No, I think you did the right thing there," I said, trying to sound calming and positive. This wasn't easy. "And I think you tried as hard as you could to be a good mother. Perry being gay doesn't mean you were a bad mother."

"I got him through the emotional problems and the drug abuse," she said plaintively. "It seems to me it ought to be time for him to settle down like everyone else."

I was speechless. Since Perry had discussed the orientation he'd finally revealed to himself, I had been wondering if maybe his emotional upheavals and substance abuse had been attempts to obscure it from himself. I had no idea what to say to Sally.

"Perry's a good guy," I told her. "He's well into adulthood, and he has to make his own life. You know he loves you."

Those were true things. I wasn't sure that they all tied together, but Sally seemed to gain some comfort.

She began to talk about other topics, and everything Sally said was absolutely lucid and intelligent. I began to wonder if that episode in the library had really happened.

I invited Sally in to meet my brother, and she looked over the house with interest while I talked to Phillip.

"That Pascoe guy called again," Phillip said. My brother seemed to be getting a little restless, which was what I had feared. He'd caught up on his sleeping and eating, he'd watched television and answered the phone, and now boredom was setting in.

I thought hard while I sat there, supposedly studying the list of callers. Phillip had spiky, tight handwriting, but it was legible after you'd looked at it for a minute.

I got out the Lawrenceton phone book and looked up a number I'd called several times before, but always in an official capacity. Josh Finstermeyer answered the phone, which was lucky for me.

"Josh, this is Ms. Teagarden," I began.

"I don't have a single overdue book!" Josh said anxiously. "I swear!"

"I know that," I said, trying not to sound irritable. "I have a favor to ask. If your mother doesn't have anything for you to do today, that is." Parental tasks took precedence over anything else.

"No, ma'am, my mom's at work anyway," Josh said. He sounded curious.

"You have a car, right?" He'd just earned the right to drive by himself.

"Yes, ma'am." Now he was even more curious. The good thing about Josh, whom I'd known from birth, was that he was a voracious reader. The bad thing was that he forgot to return books. We'd had our ups and downs

"My brother is here with me, and I need to send him shopping," I told Josh. "I have to go back to work, so I was hoping you could take Phillip to the grocery store and to Wal-Mart. And if there's anything on at the Global you haven't seen already, that would be okay, too."

"So who's paying?" Josh was nothing if not businesslike.

"Gas money and movie money."

"Done. How old is this dude?"

"He's fifteen," I said.

"He's not weird looking, right?" Obviously, Josh wanted to know if Phillip was going to be an embarrassment.

"Not at all," I said gravely. "In fact, you might want to bring your sister." Josh had a twin sister, Jocelyn, called Joss. She wasn't much of a reader, unlike her brother, but she had seemed okay when she was in the library doing research for school.

"Okay. When?"

"Anytime. You know where I live? On McBride?"

"Yes, ma'am. Where's your brother from?"

"The Los Angeles area," I said grandly.

"Oh. Cool."

"So I'll leave him the money."

"Gotcha."

Of course Phillip had been listening to my conversation, and he seemed half-excited and half-scared at the idea of spending the rest of the afternoon with kids his own age who didn't know him. I could understand that. But I knew what Phillip was capable of—taking off cross-country alone—and I wanted him busy. I peeled some money out of my purse, and while Sally and Phillip talked about southern accents, I worked on a grocery list.

After Phillip vanished into the bathroom to spruce himself up, Sally and I made sandwiches from the cold-cut tray, which had enough processed meat and cheese for maybe ten people. I rummaged in the refrigerator for mayonnaise, mustard, and pickles; meanwhile, Sally was being complimentary about Phillip's manners and looks. We had a pleasant conversation while we ate, though it was strangely nonspecific. I noticed that Sally said things like "my boss" for Macon Turner, whom I knew well, and "last week" instead of Wednesday or Thursday. But this was hardly conclusive. I was just thinking maybe I had imagined Sally's earlier reality blip, when she said, "I really ought to be getting back to work." We had put all the food away, and I fished my keys out of my purse.

"Okay," I said. I needed to be getting back to work, too. "Where's your car?"

Sally's face went blank.

For a moment, I thought she just didn't understand me. "I mean, is it at the newspaper, or did you drive down to the library?" I asked.

For one horrible moment, Sally looked frightened.

"Oh, just take me back to the library," she said with a nonchalance assumed so swiftly and smoothly that I almost didn't catch that moment. If my back had been turned, I would have swallowed her act.

Sally really didn't know where her car was.

Chapter Five

I had taken a circuitous route to make sure Sally's car was indeed at the library. It was, and I dropped her off right by it with some relief. I watched her unlock it and climb in the driver's seat. I wondered what to do, and then I realized that it wasn't up to me to do anything. This situation was Perry's responsibility, and all I could do was be a friend to him so he could talk if he needed to.

I patted him on the shoulder when I passed him in the employees' lounge, and he looked up at me and nodded, a short, jerky nod of acknowledgment.

"I made an appointment with Dr. Zelman for her next week," he said. "She tries to cover it up, and she's pretty good at it, but it's getting worse and worse."

There really wasn't anything else to say.

The two remaining hours of work flew by. There were lots of people coming in and out, lots of computer use, and the book order to complete. When it was time for me to clock out,

I was actually glad. There were so many ways for me to go, I couldn't pick one.

My plans for the rest of the afternoon took an unexpected turn when I went to the employee parking lot and found Bryan Pascoe leaning on my car. His office was within easy walking distance of the library; it was in the old, ambience-laden, inconvenient Jasper Building, which also held Cartland Sewell's office. So it had been easy for Bryan Pascoe to get where he was. The question was why he was there.

"Ms. Teagarden," he said.

"Hello, Mr. Pascoe," I said, and even I could hear the question clearly in my voice. It was a relief not to have to tilt my head back to look Bryan Pascoe in the eyes.

He held out his hand, and I shook it. He had fine bones. "Please call me Bryan," he said politely.

"Bryan," I murmured, and retrieved my hand. "Aurora," I said after a moment.

He nodded.

"My brother, Phillip, said you tried to call me? I would have returned your calls." I wanted to be sure Bryan Pascoe marked the fact that he was pushing.

"Yes, but I wanted to talk to you face-to-face."

"All right," I said hesitantly when he'd been at a full stop for a long moment. "Did you want to go to your office?"

"Can we walk around the block? I've been shut in my office all day."

It was brisk, but not truly cold. "Certainly," I said after an uncertain pause. What the heck was going on here? "My legs are short, I don't go at a very quick pace." Robin always seemed to be two paces ahead of me. Thinking about Robin instantly made me feel bad.

"Your legs are fine," he said, again catching me off balance, and off we went.

"Has something come up about John David?"

"Of course I've talked to Miss Burns. For the moment, she backs up John David a hundred percent. She says he was doing legal work for her."

I glanced sideways at Bryan, and he smiled at me. He had gleaming white teeth. "She's been drawing up her will, she says," Bryan added in an absolutely neutral way.

"If Poppy were alive, Romney Burns'd need it." I found myself smiling back.

"That's interesting. Did you see your sister-in-law as a jealous woman?"

I mulled that over. "I don't think she would have wanted to be humiliated, if John David decided to divorce her, or something about his little relationships became flagrant. Like him taking Romney to the company Christmas party, or something like that," I said finally. "I guess that's different from being gut-jealous."

"How do you feel about that?" the lawyer asked.

I felt like that was a strange question.

I stopped and faced him. Luckily, we were on the sidewalk by the side of the little downtown movie theater, and no one was going in or out at the moment.

"What difference does that make?" I could feel my eyebrows drawing together in a frown.

"Personal curiosity," he said.

"I don't know why you want to know." But I could see no reason to refuse to tell him, either. "I thought it was really . . . distasteful," I said, selecting the mildest word that would fit. "Though I'm not an angel myself, for sure."

"Why are you giving me your opinion in such a tentative way? You don't have to attach disclaimers."

"I don't know you. For all I know, you cheat on your wife every day," I said bluntly. "I hate to sound holier-than-thou."

94

"Why did you call me yesterday?"

"John David thought of you. You're the best, I hear."

"I am, Aurora."

I felt like I was missing something here. "I'm glad to know you're so confident," I said a little dubiously.

"I was glad to hear your voice on the phone yesterday. I've had my eye on you for quite some time."

"You think I've done something illegal?"

"No, I want to date you."

"I thought you were married, Bryan," I said, genuinely astonished. Come to think of it, he had mentioned "ex-wife" yesterday.

"I was, for five years. We got divorced over a year ago."

"Uh-huh," I said, feeling like he'd just smacked me in the head with a dead fish, or something equally startling. "Well, Bryan, I'm real flattered, but I've been dating Robin Crusoe."

"I know." He smiled again. His smile managed to be confident, predatory, and hopeful, all at the same time. "But my sources tell me he's been flirting with Janie Spellman."

"Ouch," I said sharply. "That was below the belt. Who's your source?"

"I'm not bound by law to cover for her. My source is Janie Spellman herself, who is my cousin once removed."

"Janie is not too particular about whom she flirts with."

"I'm sorry you're angry, but you can't deny it," Bryan said unequivocally.

"I don't have to reply any way at all, deny or admit or any which thing." I glared up at him. "In fact, this part of our conversation is over." Suddenly, I thought of the gas station receipt in my purse. I couldn't let anything slip by just because I was irritated with Bryan. "Now, I need to talk business."

"Talk away." If I'd in any way ruffled Bryan, he wasn't letting it show.

I explained about finding the receipt that morning, about its significance, and told him the names of the people who'd been in my house. Then I looked at my watch and exclaimed, "Oh no! I have to be at Poppy's right now!"

"What for?" Bryan had listened to my account very carefully, which had made me feel better about him.

"The Scene Clean guy is supposed to be at John David and Poppy's house," I explained. "Someone called from SPACO-LEC to say the house had been . . . well, released. So I called Zachary Lee and confirmed."

"I need to see the crime scene anyway. Can I come with you?"

"I guess so," I said ungraciously. We walked back to the library parking lot and I unlocked my Volvo. Bryan talked about local politics all the way over to Swanson Lane. I felt the touch of his attention every time he looked at me, and he looked at me a lot. My cheeks were hot by the time we parked behind a bright yellow van with SCENE CLEAN and a logo on the side. At least there were no macabre graphics. I fussed with my keys, yanked at my purse, anything to avoid looking into the eyes of the man beside me. We got out of the car and stood at the end of the walkway leading up to the front door. A young man with Asian features was waiting for us. He was absorbed in a book.

I was nervous about going into the house again. "I'm glad Arthur released the house," I said, just to say something.

"I'll bet Arthur has had a rough couple of days," Bryan said, clearly inviting me to ask why.

"Any murder investigation . . ." I said slowly. "But that's not what you're implying, is it?"

"I'm sure you have heard that Poppy used to see him. A couple of years ago?"

I thought I was going to pass right out. I could actually feel the blood rush from my head. Bryan put his left arm around me and held on to my right hand with his.

"Good God," I said, trying to gain some time. "But then he should be the last man on earth to be involved in investigating her death!"

Bryan said, "Do you feel all right? Wasn't he your fiancé at one time?"

"No," I said, shaking my head to clear it out. "No, we never . . . Did you do that on purpose? Spring that on me? Why?"

"You did date him."

"About a million years ago. Way before I married Martin." I gave him an incredulous look.

"I wondered if Arthur had a thing for the women in your family."

"You're confusing me." I stepped away from his arm and walked up the sidewalk to the door, just as I'd done yesterday. I faltered for a moment as that comparison hit me, then picked up my stride.

Bryan was beside me by then. "Hello," he said to the young man waiting on the ornamental bench outside Poppy's front door.

"Zachary Lee?" I asked as he rose. Zachary Lee was much taller than I'd expected, maybe six feet, and looked like a very happy mix of Caucasian and Asian.

"That's me," he said happily. "Zachary Lee, Scene Clean, at your service. I'm a certified crime-scene cleaner, and I've had extensive experience with the Atlanta Police Department. I took a course to learn how to do this properly, and I follow all safety and health regulations."

He beamed at us. Apparently, Zachary Lee enjoyed his work.

"Did the police give you the okay?" I asked.

"Yes, ma'am, and Mr. Queensland, the husband of the deceased, gave me his permission to do the job. By the way, he said to tell you thanks." Zachary's teeth were perfectly straight and white, and his eyes tilted pleasantly when he smiled, which seemed to be most of the time.

"I'm Aurora Teagarden," I said, "and this is Bryan Pascoe, Mr. Queensland's lawyer."

"Pleased to meet you" was said all around.

"Let me just show you the, um, site," I said, fumbling with the words. "Mr. Pascoe wants to have a look before you clean it. I'll wait here until you're through, then lock up after you."

For the first time, Zachary Lee looked less than happy, probably at the idea of us sitting around the crime scene while he worked. But I wanted to see him off the premises, and just generally keep an eye on him. The young man was probably perfectly all right, but we knew very little about him.

The house had been closed, and it smelled less than wonderful. Poppy would have been embarrassed. There was the awful smell of blood, and the more mundane odor of a much-used litter box. Once again, I was distressed that Moosie hadn't been found. Somehow, the cat's disappearance was an insult to Poppy.

"Tell me what you did yesterday when you came in," Bryan said, and I thought maybe he was distracting me. I was grateful.

"I went upstairs," I said. "No one was there. I came back down and went toward the kitchen." I guided him down the short hall into the kitchen, where everything was the same as it had been, except for fingerprint powder. We stepped around the counter, and I waved a hand weakly toward the spot where Poppy had lain. The gesture was hardly necessary. The blood was a powerful testimony. In fact, seeing it like this—dried and dark—made its impact somehow more violent.

While Zachary Lee went over to the sliding glass door to have a look outside, I felt that my head was buzzing just a bit. I put a hand out to Poppy's breakfast bar, which was laden with bright cookbooks and dried flowers, to steady myself.

Instantly, Bryan steered me out of the kitchen/dining room and into the living room. Instead of depositing me on the couch, he put his arms around me. And he didn't say a word. His left hand stroked my hair.

I really liked that silence. Robin, since words were his livelihood, never quite seemed to know when they weren't necessary.

"So, there's nothing upstairs?" Zachary Lee asked from the doorway.

I began to pull away, but Bryan Pascoe's arms tightened. "The fingerprint dust," he said. "No blood."

"Okay," the cleanup guy said, happy once again. "Why don't you two sit out by the pool? It's a beautiful day. I've got to go suit up and bring in my gear."

Bizarre as it seemed at first, that turned out to be excellent advice. As we walked out the front door and around to the gate at the side of the house (rather than crossing the bloody threshold of the sliding glass door), Bryan gave me rather unnecessary help. I have to confess I enjoyed it, after coping with Phillip and the assorted shocks of the past twenty-four hours. Sometimes I just didn't understand myself. Half of me wanted to stand upright and independent, and half of me wanted to lean against someone stronger. Possibly the answer could be found in a good partnership, in which one could take turns leaning.

In one of those unexpected little moments of clarity that make life so frightening, I realized (as I sat by the pool of a murdered woman, being comforted by an attentive lawyer) that my first marriage had not been such a partnership.

"All right?" Bryan was saying anxiously.

"Yes, I'm fine." I sounded like a polite robot. I shook myself a little. "Thank you for asking."

At that awkward juncture, another presence made itself known. Teresa Stanton, Uppity Woman par excellence, swept through the patio gate.

"Poor Aurora!" Teresa called. Teresa was a terrifying woman. I hadn't known that a pantsuit with matching jacket was the appropriate outfit to wear to the house of a murdered woman; until I saw Teresa, that is. She wore one, dark burgundy with golden brown touches, and so that was exactly the right thing. Teresa's dark hair was beautifully cut and blow-dried, so the short sides fanned back from her face, her makeup was discreet, and her teeth were perfectly white. Intelligence gleamed through her contact lenses.

"Teresa," I muttered. Bryan, of course, stood. I suddenly remembered that the woman to whom Bryan had been married was the newly rewed Teresa Stanton. Teresa Pascoe Stanton.

"I've had the devil's own time catching up to you," Teresa said.

I hardly felt I needed to apologize. "This has been a very busy day," I said noncommittally.

"Oh, of course! No doubt! Hello, Bryan." Teresa made sure we knew she was adding the greeting as an elaborate afterthought.

"Teresa, good to see you," he said, his voice cool and uninflected.

I tried real hard to think of a good excuse to get up and run away, but none popped to mind.

"What's that man doing there?" Teresa asked, distracted by Zachary Lee, who appeared to be wearing a space suit. He was working right inside the sliding glass door.

"He's cleaning up the blood," I said. Of course, that didn't faze Teresa.

"I'm so glad you were able to find someone who does that

sort of thing," she said conversationally. "Where's your Mr. Crusoe?"

"I don't know." I refused to explain or elaborate. I wondered what she would do if I asked her where Shorty Stanton was. I was so powerfully tempted that I actually opened my mouth, but then common sense prevailed.

"Of course, all the women in the club want to know what we can do to help," Teresa said.

"Maybe Melinda needs some baby-sitting," I suggested. "Since she's got her own two kids and Poppy's boy, too."

Teresa wrote this down on her little pocket notebook. "What else?" she asked. "We've already taken food to your mother's house."

"I'd rethink backing Bubba Sewell for representative."

"Do you think he is involved with Poppy's death?" Teresa was nothing if not direct, if she thought directness would serve her purposes best.

"No, actually, I don't, but I think his reputation may take a beating if the investigation ends in a trial."

"So it's true: He was messing around with Poppy." Teresa looked very cross.

I didn't meet her eyes.

"Someone who can't keep his pants zipped," Teresa said flatly. "We don't want that in a public servant. I think we've all seen enough of that."

"True," I said.

We all fell silent, and in that sudden hush I could hear the splash of the pool across the privacy fence. Some music was playing, too; it sounded like Handel.

"Cara!" Teresa called. "Are you doing your laps? Can you take a break?"

"Is that Teresa?" a high voice hooted back.

"Yes, girl. Come over here!"

There was a little-used gate in the high privacy fence between the two properties. It made a high-pitched squeak as Cara Embler pushed it open. Cara was pulling off a swim cap as she walked toward us, and she'd wrapped a big towel around her because it was a brisk, cool day. Her hairstyle had been chosen to complement her athleticism; she wore her blond hair (now mixed with gray) short and straight. Cara had been a champion swimmer in high school and college, and someone had told me that she was training for a seniors competition. Lawrenceton people were bemused by Cara—swimming in all temperatures, goal-oriented—but they respected her dedication and her excellent physical condition. Married to a cardiologist who seemed always to be on call, Cara had a lot of time to shape as she pleased.

Though the Emblers had a son, who was studying to be an environmental engineer or something equally laudable, he was in college in northern California and seldom came home. So Cara swam, ran, dabbled in political causes, tutored kids at the junior high, and organized the annual fund-raising drive for the United Way. She had a couple of dogs, schnauzers; she was famous locally for going to any lengths to help the pound raise money, and she was ferocious about turning in animal abusers.

I couldn't understand why she hadn't been on the list for Uppity Women years ago, but I figured that by now she should be fairly close to the top of the list.

"How's John David?" Cara asked me. She plopped down into one of the lawn chairs, draping her head and neck with yet another towel. The day was cool enough that I would have been shivering had I been wet, but Cara seemed impervious to the temperature.

"About like you'd expect." Actually, I hadn't seen John David since yesterday, and I had no idea how he was holding up. But somehow, that didn't seem the right thing to confess. I was a little surprised that Cara asked. I hadn't been aware she'd ever had a conversation with John David.

"This is just awful, and in the house right behind me," Cara went on.

I hadn't thought of that. I would sure be scared, too. In fact, I'd be shaking in my shoes. But Cara seemed concerned, not frightened.

"Did you hear anything peculiar?" Teresa asked.

Cara, who was somewhere between forty and fifty, shrugged her muscular shoulders. "No, the day was just as usual. Swam in the morning, decorated the house for Thanksgiving, went to lunch with a friend, came back, did my second set of laps—that's when I heard a lot of coming and going over here—and then in the late afternoon, I made plans for a Christmas party my husband and I are giving."

I was sure that Cara Embler's plans for a party would be somewhat more sophisticated and complex than mine would be. Probably the guests would be more sophisticated, too, if they were from her husband's workplace. Did you entertain cardiologists and hospital administrators the same way you did, oh, say realtors and librarians? The wine would have to be better for the hospital people. . . .

"Aurora," Teresa was saying none too gently. "Are you listening to me?"

"No," I said. I saw Bryan turn hastily to one side to conceal a smile. Maybe I had been a tad blunt. "Sorry, I was drifting," I murmured. "What were you saying?"

"I was reminding Cara that she was next on the list."

The day after Poppy had died.

Teresa was not Ms. Sensitive, but this was callous, even for her. We all regarded her in a long moment of silence.

"What?" she said.

"The circumstances take most of the zest out of becoming

an Uppity Woman," Cara said finally, looking past Teresa's shoulder as she spoke. "Give me a call to let me know the time and place. If you leave it on my machine, I'll write it down. I can't remember anything if you tell me away from a pad and pencil."

"I know how that is," Teresa agreed. "I live by my Day Planner." She was quite oblivious to her offense.

"Who on earth is that?" Cara asked. She, too, had caught a glimpse of Zachary Lee in his space suit.

Bryan took on the duty of explaining,

What a long day it had been. And there was more to come. But I roused myself to ask Cara if she'd seen Moosie.

"I'll keep an eye out for him," she promised. "He's a cute cat. I personally don't believe in declawing, but I know the rationale was that declawing would keep him from climbing the fence and wandering the neighborhood. I guess Poppy's heart was in the right place."

"She didn't have Moosie declawed," I told her. "She adopted him like that. He was in the animal shelter. Just give me a call if you catch sight of him. I know John David would like to know Moosie is safe." If John David had had a chance to think about the cat at all: In his place, I wasn't sure I would.

Cara excused herself and went back to her side of the fence. Before she left, she glanced once more at Zachary Lee, who'd opened the sliding door to clean its runners.

"You know," Teresa said in the hushed voice you reserve for passing along scandal, "Stuart Embler used to drop by to see Poppy before he headed home, at least before Poppy had the baby."

I hadn't heard Cara splashing in the water, and I hoped she was not standing right on the other side of the fence, listening. To my relief, I heard her dogs barking as she slid open her own glass patio door. They were welcoming her back into the house with rapture, it sounded like. Maybe I should get a dog, I thought. Then I thought about what Madeleine would do to a dog, and I canceled the idea.

Bryan had a certain amount of distaste in his face as he looked at his former wife, but he also looked interested. "I wonder where Stuart was yesterday around eleven," he said.

"That should be easy enough to find out. But I'd be extremely surprised if Stuart had anything to do with this. His affair with Poppy was stale, and he wouldn't care if there was a little scandal anyway. Cardiologists can call the shots. I mean, if you had a sick heart, and this guy was the best chance of your surviving, would you care if you heard he'd had an extramarital roll in the hay?"

I could see Teresa's point.

"By the way, Aurora, speaking of extramarital affairs," Teresa began, and my eyes fixed on her. "Rumor has it that you saw someone leaving this house yesterday as you pulled up."

How the hell had such a story started making the rounds?

"I'll bet it was a man. Or the wife of some man she'd been carrying on with." Teresa's face was avid.

"No," I said, my voice as cold as a Tastee-Freez Coke slush. "That is not true."

"Well, my goodness, I'm sorry, I didn't realize I was hitting a nerve. We all figured you'd about got this solved."

I don't think I blinked at all as I glared at her.

Bryan said, "Isn't there somewhere you need to be, Teresa?"

She stopped dead, her mouth open.

"You've come by, you've given your condolences, and you've gotten some suggestions of ways the Uppities can help. I'm sure you have another errand or appointment?"

"I do need to stop by the store, and phone the committee members," she said slowly. Her face was red. "Good-bye, Aurora."

Gosh, I just *loved* seeing Teresa upbraided. Not the most pleasant side of my character, I'm afraid. "Good-bye," I said politely and distantly, and Bryan stood as Teresa did, then opened the gate to the front yard for her.

"She can't help it, you know," he said when he sat in the chair beside mine.

"I realize that she has many fine qualities."

He raised one eyebrow.

"She runs the Uppity Women smooth as a whistle," I told him. "She's organized and focused, and we do a lot of good under her leadership."

"I was married to her. I know just how organized and focused she can be."

"You said you've been divorced for a year?" Was it tacky to mention that?

"She married Shorty Stanton about seven months ago."

"He works at one of the banks, right?"

"He's the president of Southern Security," Bryan said a little dryly.

"Oh."

"Yes, big money."

I forbore remarking that Bryan himself couldn't be hurting for a healthy cash flow, unless he had a secret vice like gambling or drugs.

"Tell me about the car." His voice was quiet.

I stared at the crouching, dim figure of the crime-scene cleaner. He was working on the glass again now. I considered and discarded several responses.

"I didn't see any car," I said very carefully. "But I did find evidence that someone had been here before we got here."

"You know who it was," Bryan said.

I looked at him sideways. "No wonder you have such a good reputation as a lawyer."

"It's deserved, I promise you. Who was it?"

"I can't tell you that right now."

"Do you care more about this person than about your sister-in-law?"

"Yes."

That took him aback, but the lawyer rallied.

"You don't trust me?"

"I told you about the receipt," I remarked mildly. "And I'll tell you something else."

He turned his hand palm up, meaning, Give.

"Someone's been in the house since yesterday."

"This house?" He pointed at it, startled.

"Yes."

"How do you know?"

"The upstairs curtains are closed. They were open yesterday when I was up there."

Bryan stared at the curtains in the master bedroom as if they could tell him why they were pulled together. "Maybe the police closed them last night, so no one could see what they were doing," he suggested.

I shrugged. "Maybe."

Bryan seemed to give up. "Let's go check it out. I believe the man is telling you he's finished."

In fact, Zachary Lee had emerged from the house, unsuited, looking cheerful as ever. "I've got the rug rolled up and in my van; here's a receipt," he said. "I'm going to take it back to the shop and work on it. Everything else is done. You'll need to call a regular housecleaning service to get everything else back to normal."

I could feel that little frown of confusion contracting my brows. "Excuse me?"

"The upstairs. I went up to clean up the fingerprint powder."

"What about the upstairs?" I cast a sideways glance at Bryan.

"This wasn't a homicide during a burglary?"

"You had better show us what you mean," Bryan said.

This time, I walked through every room of the ground floor, and it all looked normal. Upstairs, though, was a different story. The room that had received the most attention was the master bedroom. Everything was tossed around, as if a demented child had had a field day.

"It didn't look like this when you found the body?" Bryan asked, his eyes missing nothing.

"No, it looked like a home." I couldn't think of anything else to say. "Surely the police wouldn't do this?"

"They would take the bedding to check for evidence," Bryan said. And they had. "But they wouldn't do this." Drawers were pulled out of the chest of drawers, the dressing table, the lingerie chest, the jewelry chest. Poppy's side of the small walk-in closet was demolished. Out-of-season shoes had been dumped from their neat stack of boxes, and a set of stacked cubes that had held sweaters had been disassembled and lay strewn on the floor.

This was horrible. I felt like Poppy had been violated all over again.

I told myself instantly that this was a dumb reaction. What I was seeing was just a rummage through her things, not nearly as bad as sinking a knife into her, for goodness sake! But the invasiveness of it . . . I thought of how much I would hate someone going through my personal stuff, and I had to sit down abruptly on the needlepoint-covered stool that was intended to occupy the kneehole of the dressing table.

Bryan did a big production number about how I was feeling—asking if he should call the paramedics (which horrified me considerably) and muttering various things about how terrible a shock I had sustained. He had called the police already, so I let him run on for a bit. Was he trying to impress me with his empathy, with his regard for me as a delicate southern flower? I was a pretty wilted blossom, if so.

I wished Robin were there. Then I slapped myself mentally. No point wishing for that. He was flirting with Janie.

Anger stiffened my spine once more.

Chapter Six

I was fit company for neither man nor beast.

It was already late afternoon, and I suggested to Bryan that we wait until the next morning to find the gas station that had issued the receipt. That way, I pointed out, probably the same attendant would be on duty—if you could talk about attendants being on duty at gas stations anymore, which was doubtful. I could tell that for about a half cent, Bryan would take the receipt and ask the questions all by himself. I tried to impress on him how dimly I would view such behavior.

I drove Bryan back to his office, then stopped by my mother's to check on the well-being of my extended family. Melinda and Avery were at their house, and Poppy's baby was with them, just as Melinda had predicted. John David was sitting in a morose heap in Mother's den. Across from him was Arthur Smith.

What was he doing? Obviously, he was still on the case, which I found incomprehensible. Granted, Lawrenceton is a smallish town, and the police force is probably pretty stretched, especially considering murders are not the norm in our town. But you would think, even in Lawrenceton, the chief of police would remove the deceased's former lover from the list of investigating officers in a homicide case. No one had whispered in his ear yet, I presumed.

"Can you think of any reason someone might have broken into your home?" Arthur was asking. "Do you know of any particular hiding place your wife used, for important papers or—?" This was certainly a quick response to Bryan's phone call.

"No," John David interrupted. "No, Poppy had nothing to hide."

My mother was standing at the kitchen counter, reading the heating instructions on the casserole Teresa had brought by that afternoon. I knew the writing at a glance. When John David made his amazing statement, my mother's eyebrows flew up, expressing exactly the same incredulity as mine did. If John David believed what he was saying, he was a fool. If he believed he was fooling anyone else about Poppy's true character, he was also a fool.

I drifted around the counter so I could stand across from my mother. She was, as always, perfectly groomed, but she looked weary and worried.

"The bad thing is," she said in a low conversational tone, "that Poppy was a lot of good things, too, but no one's thinking about that."

"It does seem as though the, ah, negative side of her character is probably what got her killed," I said. "But I agree, Poppy had a lot that was good in her. She was intelligent, she was entertaining, she loved Chase—oh, did she love that baby—and she was willing to work hard on projects she believed in." There were a lot of people with better reputations than Poppy's, but it would be hard to think of so much good to say about them, I realized.

"Have you had a falling-out with Robin?" Mother asked. The question was so abrupt and so out of character for her that I hesitated before answering.

"Yes," I said. "He didn't call me to tell me he'd gotten back early from his book tour, and he was flirting with Janie Spellman."

"Flirting," my mother said, her voice blank.

"Yes," I replied, feeling my cheeks redden. "Practically holding hands."

"In the library?"

"Yes, in the library!"

"Where nothing could possibly happen, under the eyes of a dozen people."

"But why would he do that?"

"Maybe Janie wanted to flirt a little. You're not the only woman in the world who finds Robin attractive, Roe. Maybe Robin felt like flirting back, just a little. Did he ask her out? Did he kiss her? Did he tell you he didn't want to see you any more?"

"No."

"Did you give him a chance to talk to you about it?"

"No."

"Have I miscounted the days, or did he not cut short his tour to get back to you early?"

"Yes." I felt embarrassment creep up my cheeks in a red tide.

"Um, um, um." My mother shook her head. "That evil, evil man. He's been mistreating you so badly, I may have to slap him."

"Okay, you made your point."

"I'd have thought you would know the difference, after that one." Mother nodded toward the den. She meant Arthur, not

John David. Mother would never forgive Arthur for humiliating me so publicly. He could save ten kids from drowning and foil a dozen bank robberies, and she'd still loathe him. It was kind of nice, having someone that firmly on your side, no matter how mistaken she might be.

After I'd spoken to John and patted his hand and seen for myself that he was better today than yesterday, I left without speaking to John David or Arthur, who were still deep in conversation.

On the short drive home, I thought about what Poppy might have hidden. If it could have been in a shoe box, obviously it was something small. Would Poppy have blackmailed anyone? I thought not, even as disillusioned as I was about her proclivities. But something she had had in her keeping had scared the hell out of someone. Perhaps the searcher had found the item in the upstairs bedroom, perhaps not.

So, we had a mysterious gas station receipt, a murdered woman, a philandering lawyer, a philandering husband, a past lover or three, a searcher, and a detective who shouldn't be on the case at all.

I wasn't surprised at all to walk into my house and find my brother and Robin waiting for me. They turned almost-accusing eyes to watch me come into the room. They'd been watching football. What a surprise.

"Hello," I said, keeping my voice cool. "How long have you been back, Phillip?"

"About thirty minutes. Robin was waiting for you."

"Out in the driveway?"

"Yes." Phillip had clearly switched his allegiance, based on his thirty minutes of renewed acquaintance with Robin. "In the cold."

"Was I expecting you, Robin?" I sure didn't remember inviting him over. I made an effort to draw my righteous indignation back around me. Robin had a key, but I suppose he hadn't felt welcome to use it.

"Um, no. I was just hoping I could talk to you. I missed you."

"Let's go in the office. Phillip, did you eat? Do you need anything?"

"Josh and his sister took me to a Pizza Hut," he said. "I'm stuffed. Robin, the Broncos are ahead by seven!"

"I'll be back," Robin assured him. He glanced sideways at me and added, "I think."

We trailed down the little hall to the office, a wonderful room lined with bookshelves. Robin had been working over here quite a bit, since he had a neighbor working the four-to-midnight shift at Pan-Am Agra, and this neighbor got up at nine o'clock expressly to tune his truck.

And before I'd even moved into the house, right here on the rug, Robin and I had . . . I blocked the thought.

We sat in the two wing-backed chairs after Robin had pulled his around to face mine.

"Tell me what all this is about," he said. He didn't look angry, or guilty. He looked determined.

I was too grown-up to keep hugging my grievance.

"Robin, I've been up to here"—I made a gesture across my throat—"with the infidelity of Poppy and John David. I hate cheating anyway, and the last two days have just been full of it. So when I saw Janie flirting with you, and you flirting back, I just got . . . very angry." It still troubled me to think of the wave of unreasoning anger that had swamped me. When I stood back and looked at it from a distance, that huge rage just seemed . . . odd.

"Janie is a cute girl. But she's a girl, and she's ready to flirt with anyone. Being rude to Janie would be like being mean to a fuzzy puppy."

I raised an eyebrow.

"All right, I flirted back."

I raised the other eyebrow.

"You're a *woman*," Robin said firmly. "Jane's a girl. I'm way too old for Janie. I wouldn't know what to do with her even if I was interested."

I had nothing left to raise, so I tried a skeptical sneer.

"Okay, I flirted back a lot." Robin looked down at his big hands. "When I go on tour, my ego inflates, and I was nominated for the Anthony, and I was thinking big thoughts about myself."

I waited.

"But now I'm regrounded." He looked up at me directly.

"You sure?"

"Yeah."

"So what you're saying is . . ."

"I'm supposed to make a mission statement?"

"It would help."

"I'm not planning on seeing anyone else."

"Bryan Pascoe asked me out," I said, though actually Bryan had actually just indicated that sometime in the future he wanted to ask me out. However, I couldn't think of a way to turn that into a concrete statement.

"Are you going to go?" Robin's face was all shut down. "I don't know Bryan Pascoe. He might be the guy for you."

I thought about that. "He'd be more in the category of a fixer-upper," I said. "I think it might be safer to say that I only want to date you right now."

Robin seemed bigger suddenly, as if he'd been holding himself in a smaller space than he normally occupied.

"I like your brother," he said. "He seems like a pretty independent young man."

"He's definitely feeling his new manliness," I said. I lowered my voice and told Robin about the two girls Phillip had hitched a ride with on the last leg of his journey, and the condoms I'd found in his wallet.

"Better he have them and use them than not have them and need them," Robin said wisely. "Maybe he was just carrying them because he wanted to need them."

I worked that through. It was an interesting idea. "What I'm hoping is that he didn't buy them after the fact," I admitted. "I mean, maybe he had sex and enjoyed it and then thought, Gee, if I'm going to have some more, I better be prepared."

"I'll try to find out, in a very manly way," Robin said. "If you have to work tomorrow, I'll take Phillip out to eat or over to my apartment or something."

"Sounds good. I don't have to work, but I'm supposed to go to a gas station tomorrow with Bryan Pascoe."

"An original first date," Robin said.

"Not a date. A clue." I told Robin about the receipt I'd found on the floor, and then I told him about what had happened to the upstairs of John David and Poppy's house.

"That's mysterious," Robin said. "The house wasn't broken into?"

"No, and that makes it even stranger. I unlocked the front door for the Scene Clean guy myself. The sliding glass door uses the same key. It was locked, too, or at least I guess it was. Zachary Lee just had to turn the latch inside and open it while he was cleaning. I never thought to check to see if it was locked to begin with. I never asked him, after he showed us the state of the upstairs."

"So the patio door may have been unlocked all along."

"Well, it might have been left unlocked by whoever rifled through the upstairs. I'm sure the police wouldn't have left the back door unlocked. If I were breaking in, I'd pick the back door. You wouldn't even have to show your face on Swanson Lane. You could creep through the Emblers' backyard, and

ou'd better check. Maybe your folks could come over here
a glass of wine after dinner?"

"You want my mother to meet your mother," I said, suddenly
tting his drift.

"Yes."

I couldn't think of a thing to say. "Oh. Okay." I looked anywhere but at Robin. "Um, how long is your mom staying?"

"Until Monday," he said. "I'll bet by then she'll be ready to
leave. In fact, she'll be anxious."

"I'm glad she's got other children besides you," I said, laughing.

"She loves all of us, but she's most comfortable in her own
home with her dogs, and her buddies," he said.

A plaintive meow outside the door told me that Madeleine
was waiting for her breakfast. She wasn't used to the bedroom
door being closed.

"I have to go feed the Mongol horde," I said, making myself
get up from the warm bed and pull on a bathrobe. It was an
effort, because I wasn't feeling so great. An overload of emotion? I was a little achy, a little tired.

"I'll call you later today," he said. "After I feed Phillip and
plumb his darkest depths, I'll go get my mother at the airport.
Then we'll talk about tomorrow."

"Sounds good," I said, thinking of all the things I had to do
today. I had to run the strange errand with Bryan Pascoe. I was
supposed to work for a few hours. I had to go to the grocery
store again. I wanted to spend some brain time thinking of
what could have been hidden in Poppy's closet, something so
valuable that it was worth breaking into the murdered woman's
house before it had even been cleaned of her blood.

And, most of all, I needed to talk to Lizanne, who had been
outside Poppy's house the day she was killed.

Melinda and I had kept silent about Lizanne's presence at

Cara is on the phone in her home office half the time. You'd
have to check to make sure she wasn't using the pool. Her
husband's hardly ever home. You'd just have to make sure the
dogs were shut up in the house.

"Or, if you didn't mind a higher risk of being seen, you
could cross Poppy's front yard and enter the back by the patio
gate to the side of the house. The point is, once you're in the
backyard, the privacy fence is so high, you're practically invisible."

"Didn't you say Dr. Embler had spent time with Poppy?"

"That's what I heard."

"But not recently."

"You're saying that passions would have had time to cool?"

"I would think so. I mean, even if Cara had discovered her
husband's little fling with Poppy, she had to know by now that
it meant nothing, in terms of consequences in her own life."

I felt that we'd left my brother by himself long enough, so
we moved back to the family room, to find him asleep on the
couch, with the game still blaring.

I managed to wake Phillip up enough to send him to his
own room. He stumbled off, mumbling that he'd see me in
the morning. Robin and I were left looking at each other.

"Would you like to stay the night?" I asked, just as Robin
said, "So, can I stay awhile?"

We laughed a little, but then he put his arms around me,
and it wasn't time for laughing anymore.

Chapter Seven

Robin was sitting on the side of the bed, pulling the sleeves of his shirt back through the right way when I opened my eyes. I reached over and trailed my fingers down his long, bare back, making him shiver.

"Morning," I said, my voice still hazy with sleep.

He turned and bent to kiss me.

"Morning, Roe."

His hair looked like a haystack. He hadn't put on his glasses yet, and his eyes were blue and soft. He looked good enough to eat.

"Are you in a particular hurry?" I asked.

"Just wanted to get out of the way before your company wakes up," he said.

Oh hell. I'd forgotten all about Phillip's presence in my house, to say nothing of the Wynns. I gave a big, windy sigh.

"I'll come get him about eleven-thirty, after I've worked a few hours, and take Phillip to lunch." Robin stroked my hair

back from my face. "You know, tomorro

"You're going to eat here, right?"

"We planned that, didn't we? Remember in this afternoon?"

I pulled a pillow over my head. I didn't wa meeting Robin's mother for the first time on day, when food was the main focus of the day. confident of my cooking.

I'd just have to suck it up and act like a woman.

"She wasn't planning on flying in and cooking, l asked, just to make sure, not wanting to start out beh the woman.

"No, I told her I had made plans for us." Robin lo hopeful. "What can I bring?"

I laughed and pulled the pillow away. "Oh, okay, I guess I up to it. Let me think. I picked up a turkey breast at the stor the other day, thank God. I thought a whole turkey would be too much for just us. So that leaves sweet potatoes, peas, rolls, and cranberry sauce. And dessert."

"I can get rolls and the peas," Robin offered helpfully. "And I can bring some wine."

"That's good. Okay, I'll get the sweet potatoes and fix them, and the cranberries, and I'll make a pie or two. That'll work out."

"What about your mother and her family?"

"I don't know what on earth they're going to do. I think Melissa and Avery are going to Melissa's parents, and I guess they'll take their kids and the baby with them. John David will probably go to my mother's, whatever she's up to doing. They have enough food there to last them through the winter, I think." When I'd been at the house this afternoon, the refrigerator had been full to overflowing.

Poppy's that day, and we'd struggled with our decision for all of thirty seconds. Both of us believed that there was simply no chance at all that Lizanne had stabbed Poppy. But we did need to talk to her about why she'd been there. I guess I had a tiny, tiny sliver of doubt that needed to be erased by hearing Lizanne tell me, in person, what had happened that day.

I called Melinda to ask her to go with me. She was very busy, as you can imagine, but she agreed to go. She wanted to hear what Lizanne had to say as much as I did.

The yard had not been put to bed for winter at the sprawling ranch Cartland had bought when his practice had begun flourishing. The flower beds needed weeding and more mulch, and the grass hadn't gotten its final mowing. Someone had given up just a little too soon. A fenced-in area was strewn with little kids' toys, bright plastics that would crack in the coming cold. But the smell of corn bread rolled out of the back door when Lizanne answered our knock.

"Come in," Lizanne said placidly, her arms full of baby. "Let me just pop Brandon in his playpen, and Davis is already taking a nap. Then I can get the corn bread out of the oven, and we can talk."

Melinda and I came in cautiously; I thought we were both taken aback by Lizanne's casual air. She had to know why we were there.

Brandon was deposited in his playpen with absolutely no fuss, and he sat up and watched with interest as his mother, still one of the most beautiful women I'd ever known, despite having popped out two babies in almost instant succession, slid a pan of corn bread out of the oven and set it on top to cool.

"For the dressing," Lizanne explained, poking it with a finger to test its doneness. I figured that might be a sign of nerves; she certainly didn't need to tell us that. In a bassinet against the wall, Davis gave a little sound and went back to sleep.

"Do you fix yours in a separate pan or in the bird?" Melinda was serious when she asked this burning question. Melinda had been on the quest for the perfect dressing for the past two years.

"Both. There isn't enough, if you just stuff the turkey. And I put some sausage in."

Melinda's eyes lighted up with interest, and she began to talk apples, oysters, and chestnuts. They might have been sitting there for an hour, talking food, if I hadn't interrupted.

"Listen, Lizanne, we found the straps."

"Oh." She looked quite unsurprised. "Why didn't you give them to the police? You should have."

"What were you doing there?"

"Well, I was getting tired of Bubba going out at night and making these silly excuses," Lizanne said. She would never call her husband Cartland, not in a million years.

"So, you confronted Poppy?"

"I was ready to." I watched Lizanne's hands, long and thin, clench into fists. "I didn't get the chance. She never came to the door. And the kids got hungry, and they started crying. I couldn't stand to have anything of hers, so I took the pacifier straps and threw them down in the driveway so she'd know what I thought of her. And I came on home."

"What were you going to say to her if she'd come to the door?" I asked out of sheer curiosity.

"I was going to remind her that since, at Bubba's request, I quit my job after we got married, he is the boys' and my sole support. I was going to point out to her that there are better fish in the sea than Bubba."

Melinda and I exchanged glances. "What do you mean?" Melinda asked. Lizanne was measuring sugar into water to make cranberry sauce.

"Poppy was more serious about Bubba than she was about

122

the other men," Lizanne said after a long pause. "I don't think she wanted to divorce John David and marry Bubba, but I don't think she'd completely dismissed the idea, either. But she might have just been stringing him along. I don't understand people like that." Lizanne turned to us, a half-cup measure in her hand. Her face was white and disturbed. "She just didn't seem to care whom she hurt. She would have what she wanted, and everyone else could just go to hell."

Had Poppy really been that careless, that conscienceless? I had never crossed Poppy. I had never had anything she wanted. Melinda, I noticed, did not look shocked at all.

I was dismayed and a little mortified by my lack of acuity.

"So you just pulled up to the house . . ." I said, hoping to prod her into a more complete account of her actions.

Lizanne poured a whole bag of cranberries into the pot. She was going to have a lot of sauce, and lot of dressing, too. I wondered how much company she was having. It reminded me that I needed to get home and start working in my own kitchen.

Lizanne, having given the berries a stir, turned back to face us. "You all want a drink of something?" she asked politely.

"No thanks," we said in chorus. She laughed, and we all relaxed a little.

"I pulled up to the house, and the boys were in their car seats in the back of the minivan," she said. "I knew Bubba was going to be giving a speech that day, out of town, so there wouldn't be any danger of him driving by and seeing me. John David would be at work. I figured it would be a good time to talk to Poppy. I just wanted to let her know that I knew all about . . . them, and that I wasn't going to divorce Bubba without as much stink as I could raise." Lizanne said this with absolute sincerity. "I know Bubba thinks I'm dumb, and I am about some things." And you could tell she didn't care. "But I know how it'd look in the papers. Mother of twins, orphan of murdered parents, abandoned by her lawyer husband for another woman. And you know what else?"

A little stunned, Melinda and I shook our heads.

"The second I learned about this affair, I started taking the kids to church every single Sunday. I wasn't so consistent before, but I haven't missed a sermon in five months. Wednesday nights, too. And Bubba hasn't gone with me twice, I bet."

Lizanne was going to use God as a character witness.

"*And* I go to the same Sunday school class as Terry McCloud." Terry was another attorney in Lawrenceton. He was my mother's lawyer, so he would be conservatively excellent. "I speak to Terry every Sunday. I make a point of it."

By this time, I was gaping at the woman I'd thought I'd known. I didn't know if I admired her or if I was horrified. I didn't dare look over at Melinda.

"But I don't really want to get a divorce," Lizanne explained, never stopping her little tasks around the stove and sink. "I get along okay with Bubba, and we have everything we need. I'd have to go back to work if we got divorced, and I like being home with the boys." She beamed over at Brandon, who smiled back. He seemed to have inherited his mother's placid nature. "So I went to see Poppy, to try to talk some sense into her. I knew Poppy was at home because her car was in the garage. But she never came to the door." Lizanne blew on a spoonful of cranberry sauce, then held it away to examine the color and consistency. "After a minute, I went over to the fence, thinking I'd go through the gate and knock on the sliding glass door on the patio."

"And did you go into the backyard?" I asked, sitting on the edge of the kitchen chair.

"Oh, no," Lizanne said, her voice once more serene. "There was already someone there, so I went back to the car."

124

"There was someone there," I repeated.

"Yes, I could hear them talking."

"Them?" Melinda said in a croak.

"Yes, them. Poppy and someone else."

"Who was it?" I felt as if the air in the kitchen were vibrating.

"Oh. I don't know. The radio was on, so I couldn't hear very well, but I could hear two voices, and the louder one was Poppy's."

"What did you do?"

"I went back and sat in the car. After about ten minutes, I went and knocked on the door again. But she still didn't come. So after a little bit longer, I threw the straps out of the van and drove away." Lizanne turned back to the stove and stirred.

"You heard her killer," Melinda said.

"What?"

"You heard the voice of the person who killed Poppy," I said.

"Oh, that's . . ." On the verge of saying "ridiculous," Lizanne stopped speaking, stopped moving. Her lips lost their color.

"I could have saved her," Lizanne said finally. "I could have saved her life, and instead I went back to the van and sat."

"Or," I said, not liking the way her color had changed, "you could have gotten killed right along with her, and your children would have been left out in the van all by their lonesome selves."

Lizanne sat down across the table from us. She looked positively punchy with shock.

"Oh," she said, and that was all, but it spoke volumes.

I'd been sure that Lizanne wasn't as hard-hearted as she'd been letting on, and I was right. But she'd felt better when she'd acted tough.

"Could you make out who it was?" I asked after a pause to let Lizanne gather herself.

"No, I was so wrought up, and the radio was playing, and I was so angry . . ."

"Could you tell if the voice was a man's or a woman's?"

Lizanne's large dark eyes focused on me. "Surely it must have been a man's?"

"Look at how angry *you* were," I said. "Do you think you were the only angry woman?"

"No, I reckon not," she said. "I assumed at the time it was a man's voice. Poppy's radio was on so loud—she was listening to NPR, like my daddy used to. Remember, Roe?"

Truthfully, I didn't remember what radio station Lizanne's dad had listened to, though I remembered Arnie with great fondness. But I nodded anyway.

"So, I guess I'll have to go to the police," she said after a moment. "I mean, if I really did hear . . ."

"You ought to," Melinda said, trying to make her voice gentle. Davis squawked, and Lizanne got up and handed him the pacifier that had fallen from his mouth. He resumed sucking and fell back to sleep. Brandon watched us as if we were performing in a soap opera. To my eyes, both children looked like little Bubbas. If Lizanne did divorce Cartland Sewell, his face was still going to be right in front of her for the next sixteen-plus years.

"I guess I wouldn't be telling anyone anything they didn't already know," Lizanne said. I thought she was backing out of going to the police, but finally I decided she was thinking of having to tell the police that her husband was cheating on her. "The way things spread in a small town. Why did Bubba think he was fooling anyone?"

There were probably people in Lawrenceton who hadn't known that Cartland Sewell and Poppy Queensland had been having an affair (me, for example). But while I told myself that I enjoyed juicy gossip as much as the next person, this wasn't entirely true. Illnesses, inheritances, land transactions, job promotions—I was interested in all these bits of information. But sexual misdeeds, no, I didn't want to hear about them. I only knew the cast of John David's couch because Melinda had told me one afternoon when we were driving to Atlanta to shop, and I couldn't get away.

"Do you want Arthur to come here?" I asked, trying to sound offhand.

"That would be good. I have a lot of cooking to do; plus, I don't want to take the boys down to the police station," Lizanne said. She brightened considerably. "Oh, do you think he would?"

"Yes, I bet so," I said. Melinda handed me the phone, and I placed the call. Arthur didn't sound very glad to hear from me, which I could understand. I explained as neutrally as I could.

As I expected, he was angry with me. "You knew all along that Lizanne had been there that day," he said unequivocally. After all, that was the absolute truth.

"Well, we suspected." I was trying to sound mild and intractable, but that's hard to pull off. I just sounded stubborn.

"You're lucky I don't put you both in jail for obstructing an investigation."

Melinda was leaning close enough to hear that, and she looked at me with alarm written large in her brown eyes. I shook my head. No way was Arthur going to do anything like that. "On the other hand," I said, still trying for mild, "we happen to be over at Lizanne's right now, and we happen to know she has some information for you."

"Maybe I'll just arrest her," Arthur said. "She had plenty of reason to kill Poppy."

"Well, if she loved her husband, that would be so. But that's not the case," I snapped. I had run out of mild. "Arthur Smith, you know a woman with two babies in her van is not going to go in and stab someone to death!"

"Still waters run deep," Arthur said portentously.

"Still waters, my round rear end." Now I was sounding like a real Upppity Woman. But as I thought twice, I looked at Lizanne's placid and beautiful face, and read nothing there but polite interest in the outcome of my conference with the detective. Maybe Lizanne was deep water, and maybe she was only a shallow, still, pond. Either way, she was my friend.

"Are you coming?" I tried to sound more moderate.

He sighed, a deep and unhappy exhalation. "Yes, I am. But I'm going to pretend she called me herself, instead of you, and I want you and Melinda gone by the time I get there."

"Okay," I said unhappily. "Let's try to make it a trade-off." I didn't want Lizanne to be alone for very long at all. She was having a tough time, and being alone might sap her good resolution to come clean.

"I'm bringing Trumble with me," he said, and for a second I drew a blank. Then I remembered that was the name of the detective who'd interviewed me. "I'm leaving here in five minutes."

So Melinda and I talked babies with Lizanne for the next ten minutes. That was easy for Melinda, but not for me. I've never had a baby, and I never will. The elderly OB-GYN I'd consulted in Atlanta had been pretty clear that the chances of me conceiving were infinitesimal. I have a tilted womb (charming, huh?) and I don't always produce eggs, which makes me feel like an inferior chicken.

I suppressed a familiar ache and listened with a smile to their swapped stories about teething, walking, crawling, and sleeping patterns. This is the small talk of women of a certain age, and not only was I getting past that age; I'd never learned the language.

I quit feeling sorry for myself when I passed Arthur and Cathy Trumble on the sidewalk to Lizanne's front door, and reflected on how much I had to do between now and tomorrow. It was incredibly fortunate that I had to work only three hours today, and the library would be closed tomorrow and through the weekend for the Thanksgiving holiday.

When I pulled up to Melinda's house, she persuaded me to come in for a minute and talk to John David. He didn't want to go back to the house he'd shared with Poppy, cleaned or not, and he was taking very little care of his son. Melinda hadn't spoken to him about it yet, but she was going to, she told me. "It's not that I don't care for the little guy; he's cute as he can be," she said, guilt written large on her face. "I just feel like I have enough to do."

"Of course," I agreed promptly, because to do less would have been insulting. I realized that no one had suggested that I should take Chase. And I realized that I was relieved. A couple of years before, I'd had the care of a baby, with absolutely no preparation or warning. Going into it cold was simply terrifying. "John David should be able to take care of his own son, especially if he hires a nanny," I said cautiously.

"Avery could cope with the situation," Melinda said. "He took as much care of Marcy as I did, when he was home . . . which wasn't as much as I was, of course. And he was so excited when Charles was born!" Melinda's face was transformed by a huge smile. "Avery's a good dad," she said, wrapping up a whole bundle of memories.

"I guess John David got a big bundle of charm but none of the moral fiber," I said.

She considered. "I think he likes to do the right thing, as long as it's not too much trouble."

That summed up John David pretty accurately. But maybe we both would be proved wrong.

Melinda seemed relieved to get out at her own home, where she could follow her own normal round of activities. She'd deposited the children at Mother's Day Out at the Methodist church so she could finalize the preparations for driving to her parents' home for Thanksgiving, and she told me she was determined to go no matter what happened. "It's been awful and tense the past few days," she said. I couldn't argue with that. "We don't know when the funeral will be, because Poppy's body hasn't been released yet, and this is a good time to get away, at least for a day. The kids need some downtime." I wasn't sure who needed it more, but obviously Melinda was looking forward to seeing her family, and I wished her a happy day before leaving to put in my hours at the library.

It was absolutely dead at work. A few patrons dashed in to return books, and one or two checked out audiobooks for the long drives to holiday destinations. But no one was browsing, and precious few were even using the computers. I had no compunction at all about leaving a little early for my appointment with Bryan Pascoe.

Bryan drove a Cadillac, which surprised me. He was wearing a very nice suit, and he looked as though he'd gotten a haircut. When he held the car door open for me, I smelled his cologne. It was something classic and masculine, like Old Spice—another surprise. I would have predicted a Mustang convertible, a Calvin Klein cologne, and bikini underwear. I couldn't ask him about that, but I amused myself on our ride to the service station named on the receipt by trying to imagine a conversation in which that question would occur naturally.

"I understand that Cartland Sewell has a cast-iron alibi," he said out of the blue. Bryan sounded as if that were a bad thing, and since he was representing John David, I guess it was. The more viable suspects, the better, particularly for my brother-in-law.

"I'm glad for Lizanne's sake," I said. I know this was dumb of me, but I hadn't realized I ought to tell Bryan what had happened with Lizanne the day of Poppy's murder. Now I told him in as few words as possible. After questioning me closely about the probable time of all the events Lizanne had described, the lawyer lapsed back into a silence that I chose to characterize as thoughtful.

The Cadillac was so comfortable and the heat so effective, I was nearly drowsy by the time we reached the Grabbit Kwik. Bryan came around the car to open my door just as I was about to open it myself, so I held still and let him. This world is so devoid of courtesy, I never mind receiving a little, even if it's misplaced.

He offered me his hand, and I took that, too. I was wearing off-white pants, a fuzzy blue sweater, and blue suede moccasins, so I didn't have to worry about getting out of the car modestly. He gave a little pull, and up I popped, just like a cork.

The outside of the Grabbit Kwik was like any other convenience store/gas station along any highway. Grabbits are all painted a bright green, and this one had all its tawdry Christmas regalia in place. It had probably been up since the Halloween ghosts and pumpkins had come down. The concrete outside the door was dirty, but the glass doors were gleaming. We were the only customers at the moment, which I chose to regard as a good sign.

Inside, everything was as you'd expect, too—the racks of junk food and the refrigerated cases of drinks, the raised counter, the woman in the red smock behind the cash register. Her hair was a construction of elaborate and rigid ringlets, and she was generously round. Her heavily lined eyes looked like raisins sunk in gingerbread dough.

"Can I help you folks?" she asked cheerfully. On a tiny television behind her, a talk show was in progress.

131

Bryan produced a card immediately and introduced himself. She told him her name was Emma McKibbon and that she'd worked there two years. Her eyes flicked over to me curiously, but Bryan didn't include me in this dialogue. He'd been so absolutely correct and polite up to now; it made me as curious as Emma apparently was. But there must be a reason, so I kept quiet.

The woman's face looked really familiar, though, and I kept examining her, hoping I'd make the connection.

Bryan was asking her if there was any way she could remember a particular customer who'd come by two days before, and Emma confirmed that she'd been right there behind the counter on Monday. But Emma was wary of Bryan, for whatever reason—maybe just because he was an affluent white male. Watching her face seal itself off, I had a sinking feeling that any information we could have gathered was being chucked down a well inside the clerk.

"We were pretty busy that morning, same as always on Monday," she said grudgingly. "Let me see the receipt, but I ain't holding out much hope."

I pulled the receipt out of my pocket and handed it to her. As our eyes met, a little *click* sounded in my ears. "Emma!" I said. "You were three years behind me in high school, right?"

"I sure was," she said, relieved to track down her own elusive memory. "I'm Jane's sister—Jane Pocket she was then."

"Oh, sure. How is Jane?"

"Well, she's gotten married twice now, and she has four kids in school and another one on the way. I have two myself. I married Dante McKibbon right after we graduated. My girls—one's in high school, and the other's in junior high."

"Oh, how nice," I said, smiling as brightly as I could.

"Now, you still live in town, don't you? I'm sure I saw you at the store last month."

"I do. I have a house over on McBride."

"You married?"

A black pit opened abruptly, right in front of me, and I took a deep breath, gathered my composure, and stepped right over it. "I'm a widow," I said, maintaining my smile.

"Oh, too bad! You got any babies?"

"No, I'm all on my lonesome," I said.

Emma obviously regarded this as the worst of all possible situations and cast around in her brain desperately for something upbeat to say to me. "Well, you look great," she told me. "You don't look a day older than you did when you graduated. Those kids'll put the years on you, for sure."

Bryan opened his mouth, but I got in there first. I knew what I was doing now. "You remember my mom?" I asked. Emma nodded. No one forgot my mother. "She married John Queensland, John David's dad? I know you remember John David." He would be a little younger than Emma, but he'd had a lot of success on the football field, and that would have made his name more familiar.

"Oh, sure," Emma said, relieved to be on a different topic. "That John David, he speaks every time he comes in here."

"Oh, he gets his gas here?" I leaned on the counter, as if I had all the time in the world.

"Sometimes," she said. "He was in here the other morning, the morning you were asking about, unless I'm real confused. But I think it was early, not at the time on this receipt. This says ten-twenty-two, and he always comes in before eight, on his way to Atlanta."

"You remember Bubba?"

"Which one?" she said with a big laugh, and I had to laugh right along with her. "You mean the big black Bubba who played center on the football team, or the Chinese Bubba who was so smart, or that Bubba who's a lawyer in town?"

"Lawyer Bubba."

"He comes in here, too, but not so often," she said, thinking back. "He's always in a hurry, don't talk to me."

"You remember Poppy?"

"Yeah, I hear she's dead."

"Yeah. She married John David."

"Yeah, after they fought all through high school. Were you in the cafeteria that day she slapped him upside the head?"

"I had already graduated, but I heard about it."

"She didn't hold back none, either. She let him have it. Maybe that's why somebody killed her, she mighta whomped on them like that."

"Her mom and dad are here," I said.

"Yeah, her dad is that preacher," Emma said. "My mama used to clean house for them. I was over to see Mama the other day when the radio said that about Poppy. My mama said, 'Like father, like daughter, I guess.' "

"Oh my gosh," I said, "did he make pass at your mother?" I am sure I looked as disgusted as I felt. Somehow, you're always a child when you hear about the peccadilloes of those who represented authority to you when you were young.

Emma looked sardonic. "He don't like my skin tone," she said, as if adding another mark against Marvin Wynn's tally of bad taste. "But all those woman who came to him for counseling, you can bet a bunch of them got more than prayers. Especially the really young ones."

"Ew," I said, and Emma laughed.

"I like a man with more meat to him than that," she said. "His wife is like that, too, all thin and bony. Now *she* was in here Monday around the right time, and I was surprised, because I hadn't seen that woman in a coon's age. Did they move back into town?"

I leaned more heavily against the counter, suddenly weak.

Bingo. What the hell had Sandy Wynn been doing anywhere in the vicinity? I stuffed that thought away for later examination. I hoped that no one else would come in, since we were on such a roll. "Well, I won't take up too much more of your time. I know you're at work. I don't know if you remember this, but I have a brother."

She looked puzzled.

"He's a half brother. You may not recall that my mom was divorced when I was pretty young?"

"I knew something happened, since he wasn't around anymore."

"Yeah, well, my dad remarried, so I have this brother, Phillip, who lives in California. He just hitchhiked over here to see me, and he met these girls along the way."

"I can't believe he got here alive," Emma said frankly.

"Me either. It was dumb, but he's a kid." I shrugged. "Anyway, he may have been here that morning, Monday morning. The car he was in stopped here for gas. It would have been my brother—he's about as tall as this lawyer here—and two girls, both older than he is." I dredged my memory. "He says they were in a green Impala." Though Phillip had told me he'd caught a bus into Lawrenceton, I thought it would be unfair of me not to check on him, too.

"Can't remember," Emma said after she'd turned it over in her head. "So many kids, and if they're that young and white, I don't know 'em, so I just don't recall."

"Thanks for taking the time to help," I said. "I enjoyed talking to you. You tell Jane I said hello, okay? And Dante."

"Sure will," Emma said. She smiled, but she also looked at me as though she was sorry for me.

Well, I just had to swallow that. I kept my smile steady, and Bryan and I left the store after he'd asked me if I wanted a cup of coffee, then bought me one and paid for it.

He handed me into the car as ceremoniously as he'd gotten me out of it, and I found that was a tiny bit tiresome. But I was glad to sink back into the leather seat and feel the heat blowing around me as we started back to town.

"That was a stroke of luck." I was thinking of Emma's face as it was now, trying to picture the way it had been in our high school days. I was thanking my lucky stars I'd remembered the woman, since she was a few years younger. In high school, that makes a big difference.

"That was very smooth," Bryan said, interrupting what I suddenly realized had been a long silence.

"Smooth? What?"

"Your questioning. Are you sure you don't want to be a lawyer? Or maybe join the police force?"

"I'm sure," I said, smiling. He'd sounded almost miffed, but I was going to ignore that. I had a feeling Bryan was unhappy because his own questioning had proved unproductive. "If you know someone, it's just easier to ask the right questions."

"So. Mrs. Wynn was there, Bubba may have been, although probably not, John David was there earlier, and she couldn't remember your brother," Bryan summarized.

"That's about it."

"Sandy Wynn." He shook his head, looking as stunned as I felt.

"Yes. She's so—well, she seemed so devastated when they came to my house Monday night. I could have sworn all that grief was genuine."

"But it's hard to understand how she could have just skipped telling the police she'd been in the area that morning."

"Yes, of course. Well, maybe Emma made a mistake." I'd heard older women complain before that young people seemed to regard them as interchangeable. Maybe Emma had seen another thin, fit older woman and identified her mentally as Poppy's mom, after she'd heard Poppy had been killed. That would be natural. But Emma had sounded so certain, and she had struck me as a good observer. And after all, *someone* had dropped that receipt on my floor.

"What are you going to do about Mrs. Wynn?" I asked. "Will you talk to her yourself, or will you sic Arthur on her?"

Bryan looked gloomy. "I should tell the police," he said after a thoughtful pause. "I wonder if she was the visitor Poppy was expecting, the reason she didn't ride to Uppity Women with you."

"Mrs. Wynn's phone records would show if she'd phoned Poppy," I said hesitantly. "Would Poppy's phone record show incoming calls as well as outgoing? Can you look at those?"

"After the police have . . . if they arrest John David, I can. Other than that, I haven't any legal right to see them. They're John David's records, too. He could request them, give me permission. . . . I'll think about it."

We were silent during the rest of the drive. I guess both of us had plenty to think about. But I don't think we were pondering the same things.

Chapter Eight

By the time I got back to my house, Phillip was home and more than willing to help me unload the groceries—so he could find out what I'd gotten that he wanted to eat. I'd seen about half the people I knew dashing frantically through the grocery store, and all of them looked as scatterbrained as I felt, but I hadn't been so frantic that I'd forgotten to buy some snack stuff.

I told Phillip he was going to help me cook, and he stared longingly at the television before he agreed.

"How was your lunch with Robin?" I asked.

"We had ham sandwiches," Phillip said, which was not exactly the information I was after. "He's pretty cool," Phillip added almost grudgingly after I'd put away the contents of one bag. "We had a long talk about stuff. The only dumb thing about him is his name."

"I'm glad you two are getting along," I said. I was very curious to hear Robin's account of their conversation.

"You gonna marry him?"

It would be beyond coy to pretend I'd never thought of it. "If he asks me, I'll think about it," I said.

"You could ask him."

Hmmm. "No," I said. "I just don't think I could do that." Though I was a raving liberal compared to 50 percent of the people I knew in Lawrenceton, I knew asking Robin to marry me was way beyond my possibility level, even though I was now an Uppity Woman.

"Chicken," Phillip said fondly.

"Yep," I said. "That's me. Oh, by the way, I found a gas receipt on the floor Monday night. Did your friend stop for gas on her way into Lawrenceton?"

His face turned red just at the mention. "No," he said. "We stopped for gas in Rome. Remember, I took a bus into Lawrenceton."

Phillip had no reason to lie, and he'd never known Poppy. I had enough confirmation to drop him from my list. Though Emma had narrowed the list down, I needed to talk to the other people who might have dropped the receipt. I wanted to hear their stories with my own ears.

Opening the refrigerator, I poked the turkey breast with an anxious finger. It was close to being thawed. I got the package of ready-made piecrust out so it could be reaching room temperature, then took the pecans out of the freezer for the pecan pie. I handed my little brother a recipe for pumpkin pie and a can of pumpkin. "Put all of this stuff in there," I said. I got everything required out of the cabinet and put it in a clump on the counter. I pulled out my little electric mixer and a mixing bowl and set them on the counter by his stuff. "There you go," I said briskly. I turned on both of my ovens, yanked two pie plates out of the cabinet, and patted the piecrusts into place. Then I threw together the pecan pie.

Phillip worked quite a bit slower, but once he found out where the measuring spoons were and so on, he did a creditable job of preparing the pumpkin filling.

Since Robin's mom was coming, I felt obliged to follow Lizanne's example in making my own cranberry sauce, but that's the easiest thing in the world, and I got that ready while the pies were baking. Phillip ran the vacuum for me while I cooked the sweet potatoes and put them through the food processor for the sweet potato casserole, and I decided after that was done, we could rest. Every dish went into the dishwasher, I started it running, and then Phillip and I watched a stupid game show on television. We competed with each other to see who could shout out the answer the fastest, and in general we had a silly good time.

I called out for Chinese—we considered ourselves on the cutting edge, in Lawrenceton, having a Chinese restaurant that delivered—and though it was late in the evening to be eating, I was feeling relaxed, since the house looked good, I'd gotten a head start on the cooking, and, most of all, my brother just couldn't be involved in any way in Poppy's death.

Tomorrow, I would meet Robin's mother, and while I was a bit anxious about that, I figured since Robin spoke so lovingly of her, she couldn't be too formidable. . . . And after all, I'd been a grown woman, married and widowed, for many years now.

Just when I was feeling fairly saturated with satisfaction, the phone rang. I reached over to the table by my chair, gestured to Phillip to turn down the volume on the television, and answered it.

"Aurora," Mother said.

"Hi, Mother. How are things at your house?"

"John is doing fairly well," she said, giving me the most important news first. "John David hasn't been arrested, thank

God. Melinda called. He was over at her house, and he announced he was taking the baby and they were spending the night in a motel. He said he felt like he'd been enough trouble to people and that he should spend some time with his son."

I held the phone away and gaped at it. Would wonders never cease? "That's amazing," I said, finally realizing I had to say something.

"Yes," she said a little dryly. "I thought so, too."

"Can you and John come over tomorrow to have a glass of wine with Phillip and Robin and Robin's mother?"

"His mother? His mother's in town?" Mother was shocked out of her weariness. "Oh my Lord, you should have told me!"

"Yes, she's over at his apartment now. She's coming to Thanksgiving here tomorrow." I knew Mother had too much on her shoulders right now, but it was good to hear her sounding more like her normal self. "What about you and John? If you want to come here to eat, I'll have plenty. Did John David tell you any plans he might have? Should I invite him?" Three extra adults would be stretching it, but I could manage. I had assumed that John David would be staying with John and my mother and that they'd be eating together, though celebrating would be impossible.

"Of course John and I will come over for a glass of wine, and to meet Robin's mother. But I don't think we'd be exactly up to a festive meal. I'm feeding us out of the refrigerator tomorrow, since I just couldn't work up the energy for anything else. I think we have enough food here to last us for two weeks, and we actually have a smoked turkey breast and a ham. John David is coming over here. What time would you like us to drop by?"

I had planned to serve the holiday meal at one, so we settled on three o'clock. I told mother I'd call John David at his motel and at least invite him to come eat (no matter how much I secretly hoped he would decline). I remembered one more question for my mother before I hung up.

"Has John David heard from the police about when he's going to get Poppy's body back to bury?"

"It seems as though there's a backlog in Atlanta, so it won't be until Monday at the earliest."

"Oh no." Though in a way it was a relief that Poppy's funeral wouldn't be within the next couple of days, I didn't want to think about that backlog.

"I'm so glad the Wynns decided to go back home," Mother continued. "I know they had things to take care of, because they left to come over here in such a hurry. It'll be much better if they just come back when the funeral's settled. I think they assumed they'd be making the arrangements, and it took them aback when John David told them what he was going to do."

"The Wynns are leaving? Where are they now?" I had actually forgotten about the Wynns, and to my shame, my Thanksgiving plans had never included them. I carried the cordless phone over to the door of the room the Wynns had been using and glanced inside. Their things were still there. Hmm.

"Why, I don't know." Mother sounded surprised. "Aren't they—they haven't come to your house and gotten their bags?"

"No," I said, anxiety making my voice sharp. "I haven't seen them since last night."

"I talked to them about four today," Mother said, "and they told me they were leaving. Where do you suppose they could be?"

"I don't know." I had a shameful, petulant moment of wishing someone would just do the predictable thing. I don't deal well with prolonged upheaval. "Do they have any good friends left in town?"

"You know, they didn't have a lot even when they lived here."

That was true, though I'd never posed it to myself that way.

The Wynns, tall and thin and aggressively healthy, bright and articulate, had never been the most popular ministerial couple in town. The church youth group had been popular, though, because Marvin Wynn, awkward with his own belated child, was a whiz with other people's children.

I sighed, trying to aim it away from the phone. All I wanted to do was go to bed. But I had to track down my guests, and I had to relieve my mother of this anxiety.

"I'll call around a little," I said. "I'll get back to you. Maybe they're with John David, playing with the baby. Which motel?"

I called the Lawrenceton Best Western, and John David was in.

"Poppy's folks didn't leave our key with you?" John David sounded tired, and numb. I could hear the baby crying in the background. "They wanted to get some family heirloom to take back to their house with them—something of Sandy's mother's. I told them I had no idea where it was but said they were welcome to go over there and look. They were supposed to leave my house key with you."

"How long ago was that?"

"Hours. I thought they were long gone back home."

"I guess I'll go over there and check," I said. It was the last thing in the world I wanted to do, but it was what I should do.

"Please do." There was a long pause. John David said, "I don't know what they could be doing in our house for so long. Poppy always had a very tense relationship with her parents. If you'd do this, I'd really appreciate it. I'm just not up to dealing with them tonight. This little guy is missing Poppy." I knew my stepbrother was referring to Chase, but I think he was also talking about himself.

It was pitch-black, and I didn't know what I would find over at the house on Swanson. I wanted someone to go with me, preferably someone bigger than I, or at least well armed. My dad and his wife would kill me if I took Phillip to a place where he might have *any* sort of bad experience. Robin's mother was at his place, and I hated to butt in on their time together; plus, it wouldn't make a good impression, would it—calling Robin to come help me, when his mom was in residence? Calling the police seemed a little over the top. I thought of Angel or Shelby Youngblood, who used to work for Martin and me— and then I remembered they'd gone to Florida. That left only one possibility on my list. Reluctantly, I called Bryan Pascoe. That was better than calling Arthur anyway. Why'd I call a guy? Politically incorrect, huh? Because I was scared, that's why. And I figured Melinda was busy with her kids. And I didn't like Avery.

Bryan, to my near dismay, was delighted to hear from me, and willing to go to Poppy's and meet me there.

Phillip, engrossed in his TV show, gave me an offhand wave as I left. It took only five minutes to get to Poppy and John David's place, but the lawyer was already there. Bryan was wearing jeans and a sweater, which for him was really letting his hair down.

I apologized again for getting him out of his house so late in the evening.

"No problem," he said. "I'm a full-service lawyer. Besides, all I had to do was sit around and watch a tape of *Buffy the Vampire Slayer!*"

I laughed, much to my own surprise.

"What are you doing for the holiday?" I asked, just to stave off going up that sidewalk and into the house. Sure enough, the house wasn't dark; even though it ought to have been. Sandy and Marvin Wynn were apparently still there. What on earth were they doing?

"I'm going to have dinner with my mother at the Assisted Living Center," Bryan said.

144

Again I was surprised. Somehow, I couldn't picture Bryan with his mother. "Your dad's gone?" I asked.

"Nope, he's living in Atlanta with his second wife, a very nice woman he met in his nursing home. He and my mother have been divorced for the past twenty years or so."

"And he remarried. I guess you're never too old for romance."

"Definitely not," Bryan said. "Now, what are we doing here?"

"The Wynns are in the house. They borrowed John David's key. They were supposed to come by and get their bags and leave for their home. They told my mother they'd return when the funeral was definitely scheduled. They told John David they wanted to retrieve something of Sandy's mother's, some family heirloom Poppy had. I don't believe he asked or cared what it was. They've been here much longer than that should take. And we're almost certain that Sandy was in the area the morning Poppy was killed."

Bryan considered for a minute. "So, am I here as John David's lawyer or as your bodyguard?"

I smiled again, though I don't know if he could make it out in the gloom. Poppy and John David lived in the middle of the block, and the streetlights on the corners didn't really illuminate their yard. "A bit of both," I said. "I'm worried about them. But if they're okay, I plan on being mad at them. They've been here way too long." I took a deep breath. "Mostly, this is just weird and needs to be looked into. John David asked me to do that for him."

"Clear as a bell," Bryan said.

We went up the flagstones to the front door, and after a moment's hesitation, I opened it without knocking. This wasn't the Wynns' house, after all.

Bryan shut the door behind us, and we stood in the hallway at the foot of the stairs leading up to the bedrooms, trying to make sense of what we saw. Marvin Wynn was crouched by Poppy's rolltop desk, in the small room to the right of the stairs, the room originally intended for a dining room. Both Poppy and John David used it as an office, and they each had a computer there. A large bookshelf covered one wall, and it was crammed with all kinds of books and knickknacks. Now the room was in an utter jumble. Half the books were on the floor. Marvin, crouched on the floor, was pulling the drawers out of the rolltop desk and turning them over to examine the bottoms.

He was so startled when he looked up and discovered two people observing him that he jumped, visibly. He gasped and dropped the drawer, which landed painfully on his thighs. He made another noise, this one surprising from a minister.

Poppy would not have taped a family heirloom to the bottom of the drawer.

"What are you doing?" I asked, and I didn't sound polite.

"What is it, Marv?" Sandy called from the top of the stairs. She froze when she saw us. Her large brown eyes, magnified many times by her outsize brown-framed glasses, were wide and shocked.

"What are you two doing?" I said again, with even more of an edge to my voice now. Someone had already helped himself to searching the contents of Poppy's closet and her bedroom. Now Poppy's mom and dad were ransacking the house under the guise of parental love. I was very unhappy with them. I was also angry that people I'd always respected were making a mockery of that respect by their behavior.

The Wynns appeared to be groping for an answer to my abrupt question.

"We, ah, we were looking for something. We asked John David if he'd mind."

"You told John David you were looking for an heirloom Mrs.

Wynn's mom had left her," I said bluntly. "You've been here for hours, searching this house, as far as I can see. And I'm sure whatever precious heirloom it was, Poppy wouldn't have taped it to the bottom of a drawer, or stuffed it into a book!"

The Wynns didn't seem to be able to come up with a response. Finally, Marvin said, "Who is this man with you?"

"I'm Bryan Pascoe, John David's attorney."

Sandy Wynn came farther down the stairs, the first time she'd moved since she'd called to her husband. She exchanged glances with Marvin.

"Surely you didn't need to bring a *lawyer*," Marvin said in his best ministerial voice. "After all, we're family here."

He could not have said anything more calculated to make my neck crawl.

"We are *not* family," I said clearly. "Please explain yourselves."

"Listen, missy," Sandy said. "We are thirty years older than you are, and you will treat us with some respect."

"When you deserve it."

Sandy's face sagged on its bones, making her look much older in an instant. "We were just looking for some old family things," she insisted. "We haven't found them. Since you're in such a snit, missy, we'll just leave." She said this as if it was a big threat. "We'll stop by your house and get our bags and go home. You'll excuse me, under the circumstances, if I don't write a thank-you note."

"It's very late for you to start home," Bryan said, sounding irritatingly reasonable. "Why don't you check into the motel here in town, instead, and start back in the morning?"

"No, young man," Marvin Wynn said. "I'm not too old to drive at night, and we want to get out of this town. The day I retired from my job here was one of the best days of my life."

I'd learned, years ago, that being a pastor is a *job*—a difficult and stressful one at that—but nonetheless, I found it shocking to hear the former Reverend Wynn speak in such a vicious way.

Bryan didn't respond, which was a relief. I didn't want to hear any more discussion. I just wanted the absence of the Wynns. I nudged an open book with my foot. The house was in a terrible state now. I sighed, already guessing whose task it would be to set it to rights.

Sandy and Marvin took some time getting their coats; with Bryan and me standing there, there was little opportunity for them to take anything. I hated being so suspicious, but I knew I had to be alert. This situation was completely fishy. Sandy had seemed so broken up on Monday night, but now I knew she'd already been in Lawrenceton that morning. Marvin, too, had appeared grief-stricken and miserable, at least to my eyes. And yet here they were, trashing their daughter's home.

Finally, they were at the door. Swaddled in all their winter gear (pretty much not necessary, for the night was in the fifties), the older couple looked harmless and beneficent with their silver hair and glasses.

Sandy opened her mouth to say something else insulting, but I preempted her. "What were you doing out at the Grabbit Kwik getting gas Monday morning? Have you told the police about your little trip to Lawrenceton before Poppy's body was found?"

"We never came here Monday morning," Marvin said with dignity. "I went to get my annual physical, and Sandy went to do some comparison shopping for a new stove."

"Good cover story," I said to Sandy. "Something you could spend a long time doing, with no tangible results."

If Sandy had looked tense before, she looked beleaguered now. But her lips stayed pressed together. I couldn't have wiggled one bit of truth between them.

"Key," I said tersely, holding out my hand. Sandy fished in her pocket and dropped the key on my palm, which closed around it instantly. But then I had a thought, and I opened my palm to compare this key to the one John David had loaned me. They matched.

The Wynns gave us twin glares as they left.

I sat down on the stairs when the door shut behind them. This had shaken me more than I'd realized. I was actually surprised at how much the week's events were depleting my normal energy. I'd had several of these shaky spells. Bryan sat by me. He put his arm around me, which I could have done without, but it was okay. It didn't feel sexual, not until his fingers started playing with my hair, that is.

"Do you want to call John David from here?"

"Would you?" I was just plain being weak.

"Sure," he said, but he didn't move. "What do you think they were looking for?" he asked after a moment or two.

"I don't know. Something small. And the person who was searching Poppy's closet was looking for something small, too. Something that could be hidden in a book, or a shoe box."

"Jewelry?"

"That would fit. Or documents."

"What kind of documents? She left a will. Poppy and John David both made wills when Poppy found out she was pregnant."

"John David tell you that?"

"Yes. But it wasn't the first thing he said. He didn't come out with it until I asked him that specifically."

I thought Bryan was telling me that in his opinion, John David hadn't been thinking of his possible financial gain from Poppy's death. I had never considered the fact that Poppy might have some money stashed away, and I couldn't imagine where such a stash could have come from. Her dad was a minister, so his pay had been low, and he and his wife were still very much alive. If Poppy had ever gotten any substantial inheritance from another relative, I'd never heard of it. And Poppy had worked for a few years, but working for a few years as a teacher and living off the proceeds were almost a guarantee you didn't have a lot left over. "What lawyer drew up the wills?" I asked.

"Bubba Sewell."

"Hmm. You know what I wonder? I wonder if Poppy gave Bubba a key during the course of their affair."

"I hope I don't have to ask him that in court." Bryan's hand kept combing through my hair. I moved a little farther from him, and his hand dropped into his lap.

"I can ask him." Especially after our confrontation the day before (or had it been Monday?), Bubba and I were quite ready to be rude to each other. My mind moved on ahead. "Do you think . . . do you suppose . . . that Poppy gave a key to each of her, um, men friends?"

"There'd be quite a few around, if that's the case." Bryan looked thoughtful.

"Yes." I had a lot of unpleasant thoughts circling in my tired brain. "But Bubba . . ."

"Yes?"

Suddenly, I didn't want to continue. "Nothing," I said. "While I check out the house, why don't you call John David and let him know what happened? Then we can go. I really appreciate your doing this."

"This is just the kind of thing a good lawyer does for his clients," Bryan said with a wide, sharklike smile.

"There must be a lot I don't know about good lawyers." I smiled back. I went up the stairs. The closet, of course, was still in disarray. This time, even John David's clothes and ties and coats and sweaters had been gone through. What the hell were people looking for? I was assuming that two different people (or groups of people) had gone through the house. The first

150

intruder, the one who'd confined the search to Poppy's half of the closet, had had a specific idea of where the object—whatever it was—had been stashed. In contrast, the Wynns had used a shotgun approach.

"You could find out," Bryan said, and I looked at him blankly. I'd been lost in my thoughts. I didn't even realize for a few seconds that he had followed me and was continuing the conversation. I was too slow responding. Bryan's face wasn't too happy. "Excuse me," I said. "I was wondering what they could be looking for."

"Okay. Anything else you want to do here tonight?"

"No. I'll clean it up Friday. I'll see if my sister-in-law will help."

"Then I'll call John David." Bryan went off to use the telephone.

I sat where I was and eyed the devastation around me. I didn't see how the Wynns could have hoped to conceal their depredations. They'd have had to work all night to put things back. I wondered how they'd hoped to explain it. This looked like a go-for-broke situation. If they'd found what they needed, they wouldn't *care* if they couldn't explain it. For a couple who placed tremendous importance on community opinion, they were acting recklessly. That meant they were desperate.

So, they were searching for something of vital importance, something so significant to their future that their need for it eclipsed their daughter's death.

I could not understand parents like that, though I reminded myself of the notorious struggles between the Wynns and Poppy when she was in her teens. And I recalled what Emma McKibbon had told me about the Reverend Wynn's predilection for young women. Was there proof of the retired minister's dalliance with female members of his congregation? Maybe such proof was what Poppy had concealed in her home.

I shook my head, all to myself. Why would she do that? What leverage would it give her with her parents? I couldn't imagine what she would want from them; want it so badly that she'd keep such unpleasant things. And what could those things be? Pictures? I swallowed hard, disgusted at downing such an indigestible idea.

"Are you going to be sick?" Bryan, having returned from calling John David, sounded terrified at the prospect.

"No, just thinking bad thoughts."

"I talked to John David. He's baffled. I told him they said they were going home until they heard from him about the funeral—they're reverting to the original plan—and he seemed relieved. I also called Arthur Smith again and left yet another message on his voice mail at work. So far, he hasn't responded to any of my calls. I want to tell him what we found out about Sandy Wynn, and I want to tell him that the Wynns were here tonight."

"I hope he calls back soon," I said dutifully, though in truth I found it hard to care. I felt very tired, which seemed about par lately. I dragged myself to my feet. I didn't want to ask Bryan for help. My stomach curdled with anxiety. Oh boy. Maybe I *was* going to be sick.

I managed to get to my car without disgracing myself, and after thanking Bryan for coming out and providing moral and tactical assistance, I drove home.

Phillip was on the phone when I walked in, and he was smiling broadly, so I figured the person on the other end was a female. After a minute, I deduced it was Josh Finstermeyer's sister, Joss. After ten more minutes, I grew a wee bit exasperated and gestured to Phillip to wind up the conversation. He did so willingly enough, then told me all about what the Finstermeyers were doing for their Thanksgiving celebration—remarkably, almost exactly what we would be doing. He asked if he could go over to their house tomorrow afternoon, after we'd eaten, and I told him that would probably be okay. He beamed at me.

It was the first time I'd seen Phillip look carefree, and it made him very attractive. I felt sorry for Joss. I hoped she was a self-sufficient young woman.

"What happened with the Wynns?" Phillip asked. "I was sitting here watching TV when they came stomping in like someone had stuck a cattle prod up their—like they were really fired up. They didn't even speak."

"They were mad at me," I said, realizing I should have called ahead and warned Phillip what to expect. He didn't seem unduly shaken by the incident, and I reminded myself all over again that Phillip had been raised in a different world from the one I'd been reared in. (That made me feel old, by the way.)

Robin had learned something about Phillip over lunch, I hoped, something worth telling me. I couldn't picture my dad telling Phillip about the facts of life—well, Phillip knew the facts. What I meant, I decided, was the responsibilities.

I was aware that I was absolutely exhausted. "Phillip, I have to go to bed," I said.

"Sure, Roe. Anything you need me to do?"

"No. I just hope I'm not catching anything."

"You look kind of, ah, tired."

Nice way of saying I looked like warm Jell-O. "Yeah, I am. I'm going to call it a day. Come get me if you need me." I went into my bedroom, and after a trip to my bathroom, I pulled on my nightgown and crawled into bed. No Robin to join me tonight, I reflected as I began to get drowsy (which was almost immediately). Maybe that was good. I didn't feel up to making whoopee. I felt achy all over, my skin extra sensitive. As I drifted into sleep, I prayed that I wasn't getting the flu.

Chapter Nine

I wasn't running fever in the morning when I woke up, and I felt a lot better. Of course, I'd slept an hour and a half later than I'd planned, but somehow it was impossible to get out of bed in any hurry. I was sure Phillip wouldn't be up yet. Sure enough, when I went into the kitchen in my fuzzy slippers and bathrobe, he was nowhere in sight. I made some coffee and put out some coffee cake I'd gotten the day before. It was pretty close to time to put in the turkey, so I preheated the oven before I sat down with my breakfast. It was a beautiful day, sunny, and the temperature was expected to reach the sixties, though it was about forty outside at the moment.

I sat gazing dreamily out the window into my backyard, ignoring a magazine lying by my mug on the table. A list of things I had to do was there, too, and not one item crossed off. I found it hard to care. I finished the coffee and a piece of the coffee cake. As a matter of habit, I went to pour my second cup. But I just didn't want it today. Maybe this was the way my body was trying to get my mind to agree to get up and work. Actually, I needed to go to the bathroom anyway, so I figured I might as well get dressed.

In a matter of minutes, I was in my nice suede pants and orange sweater, my tortoise-rimmed glasses on to coordinate, all made up and ready—and with lots of messy kitchen work to do. I was just going to have a backward day. Normally, I wouldn't have put on my good clothes until the kitchen had been cleaned right before my guests' arrival. But I couldn't bring myself to care about my impracticality.

I scooted up my sleeves, found the apron that provided the most coverage, and turned on the Macy's parade to watch while I worked. I like that about my kitchen and den area; and that was another change from my former life, when I'd had no desire whatsoever for anyone to watch me while I was cooking, and I'd been glad my kitchen was just a kitchen. Now, I just didn't care. My kitchen/den/informal dining area seemed just great. I enjoyed glancing at the parade while I worked, and I enjoyed the sun coming in through the big windows on either side of the fireplace. Cooking took me away from Poppy's death and the mess and chaos surrounding it. Two hours flew by before I knew it. I glanced at the clock with some surprise.

Time to take stock.

Pies ready. Cranberry sauce ready. Dressing ready, prepared with canned chicken stock just so I'd save myself last-minute rushing. I'd gotten the turkey greased and into the baking bag, and now I slid the big pan into the warm oven. Robin would bring the English peas, which just required heating with some butter, and the rolls, which only had to brown—so nothing to do on that front. He'd have the wine, and he would open that. I got out the corkscrew and the wineglasses. Only the sweet potato casserole needed some more fixing.

The sugar was already mixed in, and I tasted to make sure

I'd added enough. I'd finished adding the spices and eggs when Phillip at last emerged from the guest bathroom, shiny and dressed. He poured himself a huge glass of juice and cut a piece of coffee cake. He gave me a sleepy smile and settled on a stool at the breakfast bar to watch the parade. After a minute, he flipped open the *TV Guide* and started looking at the football listings.

Once Phillip had finished breakfast, I asked him to help me with the big tablecloth for the nicer table in the dining room. I set the table slowly, trying to make it look correct . . . but not ridiculously so. This was not an imposing formal occasion. If I turned it into that, I'd have to go put on panty hose and a dress. Yuck.

Good silver, good china. (I'd be doing dishes all day.) I kept checking the table. Salt, pepper. I got out the gravy boat. Glasses for Ice tea. Sugar. Dish for lemon wedges. Serving spoons. The smaller turkey platter.

I'd be cleaning up at *midnight.*

Suddenly, my energy seemed to leak out through my fingertips, as though my night's sleep had simply evaporated. I pulled out a chair and sat down with an ungraceful thud.

Could the prospect of meeting Robin's mother really be that frightening? Martin's mother and father had been long dead when we'd become engaged, and I'd already known his sister Barby. Arthur had been my only other halfway-serious suitor. I'd known Mindy and Coll Smith, Arthur's folks, since I was little, at least by sight. So, though I was thirty-six, this was my first "meet the parent" situation.

I rose and pushed the chair back into place, though I hardly felt better. I went back into the den and unwisely sat in my favorite old chair, close to Phillip, who was watching some sports show. In about thirty seconds, I actually dozed off. Phillip woke me up at quarter to one.

"You want to go put some lipstick on or something?" he asked a little anxiously. "It's almost time for them to be here. The timer for the turkey breast went off thirty minutes ago, and the little red thing was sticking up out of the turkey, so I got it out of the oven. I put the sweet potatoes in. Was that okay?"

"More than okay," I assured him. "You saved my life, brother."

He looked justifiably pleased with himself. Groggy with sleep, I had to absolutely push myself into the kitchen. I put ice in the glasses, a stick of margarine on a butter dish to pass around with the rolls—oh my God, the rolls! I told myself sternly to calm down. Robin was bringing them; they'd only take a few minutes. The rolls could go in after I'd gotten the sweet potatoes out. The dressing was baking in the other oven. (Following my mother's tradition, I always baked it separately.) All I had to do was make the gravy. But first, a look in my bedroom mirror was in order.

Phillip had been optimistic when he suggested I needed only lipstick. But I looked all right after brushing my hair, cleaning my glasses, and slapping on a little fresh makeup. Back in the kitchen, I buzzed around doing tiny things. I asked Phillip if he'd give some attention to his own hair, and with a dark glance, he retired to the bathroom to look in the mirror.

"And it better be perfectly picked up in there!" I called through the door.

"Yes, Mom!" he yelled back.

I stuck my tongue out, since he couldn't see me. Mom indeed.

And then the doorbell rang.

As I went to the front door, I said a little prayer, which basically went: "Don't let me do anything really stupid."

Robin's mother was really tall. That was my first impression. And she was smiling. That was my second.

Corinne Crusoe was as elegant as . . . well, as *my* mother. All I could think was, Damn. Her thick, perfectly white hair was pulled back into an elegant roll. Mrs. Crusoe wore subtle makeup, discreet gold jewelry, and a gorgeous pantsuit of some heavy, smooth blue knit that hung like a designer dress. It matched her eyes to a tee.

"Roe, this is my mother," Robin said, since you have to state the obvious some times. "Mother, this is my . . ." Robin and I stared at each other, stymied, for a long second. "This is Aurora."

"Please come in," I said, floundering for my composure in the face of such elegance. You'd think I'd be used to it, but no.

Mrs. Crusoe was careful not to stare around too obviously, but I knew she hadn't missed a detail of me, or the house. Phillip, thank God, had come out of the bathroom and was looking very creditable.

"My brother, Phillip," I said proudly, and he beamed at me. "Phillip, this is Robin's mother, Mrs. Crusoe."

"Please call me Corinne," she said smoothly, nodding at both of us.

Phillip stood a little straighter. I wasn't about to tell him he was too young to call an older lady by her first name, not in front of the older lady.

"Corinne, can I pour you a glass of wine?" Phillip said with perfect composure, and I glowed.

"That would be lovely."

"We have . . ." and Phillip faltered.

I inspected the bottles Robin was carrying. "Robin's brought a zinfandel and a shiraz," I said. "Or, if you prefer, we have some vodka and orange juice."

"No, the zinfandel, thanks."

We got that all settled, then sat in the small formal living room after I'd put the peas on. Corinne was a past mistress of small talk, and we set about getting to know one another through the accumulation of little facts—or, more accurately, tiny indicators of those facts. Corinne, I learned, was well-off, a widow who had no intention of remarrying. She was very involved with her grandchildren by her two daughters, and she was active in her church (Episcopal).

Corinne learned I was also a widow, also financially secure, still working, had two live parents, and was a steady church attendant.

Corinne learned that Phillip normally lived in California. He was here on a visit, I told her, not mentioning his method of arrival. And I hoped Phillip wouldn't, either, but if he did, so be it.

I excused myself to make the gravy and heat the rolls, and Corinne promptly asked if she could help in any way.

"If you don't mind, I'll borrow Robin, to help me with the turkey," I said. "We'll be in the kitchen. Would you like to come offer advice?"

"I'll be glad to come," Corinne said, standing gracefully with her barely touched glass of zinfandel. "But I'll just observe silently."

I laughed and led the way. We've been formal long enough, I thought. True to her word, Corinne offered almost no observations on how she prepared Thanksgiving herself, which I thought was just wonderful and amazing.

After the usual flurry of getting everything on the table, and getting everyone to sit and relax, the meal went very well. Robin carved the turkey with enthusiasm and a total lack of expertise, Corinne seemed to enjoy her food, and Phillip had seconds of everything. Robin kept casting little glances at me that I couldn't interpret.

"What are you doing tomorrow?" he asked later, when we were all sitting, replete and sleepy, our forks laid down for good.

"Oh." My contented feeling almost vanished. "I have to straighten up Poppy's house tomorrow." Robin looked surprised. I hated to explain about the Wynns in front of Corinne.

"Who's going to help you?"

"I don't know. If Melinda can get a baby-sitter, I'm sure she will." Even more than I, Melinda would not want the whole town to know what had happened, though I was sure that sooner or later the news would travel.

"I could help you," he offered.

"That's so nice of you." I was genuinely touched. Robin was no slob, but picking up and cleaning were hardly his favorite activities, and he had a houseguest. "But I expect we can handle it. If we need anything too strenuous done, I'll give you a call."

"Is there anything I can do?" Corinne asked, out of courtesy.

"Oh, no, thank you," I said quickly. "I'm sure Robin told you that my sister-in-law was killed a few days ago. As if that wasn't awful enough, someone came into her house and ransacked it. My brother-in-law just shouldn't be faced with dealing with a mess, in addition to everything else."

We all laid out some platitudes about how dreadful the world was nowadays, and no one was safe, even in a small town like Lawrenceton, where people used to leave their doors unlocked year-round. I certainly didn't remember such a time myself, but my mother had assured me that was so.

My company all helped carry the food and dirty dishes into the kitchen, and to my embarrassment and gratitude, Corinne and Robin insisted on doing the dishes. My good china couldn't go in the dishwasher, so this was a bigger task than usual. Phillip and Corinne dried while Robin washed, and I put away all the leftovers. My pants felt a little tight around the waist, and though that wasn't unusual after a large meal, I realized that they'd felt a little snug when I'd put them on that morning. Even my bra felt tight. I decided tomorrow would certainly be early enough to worry about weight gain, but tomorrow I'd definitely need to cut back.

We decided to stay in the less formal den, cozier and more comfortable and right by the kitchen. Of course, a football game was on, and Phillip and Robin talked sports while Corinne and I discussed Thanksgiving customs, Christmas shopping, how long I'd lived in my present house, Corinne's grandchildren. Maybe she wouldn't mind so much, me not being able to have any, since she already had some. The minute the thought crossed my mind, I was sorry.

I was about to ruin my own day, and I slammed a mental door on that subject and turned to more pleasant ones.

"My mother and her husband are coming to share a glass of wine in a short while," I said. "I hope that you'll stay and meet them."

"Oh, that would be wonderful," Corinne said instantly. She seemed positively delighted at the prospect.

With Corinne, Phillip, and Robin settled down in front of the television, I excused myself. When I emerged from the bathroom off my bedroom, Robin was standing there waiting. Without saying a word, he kissed me. At first, it was a sweet sort of kiss, a "You just met my mom and she likes you" kind of kiss, but abruptly it turned into a hormonal lip lock, that had more to do with ripping off underwear than Mom. In about one minute flat, we were ready to land on the bed.

"Whoa," I gasped, pulling my lips away from his.

His mouth followed mine, and for a second we dallied with

resuming the pleasurable activity, but sanity prevailed. My brother and Robin's mom were in the next room, and the television volume wasn't *that* loud.

"Can I come over tonight?" he whispered.

"Your mom!"

"She won't miss me for a couple of hours."

"But she'll know, and that makes me feel creepy. I know she knows anyway, but still . . ."

"I'll think of a very good excuse. Remember, I'm a professional writer."

"Okay," I said, giving in without a further thought.

"By the way," the professional writer said, "your brother is a normal teenager who's just gotten lucky very recently and was safe about it."

"That's all I want to know," I said, making a stop sign by holding my hand up, palm facing him. "No gory details. Brothers and sisters don't need to know too much."

Robin decided we should kiss again. It was even harder to pull apart this time, and I was still feeling a little dazed by lust as we went back into the den, where Corinne was catnapping in an ever-so-ladylike way, and Phillip was talking on the phone again.

"Can I go?" he whispered. "Josh and Joss have finished eating, and his mom says it's okay. They live about two blocks over, so I can walk. He's got a Play Station Two and some games I haven't tried yet."

I glanced at my watch. I wondered whether my mother would be relieved or disappointed to miss seeing him, then decided that relieved would more fit the bill today, and gave Phillip my blessing, along with an injunction to be home in two hours, or I'd be calling the Finstermeyers.

Phillip waved good-bye to Robin, grabbed his jacket, and was gone before I could count to fifteen. Robin and I settled on the love seat and I leaned my head against his shoulder. Our hands were twined together. It was nice and warm, and I was full. I joined Corinne in dreamland for a few minutes, and then I heard my mother's distinctive knock on the door. I couldn't believe I'd missed all the worrying about the "Aida meets Corinne" scenario, and I couldn't believe I'd fallen asleep twice in one day.

Corinne was sitting up straight, her eyes fixed on the television, so she was already alert. Good. She'd need it.

My mother was dressed in a discreet plaid skirt and a red blouse, with some gorgeous red pumps on. John was wearing a dress shirt and a tweed jacket but no tie. He looked very bluff and hearty, which was not John at all, but it made a good first impression.

The introductions went well, though Mother raised her eyebrows at me for having my company in the den instead of in the formal living room. Tough, Mom. We'd migrated naturally.

"Bryan called you at our house today," Mother said to me directly during a lull in the chitchat. "He seemed to assume you'd be at our house. I told him you'd been cooking your own Thanksgiving dinners for a while now."

Okay. Mother wanted Robin to know other men found me attractive, she wanted me to know she didn't mind me not having Thanksgiving with them, and she wanted Corinne to know that she respected my independence.

Mission accomplished, Mom.

"I'll call him back tomorrow. Today's a holiday," I said instantly, stating that my relationship with Bryan Pascoe was Business with a capital *B*. But in the next instant, I found myself wondering if he'd discovered something about the Wynns.

The visit went well, on the whole. John was not too talkative, seeming abstracted most of the time, but I was sure Corinne would understand. John had wonderful manners and was always able to think of something pleasant to say, so I knew he would improve on Corinne's acquaintance. Robin had an excellent rapport with my mother; the thought crossed my mind that he was better with her than my late husband, Martin, had ever been. Martin and Mother had always been so conscious they were close to the same age—in fact, if Martin had married Mother instead of me, it wouldn't have raised many eyebrows at all.

I tried not to compare other men to Martin, but sometimes ideas popped into my head whether I wanted them to or not.

I opened my mouth to interrogate my mother about Poppy's parents—if she remembered any specific scandal about Marvin Wynn—but I realized just in time that there was no way she'd discuss that in front of Corinne Crusoe.

"Where's the boy?" Mother asked as Corinne and Robin were telling John a long golfing story about Robin's late father.

"He's gone over to Josh's house," I explained. "You know, the Finstermeyers. Josh and his twin sister, Joss, took Phillip around the other day, to the movies and so on."

"Well, that's nice," Mother said unconvincingly. "What do you think of the boy? How long is he going to stay?"

"Dad and Betty Jo want him to come back after Thanksgiving," I said, suddenly aware that I hadn't talked to them in two days—or had it been longer? Surely they ought to have made some travel plans for Phillip by now. But how on earth would they get airline reservations this late? Weren't the airports full on the weekend after Thanksgiving? "Maybe he can stay longer," I added hastily, so Mother would never think I was tired of Phillip. I didn't exactly want to get rid of him. I loved my brother, though I realized I didn't know him that well. My problem was the extent of my responsibility. If Phillip were to stay for a while, I would have to be a little stricter; I couldn't be an indulgent big sister if he was going to be with me for weeks.

Right after my mother and John gathered their coats and left (after drinking two cups of coffee apiece, instead of wine, and each having a piece of pumpkin pie), Phillip called and asked if he could spend the night at Josh's.

What I wanted to say was, Yes, if you can keep your hands off Joss! Don't even *think* about laying a finger on her in her own house! What I actually said was, "Why don't you let me talk to Josh's mom, Phillip? Staying would probably be okay."

Beth Finstermeyer put my mind at ease by letting me know casually that her daughter was off spending the night with her best friend, so the boys could have the run of the house. And she laughed after she said that, so I knew the boys would no more "have the run of the house" than I would swallow a goldfish.

After I hung up, I could tell that Corinne was ready to go back to Robin's apartment and put her feet up. I urged them to take some pie with them, told them my brother was going to be away for the night but that he had surely enjoyed meeting Corinne, and fetched their jackets from the guest bedroom.

Robin's eyes had lighted up when he'd heard Phillip was going to be gone, and he dropped a chaste kiss on my cheek when he was saying good-bye, even as he was whispering, "See you later."

When the door closed behind them and I was finally alone, the relief was enormous. It was five o'clock, and no one wanted anything of me. The dusk was closing in outside, and I wandered around my house, pulling curtains to and picking up the odd crumpled napkin or used glass. I got out the carpet sweeper and ran it over the area rug, then swept the tiled floor that ran down the hall and into the kitchen and den.

There, that was it. All I was going to do today.

Thanksgiving was over.

I had a turkey sandwich while I watched reruns from a million years ago of a show I'd been too young to catch the first time around. I read a little, having a hard time truly engaging my mind in the convolutions of the book, a complicated psychological mystery. In another hour, I was yawning.

A discreet knock at the front door came just in time. It was followed by the sound of a key turning. I'd originally given Robin a key in case he wanted to work in my office while I was gone. A lot of his reference books were on the shelves that lined the office walls, because his apartment just didn't have room for all his books.

"Are you sleepy?" Robin asked, kneeling by my chair.

"I could probably be roused."

"Your brother really at the Fin-whatevers for the night?"

"Uh-huh."

"Oh . . . goody."

It was one of those encounters where each person seemed to want something different. I was looking for a slow, sweet session, undemanding but satisfying. Robin was feeling more fiery and acrobatic. It took a while to get in sync, but when we did, the climax was the most intense I'd ever experienced. I lay in the dark of my bedroom with Robin's long arms wrapped around me, and I felt content and safe and loved. Though I'd been drowsy before, when I felt Robin relax into sleep, my eyes were open to the darkness.

I thought about Robin and how I felt about him. I thought about how Bryan Pascoe's interest in me didn't spark any feeling in me at all, except mild discomfort. I thought of how amazing it was that I was alive and well, able to experience lying here in the arms of a tall, thin man named Robin Crusoe, whose wild red hair was even now tangling with mine on the pillow. I had this, this wonderful moment, while Poppy, a woman vibrating with life, had had it all taken away.

What had happened to Poppy along her way? What had made her so two-faced? The loving, besotted mother, the well-dressed matron and dutiful wife had also been a promiscuous and sly female. The intelligent college graduate had deliberately wed a man she knew would not be faithful to her—probably in the sure expectation that she would not be faithful to him, either. Or had John David and Poppy married in the belief they'd cleave only to each other? They must have known, even then, that faithfulness was an ideal rather than a reality, given their natures.

Maybe blind optimism could carry you further than you ever meant to go.

I turned to look at Robin's sleeping face. I lay on my side, propped up on one elbow. The night-light in the bathroom provided a faint glow, just enough to see the disheveled head and beaky nose. When I tried to imagine his head lying on someone else's pillow, it hurt deep inside me. And then I felt the surge of anger, the backlash of that pain, just at his *imagined* infidelity.

Had it been that kind of anger that had motivated the hand that had stabbed Poppy over and over? But the evidence of the search through Poppy's closet and the odd activities of her parents added another layer of complexity to the question of Poppy's death.

"Robin, wake up," I said. I folded his hand in mine.

"What? You okay?"

"Promise me something."

"What?"

"Promise me you'll never cheat on me while we're together. If we break up, okay, anything then. But while we're . . . a couple . . . no one else."

I sounded more like seventeen than thirty-six, but I was dead serious.

"Had you thought I might?" he asked with some difficulty. "I mean, have you seen me looking at anyone? You know Janie isn't anyone I'd ever really date. She's just a goofy girl." He clearly didn't want to have to go over the Janie Spellman ground again.

"I know," I said hastily. "That was just a . . . momentary craziness. I'm not saying I've seen you look at anyone specific. No. But I just want to hear you say it."

"I have no intention of going to bed with anyone but you," Robin said clearly. "I think it's completely obvious that I love you."

Well. I should wake Robin up more often.

I bent and nuzzled his neck. "I love you, too," I said, the words coming more easily than I had thought they would.

"I was hoping," he mumbled. "Now, can I go back to sleep? Talk tomorrow?"

"Sure," I said, reversing again so my back was snuggled up to his front. "Sure."

Chapter Ten

I called Melinda after I got up the next morning. It was late. Robin had gotten dressed and left about 1:00 A.M., giving me a kiss and a pat. He'd left a note on my coffeepot to tell me that he'd talk to me later. He'd signed it, "Love, your Robin."

I had to wait awhile before I had my coffee that morning. Something I'd eaten the day before, or maybe just the volume of the food, had made me a little queasy. When I had a piece of toast, I felt much better, and by the time nine o'clock rolled around, I figured Melinda would be up and dressed and safely into her morning. I poured some kibble into Madeleine's bowl while I waited for Melinda to pick up the phone. I wondered why Madeleine didn't come in, and realized I hadn't seen her the evening before, either. But that wasn't especially significant. I often missed her little visits to her food bowl.

Melinda had had a good time at her parents' home, she reported. She'd seen her brother and her sister, and their children had played with her children. She sounded as though she hadn't been ready for that little reunion to end.

"We'd been thinking of staying until Sunday, but with every-thing happening, Avery thought we'd better come back last night," she said drearily. "So, here we are. At least the kids slept most of the way back, and they went right to bed when we got home. But this morning, I think Marcy is coming down with a cold, damn it. Did anything happen while we were gone? Have you heard anything else about the funeral?"

"Not a word. So it looks like Poppy's body isn't going to be released until Monday, if then," I said. "In the meantime, in addition to someone searching Poppy's closet and making a big mess in there and in her bedroom, the Wynns were looking for something all over the house and tossed it around worse than the first burglar."

Melinda was stunned. I could hear her choking on whatever she was drinking. "Poppy's dad, the minister?" she asked in-credulously. "Poppy's *mom*? Trashed her place? I can't believe it!" She went on like that for a few more minutes, though I knew she did believe me. It was a way to handle the unpleasant shock.

Melinda got to the bottom line quickly, as I knew she would. "So, we need to clean it up," she said. She sounded gloomy at the prospect. "Well, let me call around and see if I can get a teenager to baby-sit. They're all out of school, and maybe one of them wants to do something as boring as watching kids. Speaking of babies, where has John David stashed Chase?"

"I hope you're sitting down. John David's still in the motel with Chase, and there he stays, taking care of the little fellow."

That was just as shocking to Melinda as the vandalism of Poppy's house.

"I'll call him," she said when she had recovered. "I'll just check on them. This is a good thing, but I'm just not confident of his ability to take care of that child."

"Wasn't he a help before?"

"Not as much as *I* would've liked, though I can't say Poppy complained. As I told you, Avery has been great with both of ours. Of course, everyone takes it for granted that the mom will do everything for the kids, but if a dad does a lot for them, it's a big deal." I could picture Melinda's shrug.

"I'm proud of John David," I said. "I thought he'd fold."

"Me, too. Goes to show."

I wasn't sure what it went to show, but I grunted agreeably and we fixed a time to meet at the house on Swanson, if Melinda was lucky enough to get a sitter.

As I brushed my teeth, I found myself thinking of Sally. I felt a strong impulse to call her, just to check up on her. But what would I say? "Forgotten anything important lately, Sally?" "Do you remember who I am, Sally?" I wondered if perhaps a complete physical could turn up some problem that was solvable, and not just expose the explanation Perry dreaded—that Sally was in the early stages of Alzheimer's. I made a note to myself to call Perry or take him out to lunch so we could talk about it without being interrupted, which we would be at the library.

Melinda called back to tell me she'd gotten a sitter, and she sounded much more cheerful. I got the impression Marcy's cold was making her daughter a little difficult and that Melinda definitely wouldn't mind a break. We agreed to meet at the house on Swanson at 10:00 A.M.

I wrote Phillip a note about my plans, including the number for my cell phone and the number at John David's. After I got dressed in grubby old jeans and a faded Christmas sweatshirt, both a little loose to allow me some comfort, I started out on my morning errands.

Somewhere along the way, I yielded to an irresistible impulse and drove over to the Best Western. John David was on the first floor, and I could hear Chase shrieking from outside the door.

John David looked bleary-eyed when he opened it, but he was dressed, and not surprised to have company. "Melinda already called this morning," he said, moving aside to let me in. "Listen, help me think of something to get him calmed down."

"I have almost no experience," I warned him.

"I've tried feeding him, burping him, changing him, and singing to him."

The idea of John David singing to that baby just did something to me. I'm a sucker for man who can take care of a baby, or a man who's at least trying to take care of a baby. To cover up the fact that my eyes were full of tears, I held out my arms and he put Chase in them. Chase was a wriggling bundle of misery, and he was making such a whirlwind of his little arms and legs that I was scared I wouldn't be able to hold him. I sat down in the room's one comfortable chair and held Chase so his chest was against mine, his head resting against my shoulder. The chair wouldn't rock, so I rocked for it, back and forth, back and forth, murmuring to the baby.

Chase began to relax some, and the shrieks died down to whimpers. Suddenly, there was silence. He was sound asleep, but I kept up with my movement.

"He's all I've got left to love," John David said in a near whisper. He looked thinner after only a few days of being a widower. He had shaved, and he had tucked in his shirt and combed his hair, but the spark was not in his eyes anymore.

"How can you say you loved her?" I asked. My voice was strained with the effort of containing my anger and speaking in a low, calm voice. "I found you at Romney's, and it wasn't the first place I looked."

"I always loved Poppy. I got mad at her a lot. She was a woman with a lot of secrets," he said, his voice just as low and

172

controlled. "But I loved her. Just not the way *you* think people ought to love. You're such a straight arrow. Life has no spice unless you have adventures." He even smiled, just a faint one, but a smile nonetheless.

If my hands had been free at that moment, I might have tried to throttle him. "You're right," I said, so furiously that Chase whimpered. "I don't understand. I'll never understand." I fought to keep my voice under control. "I am really glad you're taking care of Chase. But it is beyond my comprehension, how you and Poppy could live like you did."

"She was a complicated woman. She had some bad breaks when she was in her early teens," John David said. "I would have liked it if we'd been different, I swear I would. I didn't set out to be . . . like I am. But we made a pattern, and it was one that let us live together, and I thought it would be okay."

It was like we had both taken a little truth serum. I had never imagined having such a conversation. But it was actually kind of refreshing to openly acknowledge their fractured marriage.

"So," I began, then paused. "You both always knew? When the other was seeing someone else?"

He nodded, and I felt my mouth twist with distaste. Abruptly, I was nauseated by the idea of such a union, and baffled by the point of it.

The baby was getting heavier and heavier. I got up very slowly and carefully and placed him in the bassinet that had been set up by the bed. Whether John David had brought it from the house or the motel had rolled it in, I didn't know, but I was glad it was there so I could put Chase down without my back positively breaking.

"John David," I said very softly, looking down at the sleeping child, "who do you think killed her?"

"I think maybe it was her mother," he said, his voice a hoarse whisper. "I'd hate to think Sandy would do something like that, but you don't know that family. Let me tell you, any sick pattern you think Poppy and I had, she learned it from her own mom and dad. She'd never get into details, but she never wanted them here. She'd be pretty open about everything else."

"She talked about the other men?"

"Arthur most of all. He was always obsessive about her. I think it's pretty damn peculiar that the police chief has Arthur on the case, unless Arthur's persuaded him he's found a possible suspect. Arthur kind of transferred all those feelings he had about you to Poppy. He even talked to Poppy about you, all the time at first."

This was more than I wanted to know.

"And then there were others."

I shook my head. "I can't understand."

"She used them, you know," he said. He leaned forward, his hands between his knees. I wondered if he'd be able to build a healthy relationship with anyone after this. "They were always some use to her. Or after it was over, she made them useful in some way."

"What about you?" I asked, not able to think about Poppy anymore. "Is that the way you picked your . . . friends?"

"No." He shrugged. "I just wanted something *simple.*" After a minute, I realized that he was crying, and I patted him on the shoulder, gave him a little peck on the forehead, and left to search his house.

"We could have hired someone to do this," Melinda said. We were standing in the middle of the chaos in what had once been a perfectly ordinary suburban home.

"Yes," I agreed. "We could have. But whatever's hidden here, it's us that needs to find it." Ungrammatically and inelegantly

174

as I'd put it, Melinda's dark eyes widened as she considered what I'd said.

She nodded. "Whatever it is."

"It's not going to be easy. The Wynns would have found it, if it were easy. And when we do find it, no one needs to see it but us."

"The police?"

"We'll see."

"So we're like detectives?" Melinda smiled weakly. "Well, that's a new role for me. I already have so many hats, I can't wear them all at one time."

"Hey, we're more than detectives," I said, trying to make my voice bracing and hearty. "We're Uppity Women."

"So we are."

By 10:30, we were putting books back on the shelves in the study. We dusted the books first, since neither of us was capable of reshelving anything that needed a run-over with a rag. And we checked each book for enclosures, too.

Nothing fell from the pages, no matter how hard we shook. The desks were absolutely normal, too. Melinda and I were neat and methodical in our search. We didn't talk much at first, because we were intent on what we were doing, and because we were trying to move quickly.

Melinda balked after forty minutes. "It's not the work I mind," she said abruptly; "it's the fact that you think we ought to judge whether or not the police get whatever we find."

"You know that Arthur Smith was Poppy's lover?"

She nodded.

"You want him to decide whether or not something's relevant?"

"I've been wondering..." she said after a moment. "I've been wondering if Arthur didn't actually... If he might..."

"You think Arthur might have killed Poppy?" I was shocked,

but not as shocked as I might have been. "He's got an obsessive personality," I admitted. "He's got lots of know-how." Who was better qualified to be a murderer than a policeman?

I dusted the same book (a pharmaceutical dictionary of John David's) over and over as I thought about Arthur. "But you know, Melinda . . . their affair was long over. If he'd still been involved with her, I would say it might even be likely." I thought some more, trying to picture Arthur knocking on Poppy's glass door.

"I don't know," I said, not wanting to picture that any longer. "But that's why I think we need to talk about just burning whatever we find. However, first, we've got to find something."

After an hour and a half, we had the office picked up, dusted, vacuumed, and searched. We had found absolutely nothing besides the usual detritus of any home filled with busy people. Poppy had an overdue bill from Davidson's that I knew I should bring to John David's attention (it had gotten stuck to another paper with some jelly), and she hadn't sent in her latest book club notice, so I put that on top of the little pile of due bills so John David would see it first.

The most exciting thing Melinda had found was one of a pair of earrings that Poppy had been trying to find for a month or more. I remembered her telling us, in her dramatic way, how she would just *cry* if she didn't find the missing earring. We cried a little ourselves when Melinda held it up.

Figuring John David wouldn't mind, we got some sliced ham out of the refrigerator and made sandwiches, in the process throwing out some leftovers that were obviously way past their prime. Cleaning out the refrigerator hadn't been high on Poppy's priority list. I took the first full garbage bag out the sliding glass door to the large garbage can Poppy kept there. After I tossed it in, I breathed in the clear, chilly air for a minute. My lungs felt dusty from all the books. Standing there looking at the back fence jogged a memory. I turned back into the kitchen and looked around. Yes, there on the counter was a radio. I examined it to locate the on button, then punched it. The music that came into the room, admittedly on the loud side, was not the classical or jazz music I usually heard on NPR, but a classic rock station based in Lawrenceton.

Well, there was another puzzle. Lizanne had said that when she'd approached the gate to the backyard, she'd heard the radio playing loudly, loudly enough to obscure the voices at Poppy's back door. And that was when Poppy must have been murdered. But Poppy's radio wasn't on NPR.

Perhaps the crime-scene cleaner—nope, that was ridiculous. Sealed in his hazmat suit, he couldn't have heard music clearly at all; no reason for him to turn on the radio. That was as ludicrous as the idea of Marvin Wynn, right-wing preacher, turning on a classic rock station while he conducted an illegal search of his dead daughter's house.

Of course, Lizanne might have been lying. But her account had been so believable, so detailed. Why would she have lied about the radio station? It was something so easy to check.

And yet, no one had checked it until now.

Probably that was next on Arthur's list of things to do. Right?

Selfishly, I shared my worries with Melinda. She shrugged, not too interested in solving a puzzle with so many missing pieces. We'd been eating at the dining table by the sliding glass door, and I'd pulled the curtain back as far as it could go so the sun could brighten the room. Suddenly, it seemed confining, sitting in the chair. I pushed back from the table and went to stand by the glass door. I half-turned, easing a finger around the waistband of my slacks. I realized I must have horribly over-eaten the day before. I felt swollen.

Should we have reported the Wynns' activities to Arthur?

I turned my head to say something to Melinda, only to catch her staring at me in a strange way.

"What?" I asked defensively.

"Aurora . . . don't get me wrong, here. . . . We're friends, right?"

"Sure." Confused and bewildered, that's how I sounded.

"You and Robin are really close, right? Really, really close?"

I understood what Melinda was trying to ask.

"Yes. Really, really close."

"How long has it been since you had your period?" she said bluntly.

"Oh . . . I'd have to look at my calendar." I tried to remember. "Let's see, I was cutting out ghost silhouettes to put up for Halloween, and we decorate the library the second week in October, but I did those early. . . ." I shrugged. "I'm not always real regular."

"So you're not on the pill."

"No." Boy, when Melinda decided to get personal, she didn't mess around.

"But you are using birth control?"

"Melinda! Well . . . mostly." I felt my face redden as I thought of one evening a few weeks ago when we hadn't had time. In fact, we'd been in the bathroom upstairs at my mother's. It made me feel hot all over when I thought about it. "You know I can't have kids, Melinda." Robin had used condoms all the same, except for that once. Well, maybe one or two others. But it hadn't seemed like such a big deal; since I'd dated at least one man who didn't want me if I couldn't have children, I'd been very up-front with Robin about my infertility. This was a very sore subject with me, and I'd thought Melinda would respect that.

"I know Dr. Mendelssohn, whom I think is an overpriced jerk, said so. Are your boobs sore?"

I was startled all over again. "Well, sensitive," I said, thinking of how I'd had to caution Robin to be gentler the night before.

"Have you looked at yourself in the mirror?"

"What are you driving at, Melinda?"

"I'll bet your bosom is really tender, not just a little sensitive."

I nodded reluctantly.

"You've skipped using birth control at least one time, and I'd bet more often than that, and you're having sex. Your last period was six weeks ago."

Well, that had been a long time, come to think of it.

"I'll bet you've been exhausted the past few days, been dropping off to sleep whenever you sat down. You have big rings under your eyes. Did you know that? Have you been queasy in the morning?"

I covered my mouth with both hands, feeling a wave of absolute terror and delight sweep over me.

Melinda waited for me to answer, then went on when I didn't. "I've been pregnant twice, and I'd swear you should have a pregnancy test."

"Don't even say it," I told her. "Don't even *think* it." I waved my hands to erase her words from the air. I cursed the hope that sprang up in my heart. This was false and cruel.

"I'm sorry," Melinda said, looking as though she was going to cry. And she damn well ought to, I thought. "I just think . . ." Then she looked at me and canned whatever she'd been going to say. "Okay, Roe. Subject closed."

"Let's work on the bedroom," I said, holding my eyes wide so the tears wouldn't spill out of them.

"Sure." She grabbed a fresh dust cloth, a garbage bag, and the handle of the Dirt Devil. "Let's go."

It seems to be a universally held truth that people conceal their secrets in their bedrooms. If I had to hide something, I had to admit that I, too, would probably start looking for a good place in the room that was most mine, the room where I slept. Maybe Poppy, who had single-handedly organized the Christmas food drive at St. James's, had had a smarter idea, but I planned to be even more meticulous in my search of this room than I had been in our reconstruction of the study. I had observed that Sandy Wynn had picked Poppy's bedroom to begin her own search, while relegating Marvin to the downstairs room.

Unfortunately, it was a large bedroom and the closet hadn't been cleaned in a long time. Poppy'd had a lot of clothes, and so did John David, since he had the kind of job that required suits. Melinda had a problem with small spaces, and though it was a big closet, it was still a closet. So I volunteered, then went back down the stairs to fetch a step stool. I was all in favor of a job that would keep me out of Melinda's sight for a while. I needed to work around what had happened downstairs. I was so conflicted that I pretty much felt numb. Doing something physical was exactly what I needed.

In no time, I was coughing at the dust I raised. The original searcher, the one who'd been in soon after Poppy died, had left a big jumble, and Sandy Wynn had added to the mess. But I could discern Poppy's storage method easily enough. She'd kept all her dress shoes in their original shoe boxes. Those had been stacked on the shelf above her hanging clothes, with the outer end of the box labeled—"navy pumps," for example, or "black patent 2-in." I dusted the shelf, and then I began examining the boxes and shoes as I dusted and replaced them. It was time-consuming and tedious. Poppy's everyday shoes had been on a rack on the floor of the closet, and there was a section of cube-shaped storage units toward the back that held Poppy's sweaters and purses. I restacked them, examining each one.

I'd do her stuff first, then try to restore order to John David's side.

I could hear Melinda sliding out drawers to look at the bottoms and backs, checking to see if something had been taped in a hard-to-find place. She was also replacing the strewn contents of the drawers as she went, throwing away things like ancient prescriptions, odd socks, hose with runs. We had to walk a fine line here: returning things to order and neatness without interfering too much. We'd agreed to return Poppy's things to their hangers and boxes; her clothing and paraphernalia would have to be given away someday, but that wasn't up to us.

The top part of the closet was finally done, and I was hanging slacks when Melinda gave a sort of odd choking noise.

With some relief, I stepped out of the closet to check on her progress. My sister-in-law was standing by the bed, her eyes fixed on something she held in her hand. Her cheeks were flaming red.

"Melinda?"

She opened her mouth to speak, then shut it again. She shook her head violently.

"Melinda?" I reached around her to take the object from her hand.

It was a photograph. It actually took me a few seconds to comprehend what I was seeing. In this photograph, Poppy was giving someone a blow job. The picture had been taken from so close that you couldn't tell who the male was.

I can't describe what a shock it was to see a picture of someone I knew performing a sex act. In this floral suburban bedroom, the picture was even more obscene than it would have been if I'd chanced upon it in a magazine.

"I wonder who it is," I said once when I could speak. "I

mean, possibly this is some loving record of her and John David?"

"Oh, it *never* is!" Melinda said. She was absolutely outraged. "The Queensland brothers, I know from Avery, are both uncircumcised. This . . . individual, as you can see, is *not.*"

"At least she didn't keep it as blackmail." I was looking for reassurance. "I mean, you can't tell who it is, and the thing itself looks pretty anonymous, doesn't it? No big freckles, or, ah, anything unusual."

Melinda looked at the picture again, her lips pursed with distaste. "No, just a regular old wienie," she said.

We looked at each other and burst into laughter. "Look at it this way. You know it's not Avery," I said.

"And look at the hair. Couldn't be Robin," she pointed out.

True. Robin was redheaded all over, so to speak.

"I refuse to guess," I said after one final inspection. "But whoever it is, we agree that John David should not see this."

"Absolutely."

"Where was it?"

"It was taped to the bottom of this little drawer." Melinda pointed to Poppy's jewelry box, which was filled to overflowing with inexpensive necklaces and earrings. There was a pullout drawer at the bottom, so you could lay your chains inside and they wouldn't tangle. Melinda had pulled it all the way out and flipped it.

"Aren't you smart to think of that!" I said admiringly.

Melinda looked modest.

"Well, no telling how much else we'll find," I said, unable to suppress a sigh. "I guess we'd better get back to work."

The next find was mine. Taped into the lining of a spring coat Poppy had worn maybe twice a year was a letter. The letter was from the Reverend Wynn to Poppy. It was signed and dated. In the letter, he admitted he had had "relations" with Poppy when she was thirteen.

For a few minutes, Melinda and I could not even look at each other.

"Relations with a relation," Melinda said in an effort to pull us out of our nauseated reaction. She dropped that effort when it rang false. "Poor Poppy," she said sadly.

"No wonder she was so wild," I said. "No wonder she was so . . ."

"Promiscuous," Melinda supplied.

"Yeah."

"This is the nastiest thing I have ever read. I wonder why he wrote it?"

"I guess this was insurance," I said, having thought it over for a minute or two. "Maybe this was her way of keeping him away from her kids. Keeping him out of her life. She must have told him she'd tell his bishop, or whoever stands in place of a bishop in the Lutheran church." I made a mental note to check on that later.

"Do you think his wife knows about this?"

I started to deny that instantly. Then I reconsidered.

"She was searching," I admitted. I told Melinda about the gas station receipt. "She could have come here that morning and questioned Poppy about it."

"Then you'd have to assume she knows her husband did this to her daughter." Melinda brandished the letter. "If she does, how can she live with him?"

"This is a question I can't answer. Another one is, Would she have killed Poppy to conceal this? Bryan left a message for Arthur to call him back, so he could tell Arthur about the receipt. Maybe Arthur already knows."

We began a little pile.

I had to rethink Poppy's character as I worked and searched.

My sister-in-law had shown me only the tip of the iceberg, as far as letting me know her true self. I had to realize that I had seen the better, but less complex, portion of Poppy's personality. Beneath had lain monsters.

We were determined to find everything. It was not conceivable that we would let anything slip by us, to fall into the hands of a stranger, or, worse yet, someone who knew Poppy. Sooner or later, John David would give away Poppy's things to some local charity or to a friend. Or he'd search himself. He mustn't see these—what? Souvenirs? Insurance policies? Totems?

Bubba Sewell would definitely never make representative, I decided when I found the picture of him buck naked on Poppy's—and John David's—bed. He was real excited, and hardly looked like a lawmaker. In a beige photo album, that picture was slid in behind a snap of Poppy and John David on vacation in Florida. Definitely done in an "Up yours, John David" moment.

"Idiot," I muttered, and tossed it on the pile.

"Who's that?" Melinda looked up from her examination of Poppy's lingerie drawer.

"Cartland Sewell."

Melinda shook her head in disgust, not even bothering to look at the picture. She continued with her search, and made the next discovery. She found an ID tag stuck in a rectangular Playtex box with a new bra—the kind of tag you clip to your lapel. The picture on it was of a bearded, thin man, who just happened to be Cara Embler's heart surgeon husband. It was his hospital identification.

"I guess Stuart got it replaced," Melinda said. "Her back-door neighbor! Poppy had never heard about not fouling your own nest, I guess."

"He's one of John's doctors," I said.

"Daddy John?" This was Melinda's pet name for John Queensland.

I nodded.

She sighed, a huge exhalation of exasperation. "I'm sorry, heart surgeons don't get sex lives," she said. "Not with the daughters-in-law of their patients."

"Who knows which came first, though, the heart attack or the affair? If you can term it an affair, that is. Maybe it was just a—you know."

"Just a fling," Melinda said.

That hadn't been the word I was thinking of, but . . . Oh well.

"That's right, we can't know." This actually made her feel better.

"What I'm wondering is, What're we missing. If we're finding this much, what did the other searchers find? Can there be stuff that's worse?" We stared at each other, sunk in gloom.

And we heard a door open downstairs.

I don't know how I looked, but Melinda's dark eyes grew as wide and dark as tablespoons full of molasses.

"Who's there?" called a deep male voice, and we could hear heavy footsteps as someone began ascending the stairs. "Aurora, are you all right? I saw your car."

Melinda and I stared at the little pile, and, obeying an irresistible impulse, I sat on it.

We were perched side by side on the bed, looking guilty as hell, when Detective Arthur Smith came into the bedroom.

"What are you two doing?" he asked gently. He could tell he'd given us a scare.

"It's okay for us to be here, right?" Melinda voice was high and squeaky.

"Yes, we told John David he could come back to the house anytime he wanted. But what are you doing?"

"We're cleaning up," I said, all too aware that I sounded just as nervous as my partner in crime. "Have you talked to Bryan Pascoe?" I wanted to change the subject.

"And you started with the study downstairs?" Arthur asked, ignoring my question. "Surely it didn't look like that the other day?"

Arthur was far too observant. "No, no, it didn't," I gabbled. "The fact is . . ." I looked at Melinda, desperately needing some help.

"The fact is," Melinda said, glaring at me, "that Roe caught Poppy's mom and dad going through everything Wednesday night, and she threw them out. So we had to clean up the study first."

I hadn't expected Melinda to tell the truth, and I'm sure my startled face told Arthur more than I wanted him to know.

He pulled over a chair that Poppy had placed in the corner of the room, a pretty little wooden chair with a bright needle-point cushion, more of Poppy's work. I hadn't noticed it before, at least in the sense of imagining its possibilities, and I found myself planning to check out the cushion later.

Arthur plunked himself down in front of us, looking up at us as we perched awkwardly on the high antique bed. My legs were sticking out at an odd angle, and Melinda's feet were just barely touching the floor.

"What explanation did they give?" he asked. His voice was reasonable, but his expression wasn't. "And why didn't you call me?"

"I wasn't there," Melinda said, maybe a little too quickly. Coward! "Sorry," she muttered to me. "Can't help it."

"I came by with Bryan Pascoe," I said. "We made them leave, but they sure weren't about to tell us why they were here."

"What do you think they were looking for?" Arthur asked.

Suddenly, I realized that Arthur had just come in the house

without either of us admitting him. But we'd locked the door behind us. Would the police get to keep a key? Surely not, after the house had been re-opened to the family.

Arthur had a *key*. Though their affair was long over, he had a key, too.

For a brilliant red flash of a moment, I hated Poppy with all my heart. I looked at Arthur and wondered if I ought to fear him. Over the years, I had felt many things for Arthur: love, passion, anger, grief, annoyance, outrage, exasperation. But I had never thought I'd be frightened of him.

The tense silence stretched out unbearably.

"Roe—and you, too, Melinda—I did not kill Poppy. I was crazy about her, and she was about me, but it didn't last. I never said anything to the chief, because I want to catch whoever killed her. I want to catch him myself. This is the last thing I can do for Poppy. I want to do it right."

I looked at him doubtfully, but Melinda was convinced. She turned to me. "I think we should," she said quietly.

"*No,*" I told her emphatically. The news would spread everywhere. John would be hurt by this knowledge; John David would be even more wounded. Sooner or later, the little bit of mortality that was Chase would know about it.

"We have to," Melinda said, just to me.

I gave her a very dark look and eased off the bed. She took up the letter and handed it to Arthur. He put on a pair of reading glasses that he'd pulled from his breast pocket. As he read, we both watched him carefully. While he was busy, I slipped the two pictures into my pocket. Melinda watched me and gave a tiny nod. Arthur would probably burst a blood vessel if he saw them. As it was, disgust twisted his lips as he read the words scrawled on the paper.

"Even her father," he muttered.

"That wasn't her fault," Melinda said, instantly indignant. "For God's sake, she was thirteen!"

Arthur gathered himself, glancing up at us, then back to the sprawling handwriting. I couldn't read him, had no idea what he was thinking. He folded the paper and put it in his pocket.

"There was something about her," he said.

Melinda looked at me in consternation. Though she'd known about Arthur and Poppy, this sudden wistful admission from the cop in charge of the investigation threw her completely.

"Listen, Arthur," I said as gently as I could. "Maybe someone else should be in charge of this case. What about that Cathy Trumble? She seemed real able."

"She didn't know Poppy like I did," Arthur said. "I know the chief would take me off the case if he knew I'd been involved with Poppy, but I'm the best investigator on the force, and I have to find out who did this to her. She was the most exciting, the most wonderful . . . I never dreamed anyone could be as wonderful as you were, Roe, but Poppy was something extraordinary."

Melinda gave me a horrified stare. I could feel my cheeks flame red, and I turned my hands palm up. What could I say? For years after he'd dumped me (to marry Lynn, and then divorce her), Arthur had thought he loved me. For years he'd turned up at odd moments in my life, his eyes begging me to take him back. He'd never shown that level of devotion when we were dating, when it would have been appropriate and welcome.

Maybe that was the way it had worked with Poppy, too. He'd gotten hooked on her when she'd moved on to someone else.

"We were together when she shopped for that rug downstairs, the one that had all her blood on it," he said, almost conversationally. "She told me that every time she looked at it, she thought of me. We had sex on it."

That definitely fell into the category of "More than I want to know." "But she switched to someone after you, Arthur," I said. "Who was it?"

"She told me," Arthur said, "long ago . . . She told me that when she was inducted into the Uppity Women, she was going to make sure I got a promotion. Chief of detectives is coming up. Jeb Green's gotten a better job in Savannah. Poppy told me my career would take off. She promised me so much, and gave me so little."

She'd told Cartland she'd help him progress in state government. He'd been so besotted with her, he'd been willing to leave his wife and children. Poppy had been trying to be a total package: illicit lover, career advancer, wife, mother, suburban queen. I wondered if I'd ever known the real woman. What had she been like when she was alone?

"We never really knew her," Melinda said to me. She sounded as sad as I felt. She hooked her dark hair behind her ears and gave Arthur a determined look. "Listen, Detective Smith. We don't want to hear any more about you and Poppy. What we want is to know what to do about the letter. And we want to know what you're going to do about her mother."

Arthur seemed to jerk himself out of the pool of reminiscence he'd fallen into. "What about her mother?" he asked. "Does this have something to do with the messages Bryan Pascoe has been leaving at the station?"

"If you returned your phone calls, you could have picked her up already," I said, angry and somehow hurt by all Arthur's unwelcome revelations. I explained about the gas station receipt, about the attendant's memory of the day Poppy had been murdered.

"I'll go find out."

Arthur left in a hurry, determined to track down the Wynns and interrogate them. After he'd gone, Melinda and I had to gather ourselves back together for a few minutes. We were quite shaken by Arthur and his odd behavior.

"Even if it was Sandy Wynn who killed Poppy, and that part of it gets wrapped up," Melinda said, "we still have to finish this job." She waved her hand at the bedroom, still considerably out of order.

"You're right. John David shouldn't find this stuff." I stuck the plastic ID tag into my pocket to dispose of later with heavy scissors. I ripped the fellatio picture and the frank snap of Cartland Sewell into tiny bits and flushed them down the toilet. Neither of us wanted to give those to Arthur. I didn't know how I was ever going to look Bubba in the face again, as it was. "That wasn't the same person," I told Melinda as the picture bits disappeared. "In both those pictures. Different guys."

"Oh? I guess I didn't compare." She gave me a lopsided smile.

"Well, the one in the close-up picture was a lot, ah, bigger in diameter than Cartland's."

"Think of knowing that about someone," Melinda said, and, amazingly, she giggled. "You know, Avery is my one and only. Pretty rare in this day and age, huh?"

I nodded respectfully. My own list was quite short, but it did have more than one name on it. "I can't understand anyone letting Poppy take pictures," I said. "I'm feeling pretty much on the naïve side, too. It seems like common sense would tell the man that such a thing could only lead to trouble. You can deny and deny—but if the other person has a picture, denials are pretty useless."

"Avery and I sure wouldn't do that," Melinda said. "And I can't see the point. I know what he looks like. He knows what I look like. What's the point of taking pictures? Just something for the kids to find and bring out in the middle of a dinner party, right?"

"That's my opinion, too. I just don't get it."

"Maybe we're just too middle-class?"

I laughed. "Maybe so, Melinda. Maybe so."

I called my house to see if Phillip had returned. When he didn't answer, I called the Finstermeyers and got Josh's mom, Beth.

"We were just trying to call you," she said. "Listen, would it be all right if I took the boys Christmas shopping with me? The Bodine mall is having all kinds of after-Thanksgiving sales, and with these two guys for bodyguards, I thought I might come out of it alive. I'd have them back by seven or eight tonight."

"Sure, that's fine with me." Phillip seemed to be really clicking with Josh. I felt quite pleased about that. "Um, could I speak to Phillip for a minute?"

"Sure."

"Hey, Sis." Phillip's voice was deeper and more relaxed than I remembered it.

"Listen, Phillip, do you have enough money for a trip to the mall?"

"Well, I am sort of broke."

"On your way out of town, why don't you swing by Poppy's house—Mrs. Finstermeyer will know where that is—and I'll spot you some cash."

"Thanks!" Phillip sounded quite enthusiastic. "Oh, and Roe? When I went to your house to get my coat, I saw you had a few messages on the answering machine. I didn't listen to them, because I was in a big hurry."

"Thanks back at you," I told him. "I'll check them before too long."

In a few minutes, I'd handed Phillip the entire contents of my billfold, and Melinda and I went back to work.

Two hours later, we were tired and rumpled. Melinda had started sneezing from breathing so much dust. And we had found only one more memento, a stained male bikini. When I held it up, Melinda said, "I don't even want to think about that." I could not have agreed more. I dropped the shiny black thing right into the garbage bag—the third one we'd filled with the odd trash that everyone accumulates. Melinda and I were just not capable of returning 1998 sales slips, old tissues, and outdated catalogs to their original places, especially since we had no idea where those places had been.

We lifted the bare mattress and the box spring, we checked under the bed, and we shifted all the furniture slightly. We looked over, under, and inside everything.

After a vacuuming and a final look around, Melinda and I agreed that the bedroom was cleaner and more orderly than it had been before someone came into the house on Tuesday. For our grand finale, we remade the bed. The police had taken the linens to the lab.

We trailed wearily downstairs and sat at the table beside the glass doors. With the stained rug gone and all trace of the blood removed, it was a lot easier to forget what had happened on this spot. Since John David had never seen Poppy's body, I hoped he might be able to tolerate staying in the house.

"I wish we could tell some of the other Uppity Women what we're looking for. They'd help us," Melinda said.

"Yeah, it's too bad we can't tap into that energy," I said, leaning my head on my folded arms. I could not remember ever having felt so tired in my life. I must be getting old, I thought, to let some housecleaning exhaust me to such an extent. "But it would defeat the purpose of us searching if we let everyone in on why we needed to do it."

"Listen. Cara Embler's out swimming. In this weather!" Melinda shivered. It had turned into a raw day, and Cara was either dedicated or an utter fool to be out swimming in the cold, wet air.

"Better her than me," I muttered. "You know she's going to be the next Uppity Woman?"

"Oh?"

"Yes, she was next on the list after Poppy."

"And she's so energetic."

"All that exercise. She has to do something to keep busy, since she doesn't work, I guess."

"I'm glad Avery isn't a doctor. They're gone so much. Swimming is lots better than eating when you're lonely, like I do." Melinda cast a disparaging eye down at her own somewhat-rounded stomach.

"You look great to me."

"Well, I can hardly fit into the size I was wearing before I had Charles," Melinda said frankly. She was punching buttons on the phone. "I have to check in at home."

I was left staring at a wedding picture of John David and Poppy. I tried to imagine maintaining a marriage so screwed up that the partners would not be interested in each other's infidelity. My mother had certainly cared when my father had been unfaithful. Boy, had she cared! Though they would never have fought in front of me, I'd been a teen, and I'd been aware of the thick tension in our house.

I recalled John David crying that morning in the motel room, and I tried to grasp what people could do to each other short of killing each other. In the background, I heard Melinda's voice as she talked to her baby-sitter, her laughter as the girl probably passed along something cute Marcy had said.

My mind wandered back to the previous Monday, the day of Poppy's death. My phone call from her, our conversation. How irritated Melinda and I had been with our sister-in-law.

Our drive over to Swanson Lane, my march into the house. The unlocked front door.

I wondered if Poppy usually kept it locked, or if her mother had surprised her by just walking in. My eyes opened wide as I considered this new idea. Why had Sandy picked that particular time to try to retrieve the letter? It had been dated a year and half ago. That meant that when Poppy had been pregnant, she had demanded that letter from her father in exchange for—what? Marvin's never seeing his grandchild? Poppy wouldn't have known then that she'd have a boy.

Okay, back to the basic memory, I told myself. The front door had been open. I had walked in. I had called up the stairs. I had walked up the stairs. The shower had been dry, so I'd known Poppy had been out of it for a while. The room had been neat; the bed had been made. The closet door had been shut. I could even picture my feet moving downstairs in those shoes, my favorites. Then I'd seen Moosie, right? (Who was still missing, incidentally. I made a mental note to check on that.)

The cat had stropped my ankles, then run ahead of me into the kitchen. I'd felt the cold air keenly, the closer I got to the back of the house. When I'd come into the kitchen and looked over the breakfast bar to my left, I'd seen the glass door open.

I hadn't been able to see Poppy's body until I'd come around the end of the breakfast bar with its high stools. There was Poppy's body, sprawled on the floor. She lay half in and half out the door, partially on the rug under the dining table, partially on the linoleum. I'd heard Cara splashing in the pool. I'd looked out into the backyard, over Poppy's body, and seen the concrete around Poppy's own pool dotted with darker water stains. Looked down again at Poppy, horribly dead, her hands . . . I had to gulp back my nausea.

Could Sandy Wynn have done that to her own daughter?

The older I got, the less I seemed able to understand or

predict the behavior of those around me. Instead of gaining wisdom, so that people seemed simpler, I learned more about the complexity of human nature.

"So, what do you think?" Melinda's voice made me jump.

"I think that we've probably found everything there is to find," I said. "I may be wrong, and if I am, there'll be hell to pay. We didn't find anything of Arthur's, for example, and we know he was one of Poppy's lovers. Maybe that means he was already here, searching. Maybe he's the one who trashed the bedroom. Maybe he just wouldn't let her photograph him, or he was too alert for her to risk taking some little memento. Or maybe that black underwear was his." Melinda and I wore matching expressions of disgust as we considered that.

"You sure he wasn't the one in the, you know, the picture with Poppy?" She carefully found something else to look at while I tried to remember. It wasn't that Arthur had looked awful naked—quite the contrary—but I just couldn't remember. There hadn't been anything outstanding in the pertinent department.

"I just don't know," I said finally, and Melinda nodded. "To return to our original subject, I just don't think Poppy would have risked hiding anything really awful down here in the more or less public rooms. Not only might John David have found it but also she'd have realized Chase would be walking very soon. And there were other people in and out. Baby-sitters and friends, and other lovers even. I think we've found it all, or very close to all."

"But are we comfortable with stopping now? Just letting the chips fall where they may?"

Melinda was sitting opposite me, her thin hands folded together. I tried to pretend I had some energy. I sat up straight.

"Yes, I think so," I said, not sounding sure at all.

"You're right," Melinda said more decisively. She was sure

enough for the two of us. "I think she put everything, um, naughty up in their room, where she could keep a close eye on it, and I think we've found everything. I can't imagine another hiding place in that room. We looked everywhere."

"No, we didn't."

"What?"

"We didn't look in the needlepoint cushion of that chair."

Melinda knew instantly what I meant. She was out of the kitchen and up the stairs in that smooth, unhurried stride that made her look so efficient. She was back in a moment, cushion in hand.

She handed it to me, and I looked it over. Poppy had done the needlepoint for the top of the flat cushion herself. I have no craft ability whatsoever, so I couldn't have told you what kind of pattern it was, but the design was thistles on a cream background. The top was shaped like a large pancake to match the round seat of the chair. The bottom of the cushion was covered in a sage green silky material. It had turned out real pretty. Now we were about to deface it.

"I feel bad about this," I said, hesitating over the pretty thing. A dead woman's hands had crafted this, and I was reluctant to begin. I wriggled the padding in a sort of wave motion, and I felt something rustle inside the cushion.

"Oh hell, there's something in there," I told Melinda.

We looked at each other with a kind of despair. I felt dirty outside because of all the dust we'd stirred up in the corners of the bedroom—though that had been easy enough to clean up—and I felt dirty inside because of all the dirt we'd discovered in Poppy's life—which wasn't easy to dispose of at all. It was a neat parallel, and it made me sick. I never wanted to know this much about another human being, I decided. People needed their secrets. My mother had always told me that ignorance is dangerous, but the way I felt now, ignorance would be true bliss.

Melinda said, "I can sew it shut if we just cut a thin slit."

The sharpest knife we could find glided easily into the sage green material. Melinda held the cushion absolutely flat and still while I enlarged the opening. Melinda's fingers were far longer than mine, so she assumed the task of extraction. Tweezed between her long forefinger and middle finger, the piece of paper hissed like a snake against the silk as she drew it out.

I unfolded the paper with as much terror as if it had been an actual reptile.

It was the results of a DNA test. "A paternity test," I told Melinda. "It looks like Poppy took two samples in to be tested against Chase's DNA. She paid for it up front, cash. Get this—it was ordered by Dr. Stuart Embler." I looked at Melinda significantly, then returned my attention to the letter. "She told them—well, I can't figure out exactly what she told them, but subject A was not the father, and Subject B was."

Melinda opened and closed her mouth several times, as if she thought she knew what to say, then decided that she didn't. I knew exactly how she felt.

"What are we going to do?" she asked finally.

"What a good question," I said. "And I don't have the slightest idea what the answer is. Should we make an appointment with Aubrey?"

"But he'd know then. We can't have anyone knowing if we can prevent it. On the other hand, this seems like too much for us. This is really huge."

"Yes."

"Chase may be John David's son, and he may not. My God, what will happen to Chase if he isn't John David's?"

"He'll still be Poppy's son, so that means . . ."

"Her parents will get him? Absolutely not."

"But we don't have the right to lie about it!"

"No! But we can't take Chase away from John David!"

"But he has another father! A real father!"

"Maybe John David *is* the real father. Maybe John David is subject B."

We both took a deep breath. "I say we burn this piece of paper," I said. I looked at my sister-in-law steadily.

"I say we should sleep on it and talk to Aubrey tomorrow," Melinda countered, neatly reversing her trend of a few moments before.

I was sorely tempted to grab it from her hand and rip it to shreds, as I had the repulsive pictures. Why the hell had I remembered the cushion on the chair? John David would never in a million years have messed with that cushion. If it had crinkled when he sat on it, he still wouldn't have opened it up, an opinion I based simply on John David's being a man.

Well, the deed had been done, and we were the possessors of yet another piece of unpleasant knowledge.

Chapter Eleven

When I got home that evening, cooking was the bottom thing on my list of desirable activities. The day after Thanksgiving is just not a day to slave over the stove. That's pretty much been done. So I was delighted to discover, among the messages on my answering machine, one from Robin inviting Phillip and me out to dinner. I almost dropped the phone in my haste to punch in his number so I could accept.

Phillip, back from a day out with another teenager, was less excited. The company of three adults seemed less appealing to him after a long afternoon with Josh, eyeing girls at the mall. I suspected my brother was lapsing back into his normal self, becoming more relaxed around me, rather than being so anxious to mind his manners and be helpful. He'd absorbed the fact that I wasn't going to throw him out.

"Can't I just stay here and eat leftovers?" he said in a voice suspiciously close to a whine.

"No, you can not," I said in a voice suspiciously close to a direct order. I wondered again why my father hadn't called to set up the return of Phillip.

Robin's message was the third I'd listened to. The first two had been from, respectively, Cara Embler (who said she had found Moosie and would keep him at her house until we decided what to do with the cat), and the Clean Scene guy, Zachary Lee (who hoped we had found his service satisfactory and would recommend him to our friends). I looked at my watch and decided not to listen to my remaining messages. I was dusty, dirty, and badly in need of a general cleanup. I was thrilled Moosie had been found, and I made a mental note to call John David the next day and tell him the whereabouts of the little cat.

I told Phillip he looked fine. He hadn't any more clothes anyway, and I hoped Robin would take that into consideration when he picked out a restaurant. I threw my clothes into the hamper, reflected that laundry day would have to be really soon, and tossed the small Wal-Mart bag I'd brought home with me onto the bathroom counter. Maybe tomorrow morning, I thought. Now was the worst time in the world.

The shower was blissful. I was clean all over, and relaxed, and much more optimistic when I emerged. I looked at myself in the mirror carefully. My bosom looked a little different, the aureoles darker, and when I put on my bra, I noticed that I was very sore indeed.

It took all I had to walk past the small bag, leaving it unopened.

Corinne was really fond of Italian food, and there was a new Italian restaurant about halfway between Lawrenceton and the interstate, an area that was beginning to run together in a big blur of commerce. Actually, the restaurant was not too far from the Grabbit Kwik, the filling station where Sandy Wynn had filled her car's tank with gas on Monday.

I pushed the death of Poppy out of my mind. I tried not to think of all the unpleasant things Melinda and I had learned today. I forced myself not to think of the bag on the counter of my bathroom.

All that not thinking left my mind pretty empty. I'm afraid I wasn't a very good conversationalist that night. I made an attempt to be a good listener, to encourage Corinne to talk, so I wouldn't seem stupid by my silences. And I asked Robin a lot of questions. Phillip decided to talk about drug use in his school in California, to impress us unworldly southerners, I suppose. Robin reminded him in a few well-chosen anecdotes that he had spent the past two years living in Los Angeles among the movie crowd, and any stories Phillip chose to tell, Robin could easily top.

Corinne, as it transpired, had left her Chihuahua and her toy Manchester in the care of one of her daughters, and she had called to check on their well-being that very afternoon. Corinne was one of those women who had to have something to mother; for all I knew, that made her like most women. Now that her children were very much grown and gone, and her grandchildren visited from time to time but not for days in a row, the dogs had filled that gap for her. Though she was intelligent enough to realize not everyone wants to listen to detailed animal stories, she was besotted enough not to care, and we heard many anecdotes about Punky's little trick with the bouncy ball, and Percy's little wake-up routine.

That reminded me that I hadn't laid eyes on Madeleine in a couple of days, and during a lull in the dog worship, I asked Phillip if he'd seen the massive old cat.

"No," he said. "Maybe she didn't like me and so she's staying away until I leave."

"Nothing would make Madeleine miss a meal," I said.

"Was your cat named for the little girl in the books?" Corinne asked brightly.

"No, for the poisoner," I answered, abstracted. "Madeleine Smith, Glasgow, 1857."

"Oh," Corinne said.

We didn't hear any more dog stories for a while.

When Robin dropped us off, Phillip loped ahead to get in the house to watch some television show he was dying to see. Robin came in the foyer with me and shut the door behind him. He had a big, long, smoochy kiss on his mind, but when he pulled me to him, my sore chest protested.

"Not so tight," I said, trying to smile.

"What's wrong?" Not too surprisingly, he was bewildered. I'd been Passionate Woman the night before, and now I was practically pushing him away. But I was so averse to the idea of sex that I would have kicked him in the shins if he'd suggested it. I answered him by bursting into tears.

"What?" Terrified, Robin gripped my elbows. "What's wrong? Are you upset about Poppy? Madeleine? I'll look for her tomorrow, I swear, baby."

"No, not that." I wanted to tell him about my long, unpleasant day, and I wanted to tell him what I was beginning to suspect might be the truth. But this wasn't the place, and his mother was waiting out in the cold in the car for him to return.

"Your mom leaves Monday?" I sobbed.

"No, I forgot to tell you. Before she left home, she changed her reservation, because the airline called her with a last-minute cancellation," Robin said. "She leaves tomorrow afternoon. One of her best friends lost his son in an accident overseas, and the memorial service is scheduled for Sunday afternoon. Mom wants to be back for it. It's just amazing she was able to get a seat on the plane. She was on the phone for hours, she told me, but she got it done." He sounded admiring. "But tell me what's wrong."

"I can't tell you right now," I said. I wasn't actively crying anymore, just kind of giving the occasional sob or gasp. This was crazy. I had no control over it whatsoever. I was just along for the ride. "Lots of stuff happened today. We need to talk tomorrow, after you take your mom to the airport. Call me."

"Sure," he said. Hesitantly, he leaned over and gave me a peck on the forehead. That was easier for him to reach anyway.

I was almost too tired to take off my clothes. I wished my brother good night, asked him to check the doors before he went to bed, cast a disconsolate look at Madeleine's food bowl—still full—and tucked myself into bed. I thought I might lie awake a little and rehash the day, but the minute my head came into contact with my pillow, I was out.

Someone was shaking me.

Someone had hold of my shoulder and was saying, "Roe, wake up!" in a terrified voice.

I opened my eyes to sunlight. I had not slept two hours or so, as I'd assumed—I'd slept the night through, and then some. Phillip was standing by the bed, his face full of horror.

"What?" I asked, sitting up. My heart was racing and my mouth felt like a herd of something dirty—maybe mud-covered water buffalo—had wallowed in it. "What?" I asked again, more sharply this time. I was fully awake.

"My mom has gone and your cat is dead."

I started to say something, closed my mouth, and opened it again. "Say that again," I demanded.

"Those messages you didn't listen to last night?" This was definitely said with an accusatory edge. "One of those messages was from our dad. He says my mom left and he doesn't know where she's gone. He says she's gone off with some guy."

For a wild moment, I wondered if Betty Jo, too, would hitch-hike over to Lawrenceton. Then I came to my senses.

"That's really awful," I said. "But he doesn't think she's in any danger? I mean, there's no question but that she left voluntarily?" Phillip looked blank. "She arranged to run off with this man," I said, trying to clarify. "He didn't abduct her."

"Right," Phillip said, calming down a bit. "She definitely left because she wanted to. She told Dad she'd get in touch with him soon. She told him to call me. She said she knew I was safe with you."

That was rich, coming from the woman who'd whisked Phillip off all the way to California to keep him from my contaminating companionship.

"I'm glad she feels that way," I managed to say, wanting a cup of coffee more than I had ever wanted any beverage in my life. "Now, I want to talk more about that later, because I know that's definitely the more important thing, but did you say Madeleine was dead?"

Personally, I considered Madeleine much more important, but I was trying to be sensitive to Phillip's pain.

"Oh, yeah, I went out in the backyard this morning, since the weather is good, and I was like kicking around this pine-cone, and when it landed on something in the bushes around the wall"—my backyard, like Poppy's, was enclosed by a solid wood privacy fence, though mine was definitely shorter—"I went to see why it sounded so funny, and your big old cat was lying there on the ground, and she was all wet and everything, and she's dead." Phillip looked at me pathetically. He had had a tough morning, and it was only . . .

"What time is it?" I asked.

"Nine-thirty," Phillip said. "See? There's a clock right by the bed, Sis." He may have been a tad sarcastic.

"Okay, so I didn't look." I groped for my glasses on the night table and put them on. I took a deep breath, then went into the bathroom to wash my face, trying to prepare to content this day.

I'd slept until 9:30 A.M. maybe four times in my life, and one of those had been after my senior prom, when I'd stayed out all night, as was the local tradition. I was dazed by so much sleep, and wondered what had prompted it. Then, glancing at the Wal-Mart bag, I suspected I knew, but I thrust the knowledge away from me forcefully. I had enough to deal with just at the moment, thanks very much. Pulling on the heaviest bathrobe in my closet, I slid my feet into my Birkenstock clogs and ventured out into the backyard. The day was clear and cold, and my ankles stung in the chilly breeze.

Madeleine was lying under a bush. She was nearly invisible, and I wasn't surprised we hadn't seen her from the house. She looked as peaceful as any dead thing can look. Apparently, the old cat had just lain down and died.

I believed that Madeleine was now in heaven with her original mistress, my friend Jane Engle. This conviction came to me so simply and naturally that I knew I would never question it.

"Phillip, I need you to go get a shovel from the garage," I said. "You can bury her right where she is; maybe move the hole away from the bush a little so you won't hit too many roots."

"Me?" Phillip sounded absolutely amazed. "She was *your* cat!"

"Point noted," I snapped. "But the one who loves the animal least gets the hole-digging duty. I loved this old cat, and I'm really upset, and you're twenty years younger than I am, and you get to dig the damn hole!"

I spun on my heel, as much as you can do that in clogs, and stomped back into the house to listen to my phone messages.

I sniveled and wiped my eyes and nose on a napkin before I poked the play button on my answering machine. The first message (after the three I'd listened to the night before) was from my father, and it went as Phillip had said. What Phillip hadn't said, of course, was that my dad sounded both stunned and indignant, as if he'd never expected his straying from fidelity could have such dire consequences. And, apparently, Dad had never considered the fact that his wife might have followed his example. I noticed right away—and Phillip hadn't mentioned this, either—that my dad said nothing about Phillip coming home.

Hmm. Dad and I needed to talk.

The next message was from my mother, confirming that Poppy's body would be back in Lawrenceton on Saturday, today, and would be ready for burial on Monday. John David had set the service for ten o'clock at St. Stephen's, and the interment would follow immediately.

I'd have to check the work schedule and see if I needed to arrange for the morning off. At this rate, Sam would cut me from the payroll. The library budget was always tight. I'd been picked to take a course in Atlanta about computer usage for librarians, and I was very excited about it. I'd been on the verge of asking Sam if I could come back on the staff full-time. Maybe now I'd better not make that call, I thought.

Melinda had left a message to say Aubrey could see us at ten-thirty this morning.

"Oh my God," I muttered, glancing at the clock. I washed my face again and put on some makeup, though my eyes looked red and swollen behind the rims of my glasses. I wore black ones today, with gold decorations on the earpieces. These made me look serious but fun-loving, I thought. I pulled on a pair of cerise pants and a cerise-and-white-checked sweater, so I wouldn't look funereal. Then I thought I looked too cheerful, but there was nothing I could do about it. I had to go so I wouldn't be late. I hate being late.

Besides, I thought as I backed out of my driveway, the day would probably take care of obliterating any cheerfulness.

Melinda got out of her car as I pulled into the lot by the church. She was wearing sweats today, jolly red-and-green sweats that had a huge reindeer head on the front of the shirt. With this outfit, she wore cute little red sneakers with green laces, and her red coat. The Christmas buildup had begun.

"Avery's got the kids," she said. "He's pretty miffed at me because I wouldn't tell him why we needed to talk to Aubrey. He's very obviously trying to be brave about hiding it. I can't think of the last time I had a secret from Avery." She sounded mildly amused.

"Have you seen John David?'

"Yeah, he's over at our place, too. He's asking questions about baby care and what to do when. I feel like a big fat traitor, coming here to ask Aubrey if we should tell."

"It seems to me this was your idea," I said somewhat indignantly. I sure had better ways I could spend my morning, what was left of it.

"I know, I just . . . I guess I didn't foresee how complicated this would be. Emotionally."

"Well, we're here now," I said, acting ungracious and grumpy. I started down the sidewalk to the outside entrance to Aubrey's office, which was at the back of the church.

Aubrey seemed maybe a little less than delighted to be seeing us on a Saturday morning, since Saturday and Monday were his days off. Well, tough. We had a major moral dilemma.

Realizing I was definitely in a truculent mood, I advised myself to put the brakes on.

Catch more flies with honey, I reminded myself, glancing around to make sure that reminder had been given mentally rather than out loud. Since Aubrey and Melinda were discussing the Altar Guild rotation, I was pretty sure I was in the clear.

"Aubrey," I said rather sharply. "Melinda and I have run into a problem."

We began to explain.

Thirty minutes later, Melinda and I were leaving Aubrey's office, none the wiser. I had considered Aubrey pretty much unflappable, but I found I'd been wrong. Aubrey seemed to be as confounded as we were, and his parting words had been that he planned to pray about the problem and hope God would give him guidance. He had raised more questions than we already had. How could we be sure *either* of the samples had come from John David? (That one floored us.)

"This is extremely serious," Aubrey said. "We should not do anything in a hurry. I tend to think you should turn this piece of paper over to the police. If Poppy was putting pressure on the father of her son, he might have reacted with violence. But let me think another day."

Waiting for God to give us guidance seemed as good a course as any.

The only resolution I'd formed was that it would not be me who told John David what we'd discovered. No sir.

I dropped by to see my mom and John. They certainly seemed in better spirits now that the plans for the funeral were definite. Mother was just buzzed at the idea of finally having something to do, at some conclusion having been reached. True, Poppy's murderer had not been named, but at least the family could go through the ritual of burying her. John, she said, had just returned from the funeral home, where he'd gone with John David to select a casket and make all the arrangements with the funeral director.

"I offered to go with them, and so did Avery," Mother said. She was wearing a blouse and skirt featuring a lot of dark blue, and she looked as neat and elegant as always, but the sun coming through the window hit her squarely in the face and I noticed, as if for the first time, that my mother was getting an enlarged network of tiny wrinkles at the corners of her mouth and eyes. She was still impressively attractive, and I was sure she always would be, but there was no denying that age had laid its hand on her.

"I was glad to go with my son," said John very quietly. "John David was with me when I ordered his mother's casket. Avery was too upset that day. Of course, I never thought I'd have to return the favor. Poppy was so young, so full of life."

She had been. She had looked forward to every day of her existence, at least over the past few years. I was willing to bet on that.

No matter what her faults, she had been robbed. So had John David and Chase.

I said good-bye without telling Mother about my father's phone message. I'd have to tell her sooner or later, but right now, until I knew what I was supposed to do with Phillip, I thought I'd just keep Dad's marital problems to myself.

"I guess it would look bad if I went out to the club for round of golf," John said longingly as I paused in the doorway. My mother patted his hand.

"I don't think there would be anything wrong with that," she said, and I wondered again at my mother's late-in-life love affair. "You need to get out of the house, and the funeral is two days away. The exercise will do you good, if you bundle up."

"You're nagging," John said fondly.

I smiled but tried to hide it. "I have to be going," I said. "I left Phillip at home, busy doing a job for me."

"I'll talk to you soon," Mother said automatically.

"I'm sure you will." I smiled openly.

I was thinking of Madeleine on the way home. Though I felt temporarily wept out, I was grieving about the old orange cat. I had spent a lot of years with Madeleine, as many years as Jane Engle had had with her. I remembered how cute Madeleine's kittens had been, and I wondered how many grandchildren she had. Probably great- and great-great grandchildren, come to think of it.

That reminded me of Cara's call about Moosie. It wasn't right that Poppy's cat should be in the care of a neighbor, not when I could take the cat in until John David could get back on his feet. After all, I had a fenced-in backyard and cat food, though possibly my fence was low enough for Moosie to leap over, claws or not.

To get to Cara's house, which faced onto the street parallel to Swanson, I had to drive past Poppy's house once again. To my extreme irritation (I didn't seem to be able to be moderate about anything these days), Arthur's car was parked in front of the house.

This was tacky, to say the least. After all, the house had been released to John David, and he and Chase might arrive at any moment to resume living in it again. John David couldn't stay in a motel forever, and now that the initial shock of Poppy's death had passed, he might be ready to return to his very clean home.

I parked behind Arthur's car in the driveway and marched up to the front door. I still had the key I'd borrowed from John David, and I opened the door and went in.

"Arthur!" I bellowed.

He appeared at the head of the stairs, looking considerably startled.

"What the hell are you doing here?" I asked, surprising even myself.

"I'm the detective in charge of the investigation into the

death of the home owner," he said evenly. "I have a right to be here."

"Now that you've given John David the green light to move back in? I don't think so," I said with more confidence than I felt.

"Are you jealous because I came to love Poppy rather than you?" Arthur asked as he came down the stairs. I remembered that yesterday I had wondered if I should be afraid of this man, and I'd had a friend with me then.

"No, I'm not jealous of Poppy, especially over your affections. I think Poppy loved life, but I think she lived it badly. I don't think she ever appreciated what she had, or what she could do with it."

Arthur stood right in front of me, looking down at me, and he was maybe a little puzzled. "What could Poppy have wanted that she didn't have?" he asked.

Smarter lovers, for one thing.

"Poppy could have wanted stability, but instead she created instability. She could have wanted to heal from the badness in her past, but instead she clung to the . . . the emotional problems that caused her to live so . . . dangerously." Maybe I sounded a tad pompous.

"She was wonderful," Arthur said, unbelievingly. "She was smart, and she was funny, and she was pretty. Like you."

"But unlike me, she liked to sneak," I said bluntly. "Unlike me, she liked multiple partners. This isn't about how great I am in contrast to Poppy. This is about you letting go of a dream of Poppy, a Poppy who never really existed. You can't afford to pin her down this tightly, Arthur. Let her go, so you can look for who killed her."

I wondered how much sleep Arthur had been getting. He was definitely on the smelly side, and he certainly needed a shave. That curly pale hair was dirty, and his shirt was rumpled.

"Was it you who searched the house after she died, Arthur? The one who searched her bedroom?"

"I think it was Bubba Sewell," Arthur said. "He seemed awfully concerned with how long the house would be off-limits to the family. I don't know what he was looking for."

I did. "She didn't take pictures of you?" I said, unwisely.

"Pictures? What the hell are you talking about?"

"When were you with her? It's been almost two years, right?" I'd just had the worst idea in the world. I was wondering if you added Chase's age, plus nine months . . .

"Less than that," he said, and my heart sank. Arthur was a candidate for Chase's father.

"Oh, well, doesn't make any difference," I said bracingly. "What were you actually doing here today, Arthur? Were you just mooning around, or were you working on the investigation?" Poppy must have had a higher regard for Arthur than for the others, but I wasn't up to explaining to Arthur why that was so.

"A little of both," Arthur said. His voice was mild, which was a relief. "I've been talking to Sandy Wynn. She called Poppy that day, said she was coming to talk to her. She admits she was here the morning Poppy was murdered."

"Did she do it?"

"She says that when she got here, Poppy was already dead."

"Where did she park her car? Did anyone see her car?"

"The woman across the street. Almost everyone on this street goes to work in the morning, but this woman, the one who also described the Sewells' van, incidentally, was home with the runs that morning. In between trips to the bathroom, she sat in her living room and watched television, with the front curtains open. She didn't get a good look at Lizanne, but a better one at Sandy. She picked her picture out of a photo array. Sandy parked down the street, in the driveway of a house for sale, and walked up to Poppy's."

"Why would she do that if she didn't plan on doing something bad?"

"She planned on talking Poppy into giving her something, something that belonged to Marvin Wynn. Of course, thanks to you and Melinda, we know what that thing is—the letter. Sandy broke down when I showed it to her. She said Poppy forced Marvin to write that letter by threatening to tell John David and the rest of the world what Marvin had done when Poppy was a teenager. Poppy swore that if Marvin would write such a letter, she'd never tell. He did what she demanded, but as time went on, Marvin regretted it more and more. He began to lose sleep, and slide into depression. Sandy got scared for him."

"Why would Poppy do such a thing, stay silent? Why wouldn't she tell? Why make any bargain? He was in the wrong, and she was so young."

"Her word against his. No evidence. Poppy was in her thirties, way beyond her teens. Nothing would have come of it."

"Nothing but the ruin of his reputation," I pointed out. "No matter if it came to court or not, Poppy would have ruined him forever. Plenty of people would have believed her."

"But it would have ruined her, too, in the process. At the very least, it would have made her life, and John David's and the baby's, very painful for a few months."

I mulled that over. "So this way, with her demanding he write the letter, he could believe she'd never tell, and she could believe he'd never make passes at young girls again?"

"I guess that was Poppy's thinking."

"Do you believe Sandy? Do you believe she didn't kill Poppy?"

"Yes. She was too stricken to think about stepping over

Poppy's body to search for the letter that morning. I believed her when she said it just didn't occur to her. She did her best to get the letter back once Poppy was dead, but I don't believe she killed Poppy for it. I think she did walk to the gate in the front of the fence when Poppy wouldn't come to the door, which Sandy says was then locked."

But it hadn't been locked when I tried it. I was getting more and more confused.

"So she walked over to the fence at the side of the house, came in the gate, and walked around to the sliding glass doors," I said. "And there she saw Poppy's body?"

"Yes. She says she cried for a while, then left the way she'd come, and drove back home. By the time she got there, she was hearing from us here that Poppy was dead. She and Marvin packed up and returned to Lawrenceton. She never told Marvin where she'd been."

"Okay," I said slowly, trying not to get sidetracked by my rush of disgust at having put them up in my house. "So, Sandy leaves, the front door is locked, and she doesn't have the letter. Then Lizanne comes?"

"No, Lizanne came first. She, too, knocked on the front door, got no answer, went to the fence and heard a quarrel, heard Poppy's radio, decided she couldn't ream Poppy out, not with someone else here. She threw something onto the ground." Here Arthur gave me a very sharp look. "Something that later vanished. And then she left. Then Sandy walked up, left within five minutes. Then you and Melinda came, and you found the front door open."

I had a sudden idea, and I walked down the little hall to the kitchen. It was in better shape than it had been when we arrived yesterday. Melinda and I hadn't searched it, but we had straightened it and cleaned the counters and stovetop. Poppy's little radio still sat on the counter, though now it was dustless.

I pressed a button to turn it on, and when the music came on, I looked at Arthur expectantly.

"What?" he said. His voice sounded quite businesslike, brisk. He's back to being himself, I thought.

"When Lizanne described her experience here that day, the day Poppy died, she said she'd walked to the fence." I gestured to my left, which was where the gate in the fence was at the front. "She said the music was so loud, she couldn't hear what the voices were saying, but she said the music was classical, that the radio was broadcasting NPR. This radio isn't on a classical station. I checked it the other day. So if we assume that the person Poppy was talking to was the person who killed her, and Poppy therefore didn't survive after that visit to change radio stations, then it wasn't Poppy's radio that was on."

I walked around the breakfast bar and looked out the sliding glass door. Arthur came to stand beside me. We exchanged glances.

"It was Mrs. Embler's radio," he said.

"I'm guessing it was. What did she tell you about that morning?"

"Just that she swam as usual. Didn't hear or see anything out of the ordinary. Not too surprising, considering the fact that she was wearing a swimming cap and the radio was on, and there's a privacy fence in between the houses."

"But the gate in the privacy fence had to be open at some point," I said. "She's got Moosie."

"The cat? You saw Moosie in the house after Poppy was dead?"

"Yes, I did." I stared at the boards of the high privacy fence, the fence the declawed Moosie couldn't climb. "You know, Arthur, I could swear that when I was standing here, looking out, the day Poppy died, Cara was swimming then. She had the radio on."

"So?"

"Still swimming? In this temperature? From the time Lizanne got here, waited, left; then Sandy came, found Poppy dead, and left; until the time I came in and found her body?"

"That could be," Arthur said, but he sounded doubtful.

"And Moosie—who can't climb the fence because he hasn't got claws—vanished, between the time I came in the house and the time the police arrived."

Arthur stared at the back gate.

"What the woman across the street *didn't* see was anyone leaving," he said very quietly. "Anyone except Sandy and Lizanne, that is. Yet I'm fairly certain neither of them killed Poppy. So where did this talking person, the one Lizanne heard, go?" He turned to stare down at me. "I should have been taken off this investigation," he said expressionlessly. "I should have gone to the chief, I should have told him the whole story of my involvement with Poppy, and he should have put someone else on it. I thought I'd been away from her long enough, but I hadn't."

"Maybe someone did sneak out between the time Sandy took off and Melinda and I got here. Maybe Moosie got out the front door. Maybe I left it ajar while we were waiting for the police and ambulance after I'd found the body. But I don't think so. I think I shut Moosie in the house when I came out to tell Melinda. I think someone came in to check the backyard, maybe for something they'd left there, while Melinda and I were sitting out front. I think that person came through the gate in the fence, from the Embler's yard. I could hear Cara splashing while I stood here, with this door open, by Poppy's body. I remember that clearly. But Cara usually swims at ten in the morning and at three in the afternoon. Everyone knows that. When I was here, it was about one. And I know what I think I saw on the concrete of the pool area."

216

"What?"

"Wet marks. I think they were wet footprints."

"You didn't remember until now?"

"I didn't realize what they were. I was so upset at seeing the body, I didn't think too much about the splotches on the concrete. But when I think of them in terms of what we just figured out, I realized that what I saw were footprints."

"That's hardly conclusive evidence."

"I know. Did you see any when you came?"

"I was so overwhelmed by the sight of Poppy dead—I owe your family my sincerest apology. I didn't notice half of what I should have noticed, didn't ask half the questions I should have asked."

"Arthur, just get the right person now. I'm glad you cared for Poppy. I'm glad someone who cared for her was there with her." I wasn't altogether sincere, but I didn't want Arthur to spend any more time bashing himself. I wanted action. "I'll bet she came back through the fence to dry up the water," I said absently. "That's why you didn't see it. And that's when Moosie escaped."

"Maybe, if I get a search warrant, we can find the knife."

"I'll bet she threw it away. It's in the garbage right now, and today is pickup for our part of town." At every house but Poppy's, garbage cans were sitting at the curb, waiting to be emptied.

"Then I'll have to hurry to get a search warrant." Arthur turned on his heel, ready to run out the front way, but I put my hand on his arm. I could hear the garbage truck coming down Poppy's street, and next it would turn onto the Emblers'. There wasn't time. I had to do something.

"Just wait a *minute*," I said.

"What are you doing?"

"Come with me, and wait on this side," I said. I'd had a

sudden idea, and I was determined to carry it through. I remembered Poppy done to death on her own floor, in her own kitchen. I owed her this.

I walked around Poppy's pool, knocked on the gate, turned the knob, and walked through.

Chapter Twelve

Cara Embler was drying her short hair with a huge fluffy white towel. A little puddle of water had trickled down her legs and lay pooled at her feet. By her back door, there was a table piled high with identical towels, all snowy white and neatly folded. Organized, not prone to impulse, that was Cara.

She was surprised at my appearance in her yard, but not shocked. After all, she'd called me about Moosie. He was sunning himself on the patio, and when I came in, he jumped up and ran to me, stropping himself around my legs as he'd done on the day I'd found Poppy. I saw her two dogs looking through her set of sliding glass doors. They barked energetically when I walked through the gate and pulled it to behind me. I didn't close it all the way.

"Hi, Roe," Cara said, turning down the radio, which was sitting on a table by a matching chair. "I would have gotten all Moosie's stuff together and put him in a carrier if I'd known you were coming. I'd gotten him some cat food and some litter, and a toy."

She did love animals. "I just came over on impulse," I said, which was the truth. "Are you ready to come home with me, boy?" I lifted him up into my arms and scratched his head.

"I've enjoyed having him, but the dogs go nuts when he teases them," Cara said. The schnauzers were peering anxiously out of the glass door, yipping from time to time. They were beautiful animals, obviously well cared for. "Why'd you come in from Poppy's side?" Cara asked. She combed her short hair.

"I had to get some things out of the house for John David. Things for Chase," I replied, lying. I was feeling my way, and I was suddenly cold down to my heart. What had I done? But having come through the gate in the fence, seeing Cara's assurance, I could not stand the thought that she might walk free. I could not imagine why, out of all the women Poppy had cuckolded, this one would strike back, but I knew in my gut that Cara Embler had killed my sister-in-law.

"Want to come in? It's a little brisk out here." But Cara seemed to be used to it. She wrapped a white terry robe around her. She started to put on a pair of yellow plastic clogs, then seemed to reconsider. I wondered why. She swept a hand toward the house invitingly.

If we went inside, Arthur couldn't hear.

"How many times did you go through the fence that day?" I asked.

Cara looked stunned for a second. "What day?"

"The day Poppy died. When you killed her."

The words hung between us, enormous and terrifying.

Cara's eyes changed then. The veil she'd held between the world and herself dropped, and the real Cara looked out at me.

"You don't know anything," she said contemptuously.

"I found your husband's ID tag, the one from the hospital."

"You did, huh? That was where Stuart lost it?"

"Isn't that why?"

"Why I killed her? Over my husband poking his thing in her? If I killed everyone he fucked, there'd be a lot of dead women around Atlanta. That hospital is like Peyton Place. Granted, one in my own backyard is over the top. But consider the woman." Cara's face shone with malice. "She gets pregnant so easy, she doesn't even know who the father is. She thinks I don't even know my husband's had her, that that'll scare me! But at least I can be sure it's not him, because his sperm count is so pathetic, we had to adopt. You know how hard it is to get a healthy white male infant? Not as hard for a prominent cardiologist and his wife as it would be for a garbageman and his wife, but still . . . difficult, expensive, and time-consuming. And then he doesn't even love us! We brought him up as ours, we gave him everything, and he doesn't even love us!"

"How'd you know Poppy didn't know the father of her kid?" I was very uneasy at Arthur hearing this, but I had cast the die and couldn't retreat.

"She had the gall to come over here—while I was here, mind you—and ask my husband how to get samples for DNA testing! I was out of the room, of course, but I made sure I could hear every word they said. She asked Stuart to order the test through the lab his practice uses, so she could push it through without questions asked. He told me all about it. That's what he thought of your precious Poppy. He told her to get a swab from someone's mouth, or their hair with the roots on, not cut hair. Easy enough. It wasn't a court-ordered procedure. She just wanted to know."

"But if you didn't care if your husband slept with her, why'd you kill her?"

"I wanted her to die for me," Cara said. "You know, a member of Uppity Women has to die for the next person on the waiting list to get in. And I wanted in. So Poppy Queensland died for me."

I couldn't believe I'd understood her correctly. I must have been squeezing Moosie, because he protested and began to struggle. Absently, I began stroking him again, and he relaxed, bless his feline heart.

"You wanted to be in Uppity Women so much, you killed Poppy to get in?"

"You know what I gave up when I married Stuart? I was through with college—I graduated with honors—and I'd decided to go to vet school. I've loved animals all my life, and I wanted to be a veterinarian. But my husband said it would lower his status as a cardiologist if he had a wife who was an animal doctor, so I thought, Well, that's enough, being Stuart's wife. I can run the house. I can entertain. I can do charitable work. I can raise his kids. I can contribute."

"Wasn't enough?" I said in a low voice with a big quaver. Cara's face was ugly with loathing.

"It was never enough," she answered, her voice almost a growl. "We couldn't have our own children. We adopted the one baby, and Stuart decided after that, that one was enough, because he felt Henry was a lot of trouble. As if he did anything for the boy. So I took up swimming again, and I got really good, and I began winning medals, I got so good. But Stuart didn't like that, either, because he said swimming meets for seniors were silly that I should just swim for my own pleasure and have done with it."

"I hear he went with you, though, to a lot of them, right?" I was backing toward the fence. I sincerely hoped Arthur was right behind it.

"He decided it was a good advertisement—for a cardiologist to have a wife who did such a heart-healthy thing, at her age!"

222

I didn't have an idea in the world what to do next.

"So you really did kill her so you could get into Uppity Women?"

"I really did." Cara was almost proud.

I didn't believe her for a second. Maybe that was what Cara chose to believe, but I thought it went maybe a few miles deeper than that.

"You came back in your yard with the knife and put it back in the house, didn't you? And got back in the pool?"

"I dove into the water after I killed her, and I washed all that blood off me and the knife. I figured the chlorine would take care of it, and it did," she said. "And then I couldn't think of what to do with the knife. I didn't exactly want to put it back in the kitchen drawer." She looked at me and rolled her eyes, as though she were confessing a charming foible. "And I didn't want to stick it in the garbage, because what if my garbage got searched somehow?" I began to have a real bad feeling. She strolled over to the raised flower bed by the fence and scratched her fingers through the pine bark that the gardener had put in as mulch. "So I buried the knife in here. And here it is!"

She smiled at me.

It was at least a foot long, and wicked-looking. I was so creeped out by Cara that a toothpick would have frightened me, but at the sight of this knife, I was almost paralyzed.

I had time to think, Where the hell is Arthur? when he came flying through the gate, which crashed back against the fence and rebounded, knocking the drawn gun from his hand quite neatly.

Cara disregarded Arthur completely and leaped at me. She gave me a powerful shove.

I threw Moosie at her.

Moosie screeched and bit and drew blood on Cara's chest,

and the barking of the dogs in the house reached a frantic crescendo as Cara staggered backward, ending up near the lawn furniture again. Her wet feet slipped in the puddle of water where she'd been standing, and she fell heavily. As her head hit the concrete, I landed in the pool with enough force to send me right down. My glasses were knocked off by the force of the impact, and as I plummeted deeper, I looked up and saw them drifting lazily after me to the bottom.

The water was cold, cold, cold. The shock to my system was severe, and for a long moment I seemed unable to move my limbs, unable to save myself. It was fortunate that I wasn't wearing a heavy coat or boots. I shook off the paralysis and began to force water down with my hands so I could rise. My face broke the surface and I gasped for air. The first thing I saw was Moosie's face peering out from under the table by the back door, the one that held the towels. Moosie's sense of self-preservation was far superior to mine.

Arthur was scrambling to his feet, going for the gun that had skittered to the very edge of the pool. Cara was twitching, but silent. The fall had knocked the air out of her.

I made it to the side of the pool and shoved the gun toward Arthur. I was not about to pick it up. I don't know a thing about guns, and they make me very nervous. I began to pull myself up to sit on the side of the pool. I expected Arthur would throw me a towel, or give me a hand. I *didn't* expect that he'd walk over to Cara and kick her in the ribs as hard as he could.

"Stop," I said. "Arthur! Stop!" I sat and shivered, my feet still in the water. I had never trembled so violently in my life. The moderate day seemed frigid now. I simply could not get up to interfere.

I was scared of Arthur, too, scared to get close enough to grab his arm. He was almost as frightening as Cara. Cara deserved every kind of punishment for killing Poppy, but I hated watching her being beaten.

He drew back his leg again, and I screamed, "No!"

My voice penetrated the fog of rage that hung around him almost palpably.

Arthur's foot touched the ground again. He shook himself, then said in a thick voice, "Cara Embler, you are under arrest for the murder of Poppy Queensland. Anything you say . . ."

Chapter Thirteen

I came out of my own warm bathroom, toweling my wet hair just as Cara had dried hers. Only Phillip's presence in the house was keeping Robin from waiting in here in my bedroom, and oddly, I was glad of that. I needed a few more seconds to myself, more than my quick shower had afforded. I was warm now, and with the heat turned up in the house, my hair would dry fairly quickly. Short of sticking me in the oven, Phillip and Robin had done everything they possibly could to warm me up. This had been tremendously important to them.

I couldn't suppress a snigger as I thought of how they'd competed with each other to be the most solicitous. That wouldn't last long, of course, and they'd be back to their more normal selves shortly, but I would enjoy it while it lasted.

At the moment, I'd just discovered I had a whole new set of worries.

I should have gotten dressed again. I wasn't an invalid. But I felt like putting on a nightgown and bathrobe, so I did. I hadn't been hurt, but I was exhausted and achy. I'd actually thrown up after I'd come out of the pool. I'd found this acutely embarrassing, but none of the law-enforcement personnel had seemed to think much of it. They were quite busy dealing with their own embarrassment, Arthur Smith. No matter how we glossed over it, Arthur had been mooning around Poppy's house when he shouldn't have been, and Arthur had kicked a suspect. Oh, he said Cara had tried to get up and attack me again, and I'd nodded weakly when they asked me if that was so, but I could tell they didn't believe us, especially Cathy Trumble. Besides, Arthur was in a peculiar mental state, and there was no disguising that, either.

Cathy Trumble had questioned me intently for about thirty minutes, until it became obvious that I had to get into dry clothes. She sent me home in a patrol car, with the warning that she was going to come by within a couple of hours to take a full statement from me.

Cara had gone off to the hospital under guard. I pitied the officer who had to call her husband. Dr. Stuart Embler was going to be pretty unhappy with anyone who'd arrested his wife. He could afford the best lawyers, too. Bringing Cara to trial might be a struggle; I'd have to testify in court, if it came to a trial. I figured I wouldn't count on that until it happened. If there's one thing television has taught Americans, it's that justice doesn't always move at the pace, or in the direction, that it should.

My black glasses were somewhere at the bottom of the Emblers' pool. I got my tortoiseshell ones and pushed them up the bridge of my nose. With a brush in my hand, wrapped in my favorite golden brown gown and robe, I wandered out into the den. To my surprise, Robin was there by himself.

"Where's Phillip?"

"I sent him to the store for some Epsom salts."

"Epsom salts? Why?"

"It was the only thing I could think of that you didn't already have."

"Why the need to get Phillip out of the way? Don't you like him?" I was pretty anxious about this, since I wasn't sure at all that my dad meant to get Phillip back right away.

"Yes, I do. I just wanted to be alone with you for a little while."

"It's not going to take him very long to get Epsom salts."

"I did also mention that if he wanted to stop by the Finster-meyers' house to tell Josh why he couldn't come over for sup-per tonight, I was sure that would be better than calling him."

"Okay," I said cautiously. "So, here we are, by ourselves."

Robin was beginning to wilt around the edges. "Don't you want to have some alone time? So I can just sit and hold you?"

"Probably Phillip is old enough to understand that you might want to hug me or cuddle me from time to time." I said this with an absolutely straight face.

Now Robin was looking really downcast.

"But what I'd like for you to do is come get on the bed with me and hold me," I said.

He brightened considerably. "Sure. I understand you're tired and upset. I just want to be next to you."

Within five minutes, we were snuggled up in my big bed, Robin in his T-shirt and jeans, and I in my gown. I pulled a quilt up over us. I would have been utterly content if I hadn't had one long bridge to cross.

I was lying with my head on his chest, listening to his heart-beat. I was hoping that heart was feeling extra large today. I might be taxing it.

I took a deep breath, started to speak, let it out. I was just a big chicken.

"Robin," I began. Then I stopped dead.

"What, baby?"

"Exactly," I said, and didn't get any further. It was the second time today I'd been terrified. My eyes were focused on the pattern of the quilt—oddly enough, it was the Wedding Ring. I didn't dare look up.

"Are you trying to tell me about the kit on the bathroom counter?"

"Yes."

"I saw it when I started your bathwater. Did you use it?"

"Yes."

His big hand reached over and rested lightly on my pelvis. "Are you . . ." his voice broke. "Are you carrying our child?"

"Yes."

I stole a look up at his face. It was radiant. If he had smiled any wider, his face would have cracked. My own heart gave a leap, and I felt my whole body relax against him.

"You're not going to be an unwed mother," he said firmly.

Another fear discarded. I was far too traditional to face single parenthood with equanimity. All at once, I felt lighter than air.

So, naturally, being so happy, I started crying. "Not just because of the baby," I said, "don't marry me just for that."

"You know it's not just because of the baby." He scrambled out of the bed and rummaged around in the pockets of his jacket. He dove back under the covers and pressed a little velvet box into my hand. "Proof," he said triumphantly. "I've been carrying this with me for two weeks, trying to find the right moment to ask you if you'll wear it."

I hesitated before opening the box. I thought of the past few days. "It's hard to believe anything can end this well," I said. I didn't want to ruin the moment, but I was plagued by the deceptions of my sister-in-law. She had lied to everyone, offering each of us in her life just a little glimpse of one facet of her true character. In the end, she had become so splintered, she could not present a coherent whole to anyone. Maybe Poppy had lost her core.

"I love you," I said to Robin. "And I'm proud that you're the father of my baby." It was an incredible feeling, hearing myself saying the words I'd never believed I'd get to say to anyone. I opened the box, to see a lovely yellow diamond with clear tiny ones set around it. The ring was small and delicate, and I thought it was beautiful.

"Hey, Sis! What's for supper?" Phillip yelled from the living room.

I groaned, then rested my head against Robin's.

"Lest the moment get too tender and mushy," Robin said, but he didn't sound angry. He sounded tolerant.

"We'll be fine," I said bravely, and tried to call up a mental list of what was in the refrigerator.